LOST TREASURES

Also by Jazzy Mitchell

Leveling Up

Undertow

You Matter

Musings of a Madwoman

LOST TREASURES

BY

JAZZY MITCHELL

Lost Treasures

By Jazzy Mitchell

©2016 Jazzy Mitchell

ISBN (trade) 9781633040458
ISBN (eBook) 9781633040434

Launch Point Press
4804 NW Bethany Blvd, Suite I-2 #148
Portland, OR 97229

Editor: CK King
Cover Design: Michelle Brodeur

Blurb

After working at a Manhattan clothing boutique for a little over a year, Torry Hansen requests permission to design the window displays. This is a big step for Torry since she associates fashion with her mother, who died in a tragic accident. The decorations cause quite a stir, even catching the attention of Evelyn Allbright, who decides to have her magazine, *Trending*, feature the shop, its designs, and the window display designer. Recognizing Torry's talents, Evelyn becomes fascinated and decides to convince Torry to leave the boutique for bigger and better things. As Evelyn's interest in Torry transforms from professional to personal, so do her actions during her quest to keep Torry in her life.

Acknowledgements

I wrote a short story many years ago and shared it with others. I wrote more stories, and life moved on. This one story stayed with me, though, popping into my thoughts every so often and reminding me that these characters were not finished. They were worth exploring. With the help of some wonderful people, I decided to delve back into their lives.

I am grateful to Ashley, Rosemary, Sara, and Eden. All read the manuscript and provided thoughtful feedback, as well as technical writing support, which proved invaluable. They made all the difference. In addition, I am thankful to CK, Mich, Lee, and Desert Palm Press for working with me to whip this tale into publishable shape and making it look so pretty.

No acknowledgement page would be complete for me unless I thanked my family. They dealt with a temperamental, tortured writer as best they could, often not seeing me for days, while I dug in to the text and made the necessary changes. I am grateful for their not forgetting me, for feeding me, and for withstanding my absence for long stretches of time. Their love, support, and patience made all the difference.

Dedication

This book is dedicated to my wife, Peggy. Many years ago I struggled to find my path. Should I practice law, teach, write, do something else? I didn't know, and I had never realized that I had a say. Peggy helped me to determine what I wanted to do, and more importantly, she helped me to believe that what I wanted was important. She helped me take control of my life, my choices, and my voice. Her words made a difference because she helped me to recognize that my words make a difference.

Table of Contents

Chapter One

STEPPING OUT OF THE master suite bathroom Torry swept through her parents' bedroom, searching for her mom's excited face but instead finding empty space. She loved this room. The specially ordered bay windows were open so that the salty air could waft in, and Torry was able to hear the dull roar and crash of the waves hitting the rocks nearby. Streams of sunlight bounced off a hanging crystal, creating small rainbows on the back wall. The soft colors of muted greens with undertones of golds and browns made the room feel welcoming, a haven from the outside world. Family pictures Torry had stared at countless times over the years, caused warmth to spread through her body as she stopped for a moment to gaze at the newest addition—an informal family picture of her, her parents, and her sister from last summer at a dinner party. Smiling involuntarily as happiness flowed through her, Torry turned toward the full-length mirror to see how the dress looked on her. She gasped at the sight, turning when she heard an answering gasp from the closet doorway.

"Torry," her mom exclaimed, clapping her hands together. "Twirl for me."

She spun, giggling as the dress flowed around her legs, the soft material caressing her calves.

"Beautiful. Coco would be so pleased to see her creation on such a pretty young lady."

"Mom," Torry moaned. She could feel her cheeks flushing as she walked over to the mirror, avoiding her mom's eyes. The silk material molded to her form, emphasizing her toned arms, fit body, and long legs. Although the emerald color was bold, it accentuated Torry's green eyes and brunette hair. With some makeup, Torry knew she would look pretty good.

"Now, now. You need to learn how to take a compliment, honey, and more importantly, you need to believe in yourself. Have confidence." Gentle fingers curled over Torry's shoulders, as her mom joined her at the mirror. "Stunning," she murmured before clearing her throat and saying in a louder voice, "Shoulders back, chest out, chin up, young lady."

"Mom," Torry groused, as she automatically did as she was told.

"Perfect."

"I'm home," a male voice boomed. "Ruth? Torry?"

Loud footsteps echoed on the hardwood floors below, and Torry could visualize her dad walking through the small foyer to the stairway, the squeaky steps indicating his progress up the worn wooden stairs. A moment later he entered the room.

"Oh, what do we have here?" he asked, a smile in his voice. "Why didn't anyone tell me we were entertaining a movie star today?" He leaned in to peck Torry's cheek before he turned to deliver a chaste kiss on her mom's lips.

"Isn't she gorgeous, Bobby?" Ruth exclaimed.

"Yes. My baby's all grown up."

Torry tried not to fidget. *They still think I'm a little girl even though I'm entering my last year of college, for Christ's sake. Not that I've figured out what I want to do for the rest of my life. If Dad has his way, I'll end up taking the LSAT exam in a few months and eventually practice law with him at his firm. After working for him the last couple of summers to earn some extra money, I don't feel any particular desire to become an attorney. Of course, I can't rule out the possibility, since I don't want to hurt his feelings. God, I can just imagine his reaction, how disappointed and hurt he'll be. Soon, though, I'll have to make a decision one way or another.*

Refocusing on her image in the mirror, she admired the way the sweetheart neckline and fitted bodice revealed her collarbones and just a bit of cleavage before flaring out at the waist. It was a wonderful surprise when her mom decided she would allow Torry to wear one of her beloved Chanel dresses at the Summer Solstice Social being held next week at the Rosecliff mansion. Glancing at the bed, Torry's eyes lingered on the other couture spread upon it. Colors flooded her senses, a combination of hues so rich that it took her breath away.

Behind Torry, her parents shifted to gaze into the mirror at her, their smiles so loving and proud that she felt tears gathering. Shaking her head minutely, Torry pushed back at the silly sentimentality, running her hands over her sides just for something to do. They were a good-looking family. Torry had inherited her dark hair and high cheekbones from her mom, and her green eyes and height from her dad. Both kept in shape through jogging and playing tennis regularly, and Torry was glad to find that she also enjoyed exercising.

"I remember that dress," Bobby said, startling Torry out of her thoughts. "You haven't worn that since before the girls were born."

"I put it away for safekeeping, until my baby was old enough to wear it." Ruth rested her chin on Torry's shoulder and squeezed her around the waist.

Torry ignored the melancholy note present in her mom's voice, knowing not to ask. Her mom wouldn't talk about it. She never did. "Well, I love it," Torry said with a soft voice. It was one of the most beautiful things she'd ever placed on her body. Delicate, sophisticated, and fluid—the dress felt how she imagined a butterfly's wings would while brushing against her cheek.

"You'll be the belle of the ball."

"What about Katie?"

"You know your sister prefers the newest designs, and she never misses the opportunity to shop. The classics suit you, sweetheart." Ruth lifted Torry's hair off her neck. "We can pin your hair up."

Loving days like this one, days when she was the sole focus of her mother's affections, Torry basked in the moment. She knew that her mom was excited to attend the dance. Once upon a time, her mom was quite the socialite, rubbing elbows with the fashion elite. Nana was a well-known designer and, even though she had retired a decade ago, she sat on the boards of the Metropolitan Museum and the Council of Fashion Designers of America. Unfortunately, her mom and grandmother were estranged. Torry had never heard the whole story as to why. She had her suspicions, though.

"That sounds great." Torry turned away from the mirror and smiled at her mom. "Let me take this off so it won't get wrinkled." She returned to the bathroom, ignoring the low murmurings of her parents. She changed into shorts and a t-shirt before carefully placing the dress into a protective garment bag and hanging it on the back of the door.

"How about we go out for dinner tonight?" Bobby suggested once Torry reentered the bedroom, clapping his hands together and rubbing them as he wiggled his eyebrows.

"Can we go to The Wharf?" Torry asked, already salivating at the thought of having some clam chowder. She'd have to jog an extra mile or three tomorrow morning, but it'd be so worth it.

"You bet, sweetie. We'll leave in ten minutes," Bobby said, giving her a quick hug.

"Awesome!" Torry ran to her room to grab a sweatshirt and her purse. She loved when they splurged. It wasn't that they were poor. They were an average middle-class family that worked hard and enjoyed the finer things every so often like dining out. She knew they would stroll around the wharf afterward, and that was the real treat. She loved spending time with her parents, and since going away to college, she had realized how precious these interactions were. Soon she would finish her schooling and move out of her parents' home, not that they had indicated that they were in any hurry for her to leave.

She had other ideas, though. Although her mom and Nana did not speak to each other, Torry had contacted her grandmother a few years ago. After several conversations, Torry had visited her in Manhattan. Their relationship had blossomed, and Torry loved spending time with her grandmother. She often contemplated telling her parents, but she was afraid. As it was, her parents never spoke of Nana, and when Torry or her sister brought her up, the conversation was shut down. Torry hadn't even told Katie. Maybe she was just being selfish, not wanting Katie to spend time with Nana too. The relationship was fragile and forbidden. Just last week, her nana had opened the door to having Torry live with her in New York and working within the fashion industry after she graduated.

"Darling, just think about it. I can get you a spot anywhere you wish. Didn't you tell me that you were enjoying stage crew? You'll be able to do so much more in New York. Work on Broadway. I know your mom taught you about colors and materials, and you're a natural with evoking emotion through your creations. You're talented, and I want to help you."

"I know, Nana, and I am so grateful. But Dad wants me to go to law school, and Mom wants me to stay in Newport."

"What do you want, Torry?"

"I'm, I'm not sure. I just know that I love creating, but I love my parents too. I don't want them to be disappointed in me."

"Sweetie, even if they are disappointed in your choices, they will always love you and want you to be happy."

"Then why aren't you and Mom talking?" Torry winced as she weathered the silence, wondering whether her grandmother would answer the question or end the phone call. She wished she had brought this up in the spring when she had visited so she could see her grandmother's face, but she had been more focused on learning about Nana and her world, blinded by her lifestyle in New York.

"I've tried over the years but perhaps not hard enough. I said some things—made some decisions—long ago, before you and your sister were born. I was upset with your mother for what I perceived as her turning her back on my legacy. On her legacy. And I was unfair to her and your father. But too much time has passed, too many words spoken which cannot be unsaid."

"But why can't you come visit? I'm here and Katie will be here in a couple of weeks. We can act as buffers when you talk to Mom and Dad."

"I'll think about it. I promise. And I want you to think about something for me."

"What?"

"Coming to live with me once you graduate. I can help you, Torry. I want to. Will you consider it?"

Torry felt a thrill run through her, excitement and some fear at facing such a decision overtaking her, thoughts of the possible repercussions flashing through her mind. "I promise."

"Good. I love you, Victoria. I'll talk to you soon."

"Okay, Nana. I love you too."

A hand on Torry's shoulder shook her from thoughts of last week's conversation, and she refocused on the present. Nodding at her dad, she followed her parents out the door with a spring in her step, anticipating a fabulous evening. After all, eating New England clam chowder was nearly a religious experience.

***

"What do you want to do today?" Ruth asked, while they dawdled over the newspaper and coffee.

"How about going sailing? Dad's not working today, is he?"

"No. I think that's a wonderful idea, although we really should get a move on. The forecast says we might get some thunderstorms this afternoon."

"Oh, well, we don't have to—"

"No, no. We have enough time. Let me talk to your dad."

"Katie's going to be so jealous."

Ruth chuckled. "You two have been sailing since grade school. She'll get more chances once she's home."

"Well, you can remind her of that when she complains," Torry said, shooting her mom a smile.

"Don't take too long to get ready," Ruth said before leaving the room.

"I won't," Torry answered, deciding to finish reading the editorial page before she got dressed. Hopping up to get changed after she finished reading the news, Torry passed by her parents' room, slowing down when she heard raised voices.

"I don't want you speaking to her anymore. She'll twist your mind with thoughts of celebrities and fashion." The way her father hissed the last few words made Torry flinch. Why did he hate fashion so much? Was he talking about Nana? Did she reach out to her mom? Would her father hate her if she did follow a path that led to fashion in some way?

"She's my mother! I miss her. And lest you forget, I was born and raised in that atmosphere. You fell in love with me while I was a part of that world."

"We've built a life here. I don't need her telling you how you deserve so much more."

"Bobby, I chose you. I gave up everything—"

"Not that again! That's always what it comes down to, isn't it? How you gave up everything for me. How much you've suffered—"

"Don't be ridiculous. I love our life, our family. I would make the same choice a thousand times over. I love you." Silence pervaded, and Torry started to move away, stopping when she heard her mom's next words. "At some point you're going to have to trust me. You haven't had to prove you trust me because I walked away from everything, but the girls are adults, and they deserve to spend time with her. I want to spend time with her too. Please think about it. At least having her visit here instead of visiting her in New York will keep us out of the lifestyle you abhor so much."

Hurrying to her room, Torry sank down on her bed, thinking about what she'd overheard. Nana had kept her promise and reached out to Mom. If they were able to reconnect, Torry wouldn't feel so guilty about moving to New York. She wouldn't feel like she was doing something that might hurt her parents. And that conversation confirmed what she had suspected—her mom had given up everything for her dad. She wondered just how well known her grandmother was. She'd have to do some research later. She'd never thought to do it before, as she had found her grandmother's address in her mom's address book. Over spring break she had stayed with her, learning about the woman who had fostered a love of fashion in her mother. It was past time to figure out exactly what Nana was offering her.

Hearing steps in the hallway, Torry made her way downstairs, pasting on a smile. The last thing she wanted to do was to give away what she'd heard. She folded up the newspaper and placed her coffee mug in the dishwasher, glancing at her parents through lowered eyelashes. Her mom placed sandwiches and water into a small cooler before turning to Torry.

"Ready to go sailing?" Ruth asked with a falsely cheerful demeanor.

"Absolutely. Dad? You coming?"

"I wouldn't miss it for the world," he said, a small smile breaking through his serious expression like the sun burning off the morning fog.

Torry smiled with relief, glad he was shaking off his anger in favor of spending time together. He was normally a pretty affable guy, not one to stew in negative thoughts. He was easygoing, often the one to settle any disagreements that erupted in the household.

After arriving at the pier, Torry waved her parents on board and cast off the ropes before pushing the boat away from its slip and jumping on. She'd done this hundreds of times, and the routine of unmooring the boat soothed Torry's anxiousness. She chose to ignore the tension between her parents, knowing that as they enjoyed the peacefulness of sailing, their moods would soften. Once the breeze caught the sails, the boat skimmed the water, and ocean spray coated the air. The sun's rays caressed Torry's face, drying it even as more spray found its mark. The slapping of the waves against the hull soothed Torry's frayed nerves, and she smiled exuberantly at her parents, who smiled in return.

As the day passed, clouds formed, and stronger gusts pushed them across the bay. Torry donned her sweatshirt, staring at the horizon as her breath hitched in her chest. Uneasiness blanketed her as she eyed the massive cumulonimbus clouds forming.

"Maybe we should turn back," Torry suggested to her dad, who stood at the helm, while she and her mom reclined on the front deck. "The wind is starting to pick up." Thunder rumbled ominously, and a few minutes later lightning lit up the darkening clouds.

"I think that's a good idea." Bobby turned the boat to port. "Hang on," he said belatedly, as Torry and her mom slid across the bow.

Torry reached for the lifeline with one hand and her mom with the other. "Whoa," Torry gasped. "We'd better get off this before we fall overboard." They scrambled off, hurrying to help secure the boat as they attempted to beat the storm back to shore. Thunder boomed, and the first drops of rain splattered across the deck in an increasingly fast staccato beat. Lightning split the air, followed closely by thunder, and Torry wobbled over to the cockpit, nearly falling as the wind pushed her off-balance. Sheets of rain lashed at her face, and the wind whipped up the waves.

"Watch out!" she heard her dad yell, and Torry ducked as the boom swung around, wind filling the mainsail and pushing the boat toward shore. "Reef the sails!"

Noticing her mother was leeward as the wind shifted and lightning flashed across the sky, Torry yelled out to her. Time slowed down as she watched her mom slip across the deck, hands flailing. Her father reached for her, grabbing her shirt as the boat rocked. Another gust caused him to lose his grip, and her mother fell off the boat. Torry opened her mouth to scream, but no sound came out. She blinked the rain out of her eyes as she made her way over, searching frantically for any signs of her mother. *She had a lifejacket on. She'll be fine.* Torry kept telling herself that, even as she searched the swells.

"Go back!" Torry pleaded.

"I'm trying."

For countless minutes they searched the area. Waves slapped the hull, their sounds like pounding fists echoing Torry's elevated heartbeats. Torry saw her first, the bright orange lifejacket bobbing against the whitecaps. "There!" Torry yelled, pointing. As soon as they got close enough, Torry dove into the water, swimming against the tide to grab her. Her mom was unconscious, head lolling against Torry's shoulder as she paddled back to the boat. Her father helped to get her mother on the boat before grabbing Torry's arm to pull her in. She lay on her back, gasping, eyes closed against the rain, drops so sharp that they seemed to tear through her skin as she listened to her father's attempts to revive her mother. She knew it was fruitless. She had known as soon as she had pulled her mom into her arms—the dead weight, the white skin, the gaping mouth.

She'd never heard her father cry before. Never seen him shed a tear. As she lay in the cockpit, refusing to open her eyes, water hitting her again and again, Torry ignored her instinct to comfort him, giving him some privacy as he fell apart. It was only when he pulled her into a hug sometime later, only as their tears mingled and their voices cracked, that Torry realized the storm had ended. The sun's rays no longer warmed her, and she wondered whether she would ever feel warm again.

Chapter Two

ANOTHER DAY, ANOTHER DISAPPOINTMENT. Evelyn sighed, rolling her head to loosen her neck muscles while sinking into the back seat of the town car, black leather encasing her curves like a lover's hands. It had been another long day filled with incompetence and delays. In addition, she had missed dinner with Bruce last night—again. Now she was receiving the cold shoulder. At least, so she assumed. She hadn't actually had time to call him today, and he'd been asleep by the time she had arrived home last night. Asleep when she had risen for the day too. As if she had the time to lounge around in bed all day. Did it matter that today was Sunday? Certainly not.

Married for four years, Evelyn could already see the signs that their marriage was breaking apart. She didn't know what to do to fill the cracks and strengthen the foundation. She didn't know whether she had the energy to try.

Well, that wasn't really the truth. She always had energy for what she deemed important. She didn't know whether he was worth the effort. Whether marriage was worth the effort. He just kept sucking her dry, demanding more and more of her time. And when they spent time together, it was unpleasant—filled with loaded silences and pointed glares. She no longer wished to expend time trying to placate him, not when it was so clear that nothing she did, nothing she said, would be enough. In all probability, Bruce expected her to plead for another chance, to promise to do better. Well, she would not resort to such methods at this late juncture.

Ever since she had missed their anniversary dinner, he had ratcheted up the hostility, accompanied by a healthy dose of alcohol. *Liquid courage, indeed.* His behavior lately had embarrassed her, not that he cared. Last month he had become inebriated at a company dinner party and called her boss, George Walski, the CEO of Magellan-Weeks Publications, the cheap toupee guy. He wasn't even trying anymore, so why should she? He was intimidated by her power, emasculated by her fame. She had not realized just how threatened he felt by her success. And now too many words had been said, too much vitriol spewed, leading her to believe that they could not repair the gap in their relationship. Better to let it die while retaining what little dignity remained. Perhaps, if she let him go, they could remain civil during social situations, not that he would be attending any more fashion events if she had any say in it. Evelyn sniffed.

Bruce was a product of Wall Street, one of those rich, arrogant stockbrokers who brazenly took risks and made a name for himself. She had hired him five years ago to help her invest her money in the most profitable ways possible. Her then financial advisor had been retiring, and Bruce had come highly recommended. She had been lonely, driven, and in need of someone on her arm for the endless events she had to attend, if only to keep herself looking respectable in prospective advertisers' eyes. He had seemed the perfect man for the job, and he had been, for a while. Until he had realized that she would not change her focus, her hours, or her life for him.

Oh, she had made space for him within her life. She had given him free rein with redecorating one of the dens. She had not objected too loudly when he had insisted on keeping his out-of-style leather armchair once he had moved into her townhouse, or to his penchant for smelly cigars as long as he smoked them on the back patio. She knew who she was, and she'd assumed he did too. Instead, he continued to disappoint her. The sound of her cell phone ringing interrupted her melancholy thoughts.

"Evelyn. Did you hear what happened to Cynthia Smythe's daughter? It's awful. Positively heartbreaking," a tinny male voice echoed through the interior of the town car once she placed the call on speakerphone.

"Ira? What are you twittering on about?"

"Cynthia Smythe's daughter died in a boating accident yesterday. Her name's Ruth Hansen. She was sailing with her husband and younger daughter, and they got caught in a thunderstorm while on the ocean off Newport, Rhode Island."

Closing her eyes, Evelyn felt her stomach drop. She had just seen Cynthia last week at the board meeting for the Met. Hadn't she mentioned that her granddaughter had visited a few months ago?

"That's terrible. I can't imagine…" Evelyn's words trailed off as she attempted to marshal her thoughts. "Hmm. Send me the funeral details and get me Cynthia's phone number."

"Of course."

"I'm on my way in now. And, Ira, thank you for telling me."

"You're welcome. I'll text you her number."

Disconnecting the call, Evelyn sighed, rubbing her temples as she thought about their conversation. She couldn't imagine the horror of outliving a child. Of learning that she had died in a freak accident, so suddenly. No one should have to live through such a tragedy. Hearing a ping, Evelyn clicked on the number Ira provided. Evelyn hesitated when she heard Cynthia's voice before saying, "Cynthia?"

"Evelyn? Is that you?"

"Oh, yes. I apologize, Cynthia. I didn't expect for you to pick up. You must be inundated with phone calls."

"Yes. It's been quite overwhelming."

"I can't imagine. I won't keep you long. I wanted to extend my condolences and offer my assistant to help you make any necessary arrangements. I don't believe I ever met your daughter."

"We were estranged. I was intending to visit her this weekend at my granddaughter's urging. She reached out to me a few years ago unbeknownst to Ruth, and she wanted us to mend fences."

"She sounds like a lovely girl."

"Yes. She's so much like her mother. I mean…"

Evelyn grasped the phone tighter as she heard the woman's voice catch. "I really am sorry for your loss. My assistant's name is Heather. Shall I give her your number so that she can help you?"

"Well, the funeral will be in Newport, not here, so there won't be much need…"

"Mmhmm. She can help you with your travel arrangements and lodging then."

"Yes, that would be helpful. I feel so scattered right now."

"As would any mother after losing her child. Try not to be too hard on yourself. It sounds like you had reached out to your daughter, and I am certain that meant the world to her. I don't know why you were estranged, nor is it any of my business. I do know that regardless of the reason for it, the bond between mother and daughter can never be broken. Please take solace knowing that she loved you and that she was open to seeing you again."

Silence filled the line, punctuated with some sniffling. Evelyn knew the woman was fighting tears and perhaps losing the battle. Not wanting her to feel embarrassed, Evelyn said, "You'll hear from Heather within the hour. Please let me know if there is anything else I can do. Anything, Cynthia. Will you do that for me?"

"Yes. I, if you're serious…"

"Quite. What can I do?"

"I know we aren't really friends. We've served on boards together for years, and before that we interacted through our respective roles in the fashion industry—"

Recognizing the woman's anxiousness, Evelyn cut her off. "Cynthia, you needn't build this up. Please don't be afraid to ask."

"Will you attend the funeral with me?"

Not expecting such a request, Evelyn's eyebrows shot up as she thought about what Cynthia was asking.

"Her husband and I hardly know each other, and the few times I had interacted with him were disastrous. I've never even met her older daughter, Katie. Just Victoria, and only a handful of times. So you see, I won't have the familial support I'll need. I was an only child, as was Ruth. And my husband, sweet George, died many years ago. I fear that I will not be welcome there, but I want to go, regardless. It would help immensely to have someone with me. You are so strong, Evelyn. I could use some of that right now."

"I understand." And she did. Her first marriage had been filled with tension due to her mother-in-law's immense dislike of her lifestyle, her career, truly everything about her. Jeremy's mother always believed that he could do better, and she had used every opportunity to drive that point home. Thinking about how she could rearrange her schedule, she said, "I'll come with you, Cynthia. You won't be alone."

***

"Ready?" Evelyn asked, as their car arrived at the funeral home. They had not attended the wake the night before, not wanting to deal with any more unpleasantness than necessary. Cynthia, expecting many from the fashion world would have shown up to pay their respects, confided in Evelyn that she hoped today's gathering would not be as crowded. Their driver parked in the funeral line before getting out of the car to open their door. A funeral home employee asked whether they were family members, and once given Cynthia's name, the driver was directed to move the car toward the front of the line. Evelyn and Cynthia exchanged surprised glances before making their way inside.

Although in her seventies, Cynthia looked much younger. Perhaps it was her vivacious nature or lithe figure, but the woman seemed to glide instead of walk, and she held herself in such a way that she drew everyone's attention. Although Evelyn had cultivated her image as she had gained power in the fashion industry, Cynthia's allure was natural. Evelyn had found out, last night over dinner, that before becoming a designer, Cynthia had studied ballet for many years and was even offered a full scholarship to attend a prestigious dance conservatory. Turning down the opportunity had been hard, but she had loved fashion more. She confided in Evelyn that she never had regretted her decision.

Evelyn had to agree that it was the better choice. Certainly, Cynthia's vision had affected the fashion world, moving it in a direction that changed the way designers combined imagination and material. Her vision had shown others how to think more abstractly while combining colors and fabrics.

"I must apologize in advance for any impolite behavior my son-in-law may exhibit. Victoria will be welcoming, but I trust she will feel torn, and I do not wish to place her in a position where she will need to choose sides."

"Cynthia, we will deal with whatever comes. I am here to support you. Remember that we are two formidable women."

With a small smile, Cynthia led the way inside the building. They were greeted by an older gentleman who told them a private screening was being held in the back room for family. Once they walked in, Evelyn scanned the room. All dressed in black, as was customary, and all speaking in low tones. No young children were present. No smiles or laughter. A light touch to her elbow captured Evelyn's attention, and she turned toward Cynthia, who nodded toward the back of the room where an open casket was situated.

They slowly approached the casket, and Evelyn let out a small sigh of relief at not being waylaid by any of Cynthia's family members as they both sank down on the bench before it. Lowering her head, Evelyn thought about how devastated she'd feel if one of her daughters died. How heartbroken she would be if she'd been estranged from either of them. How hopeless she would feel to have one of them ripped away from her so suddenly, taking away any chance to reconcile. She sent a silent prayer that this woman's soul would rest easy and the fractures in her family would heal, before lifting her head and rising. Standing silently next to Cynthia's kneeling form, Evelyn took a moment to gaze at the deceased woman.

Coffee-colored, shoulder-length, straight hair and bangs contrasted with light skin and emphasized angular features. She was dressed in a navy-blue dress that looked more like business attire than a favorite dress. What a pity. The daughter of such a well-known, lauded designer looking washed out in off-the-rack clothing. No doubt her husband had chosen the outfit.

Glancing to the side, she saw several pictures of the woman from various points in her life. Some reflected a youth and vitality that Evelyn envied, and others a solemnity that hinted at less carefree times. A family photo caught her attention. She studied it, noting the two younger women in the picture. Although both daughters were brunettes, the taller one had mesmerizing green eyes, while the other daughter had hazel eyes. The sun hit them just right, emphasizing their eyes and smiles. Even the husband's brown eyes were devoid of shadow. They looked happy. Hearing movement next to her, Evelyn offered a hand to help Cynthia to stand. Just as Cynthia gained her footing, one of Ruth's daughters appeared next to them.

"Nana," she breathed, before pulling Cynthia into a tight hug. Smirking, Evelyn's estimation of the girl rose. Not that she'd given her much thought. She knew nothing about the girl other than that she had reached out to Cynthia in spite of her parents' wishes. With that in mind, Evelyn was sure the girl's father would not be pleased with such a public display. She knew from harsh experience how the rumor mill worked, whether it be at work or within the family dynamic. She was certain that he had turned his side of the family against Cynthia many years ago.

"Victoria," Cynthia said, her voice breaking. "It's good to see a friendly face."

"I'm glad you came."

"Well, that makes one of us," a male voice growled.

Evelyn glared at Cynthia's son-in-law, ready to defend her friend. What a disrespectful, selfish man. To think he couldn't push aside his own issues even for a day. Before she could rip the man apart, Cynthia's other granddaughter joined them.

"Hello. I'm Katie. Are you my grandmother?"

"Yes. It's a pleasure to finally meet you, dear."

Evelyn watched the interaction with interest, wondering just how rude the man would continue to be. She saw how thunderhead clouds seemed to be converging over his lowered eyebrows. His face reddened as he clenched his jaw, and she could practically hear his teeth grinding.

"How dare you show up here. What makes you think you're welcome?" he bit off.

"Dad, please," Victoria said, placing her hand on his forearm. "She's grieving too."

"Please. That woman has no heart. She disowned Ruth, cut her out of her life!"

"But they were trying to reconcile. She was going to visit this weekend."

"What do you know about that?" He glared at his daughter.

"That need not be discussed now, I am sure," Evelyn interjected smoothly. "Cynthia is here to pay her respects. You may not like her, but she was Ruth's mother and has the right to be here. I suspect Ruth would want her here."

"How dare you speak as if you knew my wife," he roared. "Who are you, anyway? Why are you here?"

"I am Cynthia's friend, and I am here to support her, suspecting how ill-mannered you might be. I am disappointed to find that I was correct in my assumption. Now it would be best if you could find a way to contain your animosity for a few hours. We will be out of your hair soon enough." Evelyn turned toward Cynthia, glad to see her two granddaughters flanking her. Before she could say anything else, an employee entered to announce that visitors were being allowed in for the funeral service. Relieved that they would be shielded from any more unpleasantness, Evelyn guided Cynthia to a seat in the front, smirking when her granddaughters sat between Cynthia and her son-in-law.

The room filled up over the next fifteen minutes. Evelyn chose to not look behind her, preferring to listen to the various conversations. She did not allow herself to gawk at the visitors as if she were some common people watcher. She loved to watch others, to guess who they were and what their lives were like. And why wouldn't she? She made a living out of creating back stories for her magazine spreads. Creating stories through the clothes she chose to showcase, the models she chose to pose, the locations she chose to use. Her imagination opened the door for others. And watching people stirred her imagination.

Only a few people spoke at the funeral mass—Ruth's best friend, a colleague, and her younger daughter, who was in the boat when the storm occurred. Her words stuck with Evelyn as they rode in the car to the cemetery.

"Living off the ocean, growing up in Newport, I loved sailing. I still do. Our family has spent so many summers together on a sailboat. I think that we forgot how the ocean is so powerful, so fickle, so unpredictable. We got fooled by our familiarity. We forgot that our world can change with one wrong action, one wrong word, one wrong thought. And I've been thinking about what happened, about what we could have done differently."

Tears ran down the young woman's face, and Evelyn felt her chest tighten. The girl's pain was so palpable, so poignant. She could see how Victoria was struggling to remain composed as she spoke.

"I can't help but believe that there's nothing we could have done differently. And I choose to believe that, because if I don't, I'll never be able to grieve fully. People say that you can learn something from this kind of tragedy and that you can rebuild while not taking anything for granted in your life. I don't know if I believe that. I think people just want to get on with their lives and put any unpleasantness behind them. To remember Mom and her bright smile and witty remarks is to remember that she was taken away too soon. She left things undone. She left people who wanted to connect with her. She left problems unsolved and situations unattended. She had compartmentalized parts of her life, you see, and just when she was starting to take away the partitions, just when she was ready to reconcile with her past and present to create a better future, she died."

Evelyn's entire focus was on Victoria and her words. This wasn't the usual eulogy. This was a thoughtful, painful, insightful expression of grief. Of lost chances. Of hard-earned wisdom.

"Mom and I spent many enjoyable afternoons, over the years, discussing fabrics and colors and art. You might not know this, but she was brought up surrounded by designs and ideas and possibilities. That was due to her mother, my nana, who is here today." As Victoria nodded at Cynthia, Evelyn felt the older woman tremble. She squeezed the woman's hand, providing support as best she could.

"Several people have come to pay their respects over the last couple of days who knew my mom when she was younger and part of the fashion world. I can't fully understand any of that, but I know this, she denied a part of herself when she turned her back on that side of her life. So, all I can do is promise to learn from that, learn from a woman who gave up everything that she held dear because she knew of no other way to hold on to what she believed to be her happy ending. I believe she never regretted her choice, but I wish…I wish she could have found a way to be happy without having to sacrifice so much that made her who she was."

At that point the tears were coming down thick and fast not just down Torry's lovely face but down the faces of those who sat close to Evelyn. She had no doubt that was true for many of the people listening to the young woman's words. Evelyn dabbed at her eyes while passing some tissues to Cynthia and Katie.

"Goodbye, Mom. I promise to do my best to not give up, to not give away what is important to me in order to make others happy."

Eyebrows inching up on her forehead, Evelyn marveled at the audacity Victoria was displaying through her words. Obviously, she was not very happy with her father. This was a clear message that she would do what she wanted regardless of his feelings or anyone else's. *Interesting.*

"She's quite something, wouldn't you agree?" Cynthia whispered to Evelyn as they watched the young lady walk toward her seat.

"That's putting it mildly."

"I've asked her to consider living with me once she graduates college. She is quite talented. We'll have to see what happens."

Humming at Cynthia's words, Evelyn returned her attention to the front as another person got up to speak. She could only hope that this was the last speaker. Funerals tended to be so macabre. Evelyn shivered. At least Victoria's speech had broken up the dismal monotony of tears and sadness for lost moments and wasted time. Although Victoria had touched on all those useless feelings, she had transformed them into a powerful message. Evelyn was content knowing that attending the funeral, at the very least, had given Cynthia some hope that she would be spending time with her granddaughters at some point in the future. They just needed to get through the unpleasantness of the burial.

Chapter Three

LOOKING THROUGH THE STORE window at the cool, autumnal day, Torry grinned with delight. She watched as a few vibrant red leaves floated on the wind, spinning, twirling, like a young girl with arms extended. That's how Torry felt—happy and carefree. Like a part of her had unfurled and brightened. She'd seen it in her eyes when she had looked in the mirror this morning. Her bright eyes had reflected her excitement, her passion—both had been sorely missing before last week. Last week when Harold McCarthy had finally, finally agreed to her pleadings to let her try her hand at decorating the windows in his boutique.

Harold's wife, Grace, usually designed the windows with the latest fashions. She did a good job, but it was apparent, at least to Torry, that she approached it as a task instead of an opportunity to connect with those who viewed the displays. Although the woman didn't enjoy that part of her responsibilities, Torry coveted the privilege, yearning to create what her imagination so vividly conjured. And now Harold was giving her that chance.

The small boutique was located two blocks south of Saks on Fifth Avenue in Manhattan's Diamond District. Every day, Torry walked past the well-known department stores and haute couture boutiques, greedily soaking up the diverse personalities reflected through their window displays. She had so many ideas on how to promote the boutique where she worked.

Once the boutique closed, Torry could get to work. Grace tended to decorate whenever she had the time, but Torry wanted to make the changes in the display without having to worry about being interrupted. Maybe she was being a bit of a romantic, a bit theatrical even, wanting to create the changes without anyone seeing her do it—as if little fairies had waved their wands or as if Santa's elves had delivered a Christmas gift to those walking by the store. No one wanted to actually see the work occurring, they just wanted to appreciate the end result. All the large department stores changed their windows overnight, and now this little Manhattan boutique would too. At least during the time she'd worked at the store, she'd earned her boss's trust enough that he'd agreed with her request to decorate the windows overnight instead of during store hours. It was perfect since she could sleep late the next day—her day off—as long as Brandon wasn't a jerk about it.

Although he worked late on the weekends, Brandon expected her to be available whenever he was. Torry frowned, not understanding why he gave her such a hard time. They'd been dating for about eight months, and she'd thought he understood how important it was for her to chase after her dream of using her talents somehow in New York. He didn't seem to get it. He didn't like her job and kept pointing out that it would not provide her with the opportunity to do what she wanted to do—follow in the footsteps of her grandmother. Torry couldn't refute his words; after all, she refused to allow Nana to open any doors for her, and her boss had no idea that her grandmother was a well-known designer.

Torry ended up working most nights and with these new responsibilities, she would be out even later. This morning, she'd arrived at work when the store had opened, and although she supposed she should feel tired by now, she vibrated with anticipation. It wiped away all the long hours spent on her feet and made her feel giddy as possibilities danced before her eyes.

Taking out a sketchpad, Torry reviewed her drawings. She had many ideas harking back to great literature from which to choose. Even if no one noticed the displays, they would make her happy. She had always loved books, the magic of falling into them, traveling to different worlds where she could experience others' lives. They took her away from her own problems, if only for a little while. Over the years books had taught her about courage and weakness, wonder and disgust. They had helped her to grow and expand her thinking. They had helped her to navigate through her own life's challenges. Torry knew she was not talented enough to touch people the way such authors had affected her, but she aspired to make a difference, somehow. This was her way of reaching out and making people smile. It was her first step toward making a difference. Skimming through her drawings, Torry thought of her conversation with Harold last week.

"Please let me try, Harold. Grace spends so much time here, and I know she'd rather devote it toward what she loves instead of decorating windows. I have some ideas I'd love to try. Just let me try this once, and if you hate it or we get complaints, you'll never have to let me do it again."

Torry trotted out her best puppy-dog look, gazing through lowered eyelashes as she clasped her hands to her chest and held her breath. She even fluttered her long, dark eyelashes, knowing that Harold would get a kick out of her coquettish behavior and her shiny round eyes so filled with hope.

A negligent wave and a loud chuckle preceded his answer.

"Sure, sure, Torry. Take a shot at it. I'm sure Grace could use the break. But only with what we've got, okay? We don't have a budget for window designs. Generate some customers, and we'll see."

It was funny to think of how she had ignored her gifts for years only to find herself firmly entrenched in fashion. It had taken months to find a job after she arrived in New York, and her father hadn't helped matters. Every conversation became an argument where he insisted she give up her 'ridiculous dreams' and get on with life.

"Come home, Torry. Or go to law school. You got accepted by some of the most prestigious law schools in the nation. And after you finish, you can practice law with me."

"Dad, you know I don't want to do that. You're great at law, but I don't think I could do it."

"Of course you could, sweetheart. You'll learn how to distance yourself from your clients so that you don't become too emotionally invested. You're great at details. You have a sharp mind. And how many law students have a job just waiting for them after they pass the bar? You can even work on some of my cases during the summers to get more hands-on training."

"No, I just need to keep trying. I'll find a job soon."

"Then at least accept your grandmother's offer to help you. There's no shame in accepting help to get your foot in the door. The rest will all be you."

Torry knew how hard it was for him to say that. Although her father and grandmother were getting along, he still hesitated when mentioning her. "You know I can't. Please, just trust in me. I can do this."

"It's not a matter of trust, Torry. Striking out on your own is hard, and doing it in New York on your own, well, it's not necessary. You have people who love you, who want to support you."

"Dad, please." Torry covered her eyes with a hand. She couldn't listen to this again. She still felt guilt plague her for turning her back on everyone after her mom's death: her father, her sister, Nana, and her friends. She hadn't been able to deal with the

family stress or her friends' awkwardness, while she struggled to grieve and process and move forward. It was only rather recently that she'd reached out to anyone after realizing how much she'd hurt those she loved most by maintaining a distance from them.

With her mother gone and her older sister married, Torry was not surprised that her father wanted her closer. He was probably lonely in that large, empty home. That didn't mean she was going to give up on her dreams.

"You know," Bobby said with a deceptively mild voice. "There's an opening at the paper. With your experience at BU, you could easily get it. John said—"

"You already spoke to Mr. Bitman about it?" Torry broke in, mortified that he and the editor in chief of the local newspaper had discussed her. "Why would you do that?"

"Oh, it was in passing. Very brief. He asked how you were and mentioned the position. Asked if you'd be interested."

Torry knew her father was glossing over the truth. "How could you do that?"

"Sweetheart, by working at the paper, you could fight the good fight, educate people, and make a difference in your hometown. Would that be so bad?"

Balling her free hand into a fist as she squeezed her eyes closed, Torry bit her lower lip to keep from snapping at him. He meant well, but these temptations only hurt her, undermined her. She knew it would be so easy to move back. Yet she yearned for more.

"I'm going for an interview at a small clothing boutique this week. Let me try by myself a little longer."

"At least let me put some money in your bank account."

Thinking about her upcoming rent and her modest clothes, Torry sighed. She could buy a new outfit for the interview, something designer. Although it hurt her heart to think about fashion, it was time to embrace her heritage again. "Okay. Thanks, Dad. I love you."

"Love you too. Talk to you soon."

But they hadn't spoken for a good week after that conversation. Torry had mulled over his words, working through her anger at his repeated attempts to get her to come home, and during that time, she'd refused to return his telephone calls and e-mails.

He didn't understand that Torry wanted to touch people's lives globally. She wanted to make her mark on the people of the world, engrave her name on their hearts. Torry snorted at such dramatic thoughts. Nevertheless, she knew that she did not belong in Newport anymore. She was talented. Someone would see it. She would find a way. And she would do it on her own.

So far, she had refused all her grandmother's offers to help her and, now that she was given permission to design the windows, she was certain she would be noticed based on her talent, her grit, and her determination. Not someone else's name, reputation, or coattails.

Torry regretted pushing away her love for colors and textures and design after her mom died, not able to deal with how the memories of hours immersed in them would overwhelm her. Ignoring those aspects of her life had been immature and impractical. How could she seriously believe that she'd be able to fulfill her promise to her mom's memory if she dressed like a street urchin? Refused to look at couture? Neglected to speak to her family? Rebuffed her grandmother's offers? She'd been delusional and immature.

Her mother would be so disappointed in her. When Torry was a child, she used to play dress up with the grand gowns and fancy clothes her mother owned. Before she'd met Torry's father, an eclectic group of artists, politicians, and writers had gathered monthly at her mother's estate, passing time trading ideas, laughing, and connecting. After she'd met and married Robert Hansen, her mother had slowly pulled away from those wild, stimulating, Bohemian days to become what his parents had deemed to be a respectable wife.

As Torry grew older, her mother had shared her love for fashion with Torry by teaching her how to combine colors, fabrics, and styles to create the perfect look. Three years and three months after her mother's untimely death, Torry still struggled to come to terms with the loss. Torry could not look at couture without remembering her. Yet, she'd finally gotten to the point where she could be surrounded by it every day.

Torry realized after she made the move to New York that her juvenile rebellion against anything reminding her of her mother, and that avoiding fashion, would not bring her mother back. She found, however, that making up her mind to infiltrate the fashion industry wasn't enough. Her independent streak and willpower were not enough. She needed to dress the part. She needed to embrace her past to make a future. Too bad she hadn't woken up a bit sooner. It was very possible that she might have found a position that would provide better access to fashion than this little shop, particularly if she'd allowed her grandmother to help. Nana had no idea where she worked. It was tempting to tell her, but since Torry had begun this journey without any help, she was determined to continue by herself.

It didn't matter now. Once Torry landed the job at the boutique, she settled into the position easily. She found herself able to connect with the boutique's eclectic clientele without much difficulty. The pay wasn't great, as she was a commissioned sales employee with a meager salary base, but Torry was able to sell enough pieces each month to cover her bills. It helped that Harold was so good about giving her as many hours as she needed to meet her financial goals. Best yet, she got a discount off any clothes she chose to purchase from the boutique.

Over the last few months, Harold granted Torry more responsibilities, sending her to designer showrooms to pick up clothes, allowing her to open or close the shop, and even talking to her more about the pieces in the store. As she had before her mother's untimely death, Torry found that every aspect of fashion fascinated her.

Shaking her head to rid herself of such useless thoughts, Torry returned her attention to her plans for the windows. If this was the only platform open to her, she was determined to affect passersby through the visual expression of her voice with a little help from literary masters. Excitedly, Torry began to catalog what she would need.

Noticing the time, Torry straightened up some clothes as she made her way to her boss at the registers. "Is it okay if I take my dinner break now, Harold?" Torry shifted and leaned against the counter. No one was in the store, and it was nearly seven. Eyeing Harold as he finished placing some new pieces on hangers, she wondered how he'd gotten into the fashion industry. In his midfifties, lanky with lily-white skin and freckles, he was good at making others feel as if he were an old friend or a good drinking buddy. Maybe it was his Irish accent or the sparkle in his light green eyes. Whatever it was, Torry felt comfortable around him.

"Sure, sure. Go ahead, Torry. It's dead in here, anyway."

With a smile, Torry retrieved her jacket and gave a little wave before walking through the door, pulling her jacket closed as a cool breeze whipped through her. Now that the sun had set, the night was becoming nippy. Looking around, Torry stood at the corner, waiting to cross. She knew she couldn't go wrong with a slice of pizza from Giovanni's, and it was in her price range. As the light changed, she stepped off, keeping pace with several strangers so as to avoid dirty looks for being too slow. She remembered with a smile how she had learned while attending college in Boston how to navigate the crowds, banishing any fears of a large city's hustle and bustle in favor of exploring whenever she could.

"I bet since you're from that little tourist-trap town in Rhode Island you probably have no idea how to cross city streets," Melanie said.

Torry made a face at her friend. "I know how to cross a street, Mel."

"Not these streets. As soon as the walk light goes on, you have to get across the street quickly, and it's better to be in the middle of the group instead of on the edge. Cars love to pick off the stragglers."

Noticing how many people were gathering on the sidewalk, waiting for the light to turn, Torry became a bit nervous. "Cars will really hit people if they don't cross the street fast enough?"

Melanie giggled. "Probably not on purpose. I mean, that would be messy, and the driver wouldn't want to waste time waiting for the police or washing the person's blood off the front bumper or whatever."

Catching the glint in Mel's eyes, Torry shook her head. "You're pulling my leg."

"Yeah, but not really. Come on," she said loudly, pulling on Torry's arm as the crowd surged forward to cross the street.

Giovanni's was crowded, but she spotted some unoccupied stools. Grinning at Johnny, she placed her order and sat down at the front. People watching was one of her favorite pastimes. Gazing through the large window, she took special notice of what people wore. For the most part, she saw business attire as people made their way home from a full day's work. Many wore matching outerwear—jackets that provided limited warmth. It

was that time of year when no one wanted to wear heavy coats
just yet.

"Here's your slice of pie, Torry," Johnny said, as he placed a
large, gooey piece of goodness masquerading as a slice of pizza in
front of her.

Twisting on the barstool, she caught his eye. "Thanks!"

"So, when're we goin' out?" Johnny asked with a smirk.

She chuckled. "You know I have a boyfriend."

"You should dump that thug. I'll treat you like a queen. Make
sure you know just how beautiful you are." Johnny placed his
hand to his chest over his heart. One of his coworkers snapped at
him with the end of a towel.

"Johnny, give it a rest. She ain't gonna give you the time of day.
She's high class."

Torry smiled widely, even as she dipped her head demurely,
feeling her cheeks flush with the embarrassment she always
experienced when people brought attention to her looks. It
happened often enough for her to know that she was pretty. Even
though she didn't have much time, she still tried to jog each
morning. She wasn't fanatical about it, but she felt better after
exercising. Not wanting to hurt his feelings, Torry teased, "Johnny,
you're such a flirt. Thanks for the ego boost." With one last smile,
she turned back to her pizza and dug in.

She loved this place. It was a hole in the wall with a friendly
atmosphere and large slices of pizza. The garlic knots were to die
for, but she tried not to eat those too often. It was bad enough
that she indulged in pizza, not to mention the hotdogs she often
purchased from the pushcart vendors.

Torry could hear the television blaring the ballgame behind
her. Cheers erupted from the present New York Yankees' fans
directly after the telltale sounds of a homerun. Several people
were sprawled around tables, heckling the other team and rooting
for their own. Torry had attended several games at Fenway Park
while in Boston, a closely kept secret since she'd moved here. She
had no real love for a particular baseball team—Boston, New
York, or any other. Nevertheless, she'd enjoyed sitting in the
bleachers with her friends. She hadn't had the opportunity to
attend a game here, but she wanted to.

Refocusing on the people walking past the pizzeria, Torry
wondered where she was going. Sure, she had a job and a
boyfriend, but it felt like so much more was on the horizon. It

scared her a bit, this feeling of anticipation. She felt like she was standing at the beginning of the next chapter of her life, and she had no idea what to expect. Perhaps it was her excitement of dressing the windows, doing something that made her heart sing. With a smile on her face, Torry finished up her meal, waved to Johnny, and strolled toward the boutique, ideas parading across her inner eye.

The bright lights of the surrounding stores and the various conversations swirling around her comforted Torry as she made her way back to the boutique. Such vibrancy was created through so many people and so many places. Nothing like her upbringing. Perhaps this was just another way in which she was like her mother who had thrived on interactions, on learning new ideas, and experiencing new adventures. Every once in a while, Torry had found her mom with a faraway look in her eyes and a small smile gracing her features. When Torry had ventured to ask what she was thinking about, her mom would relate to her some fascinating memory from her days before marrying Torry's dad.

As Torry grew older, she often wondered why her mom had married her father. He was so steady and unassuming. *Boring.* Torry cringed, feeling guilty for thinking about her father that way. Her mom had told her that he was just what she needed, that everyone had to grow up at some point, and those parties, although fun and exciting, were not conducive to starting a family. But that faraway look in her eyes had told another story. Feeling her purse vibrate, Torry stepped to the side of the boutique and retrieved the phone. With a sigh, she answered. "Hi, Brandon."

"Where are you?"

"I'm decorating the windows tonight. Remember I told you?" Torry bit back her frustration. She knew he hadn't been listening to her. She'd been so excited, and he'd shown no interest in her plans. In her.

"Wha...oh, yeah. Right. So, how long are you going to be?"

Torry could hear rustling in the background, and she wondered what he was planning. "I'll be here most of the night, probably. I can call you later, once I have a better idea. I can't start dressing the windows until after the boutique closes." She closed her eyes tightly, knowing that if he hadn't listened to her during the various times she'd excitedly talked about tonight, he was going to flip out any moment now.

"Are you fucking kidding me? What happened to going out for drinks with Tommy and everyone?" Brandon exclaimed. "Jesus! This is ridiculous."

"Brandon, I'm…I'm sorry. Go without me. Have fun. I'm off tomorrow," Torry said apologetically.

"Yeah? Well, I'm not, so what good is that?" he answered petulantly.

"Sweetie, please don't be upset." Torry leaned against the side of a building, biting her lower lip as she waited for him to say something.

"You know they'll be asking about you. What am I supposed to say? Oh, my girlfriend had to work. Again. How do you think that makes me look, huh?"

"But we can see each other tomorrow night, share some quality time," Torry said, hinting that they could indulge in some carnal activities. With their conflicting schedules, their sex life had suffered greatly. Guiltily, Torry admitted to herself that she hadn't really missed it. Not that Brandon was a horrible lover. Although he never really made sure she was ready for lovemaking or satisfied afterward, she knew how to finish the job, so to speak. She imagined she wasn't the only woman who knew how to touch herself better than her boyfriend did.

"Yeah. Whatever. It's just, I wanted to, never mind. See you later then."

"Um, okay. You know, you could come by later. I'll probably need a break at some point, never mind coffee," Torry said softly.

"Really?" Brandon said mockingly. "Now I'm supposed to be your delivery boy while you're oh so busy?"

"No! Forget it. That's not what I meant. It was just an opportunity to see you." Torry sighed. Nothing was ever easy with him. Not for the last few months, anyway. She longed for those carefree days they'd shared at the beginning of their relationship. "It was stupid. Sorry, hon. Go have fun. I'll…I'll talk to you later."

"Right. Bye."

"Bye." Torry stared at her phone for a moment before slipping it into her purse. Their conversation was nothing new. He complained, and she capitulated. The thing was, she shouldn't have to apologize all the time. She shouldn't have to feel bad about her drive to succeed, her interest in being better at her job. And, okay, so this isn't what she'd planned to do when she first came here. That didn't mean this was a waste of time. Shaking off the conversation, Torry looked through the windows, into the boutique. Ideas coalesced as her eyes roamed over the clothes. She smiled. No, this wasn't a waste of her time at all. This was where she wanted to be.

Chapter Four

PURSING HER LIPS, EVELYN focused on the view outside her town car as her driver weaved through traffic. It was the end of September, and the air was sharp with the taste of red leaves and warm apple cider. The girls had requested that they walk in Central Park this weekend to see the distinctive colored foliage—so bright as it died—nature's last wave given in farewell. A last ditch effort to be noticed before falling to the ground and becoming trampled by the multitude of people strolling about without noticing the transition of life. Like the seasons of fashion, so nature changed her clothes—beautiful, ephemeral, dead.

Perhaps relationships were not meant to last. Perhaps, like the seasons, they grew, matured, and withered. Perhaps she should just accept the fact that she could not navigate a successful relationship, if only because things changed, life changed, and, yes, even she changed, provided it was her idea and not due to some ridiculous demand. Change was the one constant in life, was it not?

Ever since her divorce, she had buried herself in her work. It was always faithful to her. It understood her. It fulfilled her. It submitted to her wishes. She controlled the changes in the fashion world. She guided the industry through each season. She chose what colors to emphasize, which designs to showcase. She knew every upcoming designer, every shift in the winds of design, every new idea created by innovative artists. Anything happening within the realm of fashion she was privy to as she sat on her throne, regally dictating to the masses what to embrace. As demanding as her work was, she thrived on the challenge.

"Andrew, stop the car." Staring through her window, Evelyn searched for the storefront that had caught her eye and pulled her away from her thoughts. "Wait here," she directed before exiting the vehicle, turning to her right, and walking north. There.

Evelyn stood to the side, mesmerized as people stopped to peer at the display of a small resale shop. Lost Treasures was a clothing store with two display windows. Evelyn had never paid much attention to it. She had never had a reason. Standing on the sidewalk, though, she swallowed her astonishment while noting the mass of people milling around or standing near the window displays, much as she was.

In front of her were two scenes directly out of *The Hunchback of Notre Dame*. One window featured La Esmeralda dancing as

Quasimodo bowed, watching. The hunchback wore a luxurious fox-mink long coat, deerskin pants, and dark leather boots. His misshapen shoulders were parallel with the gypsy's outstretched hands, his head tilted upward in supplication. Evelyn nearly smiled, recognizing the pose, the obvious deference the outcast presented to the free-spirited, young lady. The earthy colors and fabrics on the male character contrasted well with the bright, bold colors hung on La Esmeralda.

Her clothing draped loosely in cascading waves of vibrant purples and fiery oranges. The Udolfo silk tunic contrasted beautifully with the maxi skirt as it lay splayed across her lower body, while one leg was frozen in the air, bent at the knee. The head of hair on the mannequin was held back by a coral-encrusted band, and a necklace of long, dark-colored, chunky stone strands hung against the fitted bodice. Vintage, knee-high boots with wedge heels completed the Bohemian outfit. Lanterns, softly lit, cast shadows that emphasized La Esmeralda's splendor and Quasimodo's repulsiveness. And yet, Evelyn felt her heart stir with sympathy for the ill-fated hunchback. A charcoal drawing of a magnificent cathedral hung behind them, cluing in those less read to the context for the displays. Of course, Evelyn couldn't help but think that the hunchbacked man's physical resemblance to the misunderstood character would clarify the classic story well enough.

The second window boasted Archdeacon Claude Frollo arrogantly standing with a hand clutching one of the double-breasted lapels of his black, Armani pinstriped suit. He stood confidently with his head tilted slightly downward, as if he were deigning to look at La Esmeralda. His other hand was extended in a sweeping motion as the gypsy looked at him like a caged animal. A black silk, button-down shirt worn underneath his suit, a satin black cape with red lining over the suit, and black square military boots completed Frollo's elegant but menacing look. Although appearing suave and powerful, one could easily see he was an evil bully.

His superior stance was offset by the meek, attractive La Esmeralda. Her hair hung freely this time, in exquisite ringlets, and she wore a fitted, floor-length leather coat with fur lining, another long skirt, and soft, ankle-high, fawn-colored boots. The colors of her clothing reflected nature through deep greens and chestnut browns. On her wrist, an emerald bracelet hung daintily, as she held up her Donna Karan antiqued-leather maxi skirt, appearing ready to flee.

Evelyn cocked her head, as her eyes jumped over the displays. Every piece of clothing, every accessory helped tell the story. And every piece was couture. She did not try to stop a small smile from crossing her face. Whoever had designed these window displays had vision. Something so few people in the industry seemed to possess nowadays.

Breathing in deeply, Evelyn nodded and strode back to the town car. Once inside the comfortable interior, she retrieved her phone and dialed the office. "Ira, I want a write-up about the window displays at Lost Treasures to run in the next issue under Hot Spots. Make it happen." With a sigh, Evelyn closed her eyes as the display replayed through her mind. Good work deserved to be rewarded. "Intriguing," she murmured. She would keep an eye on this boutique. She hoped it wasn't just a fluke, that the designs would continue to astound and delight. Only time would tell.

As the car slowed down, Evelyn readied herself to exit. Andrew opened the door with practiced ease and, once she stepped out of the car wished him a good evening. Taking a deep breath, she swiftly entered her home, listening for any signs of where her children were. At least she didn't have to worry about a brooding husband. After two years of protracted negotiations, she was freed from an emotionally draining relationship. During that time, she had chosen to remain alone, not caring to date or cater to another man's ego. Evelyn hung her coat in the closet and wandered toward the heavenly smells in the kitchen. She knew her dinner was being kept warm for her, but before she ate, she wanted to check in with her darling girls. Climbing the back stairs to the third floor, she knocked on the slightly open door.

"Come in!"

Smiling, Evelyn noted how Jennifer was sprawled out on her bed with schoolbooks and notebooks surrounding her, while Julie sat at the desk, tapping away at her laptop. "Hello, girls," she greeted them, leaning against the doorjamb.

"Hi, Mom." Jennifer looked up from her book, smiling brightly.

"Hi, Mom," Julie said a moment later, after she finished typing out her thought.

"I'm sorry I didn't make it to dinner, darlings," she said, trying not to wince.

"Don't sweat it, Mom. We know you have a lot going on," Jennifer said.

With an explosive sigh, Evelyn sat on the edge of the bed. Twirling her rings restlessly, Evelyn had no idea what to even say. She hated leaving her girls alone while she worked, but she couldn't shirk her duties at the magazine. It reminded her of the guilt she'd felt while married to Bruce. Of all the nights she had disappointed him. The nights that had led to their divorce.

He blamed her, of course. Said she'd brought out the worst in him. As if he hadn't had a choice. No one had twisted his arm to marry her. He had proposed. Claimed he loved her and her girls, that they would be great together. He knew, or she thought he had known, who she was. But no, it had been so much easier to blame her, to use the monikers against her that the press had coined so many years ago. And although such labels might be accurate in the business world, they were misnomers in her private life. She had cared. She had wanted the marriage to work. She had wanted stability and companionship. Most of all, she had wanted acceptance and understanding. Dual hugs surrounded her, pulling her from her thoughts.

"Don't be sad, Mom. We love you," Julie said, squeezing her.

"Yeah. You have us." Jennifer laid her head on Evelyn's shoulder.

"And I am the most fortunate mother in the world," Evelyn replied, her voice light as she slid her arms around her girls, squeezing them back. "I'm going to eat downstairs. Are you nearly done with your homework?"

"Yes," they both answered eagerly.

With a small chuckle, Evelyn said, "Well then, perhaps we can watch that movie you've been begging to see." She exited the room, their excited agreement following her. She felt better already. She loved them so much. It amazed her how intelligent and affectionate they were. She often worried that her fame would negatively affect them, not to mention her poor taste in companions and her absence due to her work demands, but they became more mature, beautiful, and thoughtful as they grew older. It was a minor miracle.

Removing her food from the oven and placing it on the kitchen island, she poured some water for herself and sat on a bar stool. Not keen on reading anything for the moment, she allowed her mind to wander. Thoughts crowded in, all raising their hands, demanding her notice. Tonight she would give her mind a rest and watch a movie with her daughters. Tomorrow she would spend the day with them, as promised. The park, the zoo, and lunch near Central Park, not necessarily in that order. Although every moment was strictly scheduled at work, Evelyn refused to rush her time with the girls.

They could take Sandy, their boxer, with them to the park in the morning. Sandy loved to play with Jennifer and Julie. She was well-behaved and responsive to Evelyn's commands. The girls often played soccer with Sandy, who, in Evelyn's opinion, was a better goalie than several so-called professional soccer players who could learn a thing or two. Evelyn sniffed. They could eat at that place which allowed dogs on the patio. The weather would be warm enough. Andrew could take Sandy home after dropping them at the zoo. Tapping her lower lip with her finger, she decided to text her assistant to secure lunch reservations. And VIP tours for the zoo. And dinner at that new hot spot the girls kept mentioning.

Plans made, her mind switched to another pleasant topic: the window displays at Lost Treasures. It had surprised her, seeing the mass of people standing near the store, listening to their murmurings, their positive comments, their exclamations as they recognized the scenes from literature. She had no doubt that her girls would love the displays. She would make sure they drove by tomorrow, at some point, so they could see the window designs. She hoped that the little resale shop would present another impressive window display in the future. No doubt, with the dozens of potential clients that had entered the store, the owners would seek to keep the momentum going. She felt her lips curl upward at the thought of the publicity they would receive through *Trending*. They had earned it. Hopefully, they would not make her regret her magnanimous gesture.

***

Evelyn made a habit of viewing the window displays at Lost Treasures. Depending on her schedule and mood, she would direct Andrew to pass the boutique. If it was still open, she would note the impressive crowds that inevitably would pause to admire them and, more often than not, enter the shop. The intelligence, creativity, and heart reflected through the designs eased Evelyn's stress level.

Shortly after Evelyn had directed Ira to add a write-up about the boutique in the next issue, they had traveled to Paris for the all-important fashion week. Evelyn had been forced to face the dismal process of pushing out the current CEO of Magellan-Weeks Publications. What a tiresome task.

During that hectic, life-changing week, Evelyn had found her mind returning to the window displays repeatedly. They proved to be a balm on her frayed nerves. If this month's displays were also satisfactory, she had decided she would take steps to feature the small boutique in the January issue, including the mysterious creator of the designs.

Ira had determined that the designer and dresser of the windows were the same person. This was not a surprise given the size and stature of the boutique. Although the owners were extremely forthcoming with their information, it was clear they did not know much about this person. Evelyn's eyes flicked down toward a piece of paper with Ira's handwriting—this Torry Hansen, other than that the employee had started as a salesclerk and recently requested the chance to design and dress the windows.

Evelyn swept her eyes over her paperwork before deciding to take a drive. "Heather," she called in a soft voice. As soon as she arrived, Evelyn said, "I'll be leaving in five minutes. Push back my meeting with accounting to three, and please clean this up for me." Evelyn waved vaguely at her desk where the remains of her lunch sat to one side. Heather nodded as she picked up the plate and cup. Soon after Heather left the room, Evelyn could hear her calling Andrew. She smirked.

Nowadays, Heather was very efficient. Before Paris Fashion Week, Heather had seemed distracted, often making silly mistakes or not completing tasks in a timely manner. Evelyn had told her to stay in New York rather than accompany her to the most important fashion shows of the year. Losing her ability to attend Paris Fashion Week had crushed Heather, but really, how could she have expected to go while not accomplishing what Evelyn needed? Instead, she had manned the desks at the empty *Trending* office, communicating with the junior assistant and department heads each day to help as much as she was able. In some moment of selflessness, the junior assistant had brought back some couture for Heather. Since their return, Evelyn's assistants had worked seamlessly together, and Heather always gave her focused best. If she continued to perform well, Evelyn would have to think of an appropriate reward. Her senior assistant's time to move on was fast approaching.

Of course, Evelyn also needed to find a way to reward Ira for his loyalty. They had risen through the ranks together, and he was her right-hand man. Ira Linstein was the type of person who put everyone's happiness ahead of his own. He had given up several opportunities to become the editor in chief of his own magazine simply because she needed him as her art director. She knew the board wanted to create a magazine geared toward the male readership. She knew he would be the perfect person to create the magazine and lead it in the right direction. The position would excite him, challenge him, and fulfill him, much as she used to feel while at work each day. Evelyn shook her head, exasperated. What was the matter with her? *Trending* still excited her, challenged her. Fulfilled her, though? Not quite. Not anymore. Not like it used to. And it didn't matter what she told herself. She was restless.

Sashaying through the outer office, Evelyn accepted her purse and coat without pausing, making her way out of the building quickly. Andrew stood next to the town car, hand on the handle of the open door and a polite expression on his face, as Evelyn slid in. "Take me to Lost Treasures."

Evelyn knew the boutique would be changing its display any day now. She felt a ripple of anticipation roll through her. With all the difficulties she had faced over the last few months, this was her guilty pleasure, the bright light cutting through an otherwise inky reality.

The car stopped in front of the shop, and Evelyn looked on in shock. A large crowd milled around, many eventually making their way inside the store. Evelyn gazed at the displays, experiencing disquiet and appreciation. The displays were as compelling as the previous month's designs. "Stay here," she ordered before climbing out.

Slowly, Evelyn approached the windows, cocking her head in thought. In the left window, a tortured man in a black velvet cocktail jacket—Varvatos, she identified with approval—was seated at a table where a burned-out candle, feather quill in a dented inkpot, and letters were chaotically strewn. Old tomes were stacked, one opened at his left elbow. A hand propped up his chin, as he glared at an excellent depiction of a closed door over which a raven perched on a bust of Pallas. Words on the handwritten missives jumped out at her—raven, midnight dreary, Lenore, and nevermore. This display was filled with shadows, allowing only enough illumination to be able to see the display's key parts.

In the second window, a woman wore an ivory silk, ruffled evening dress from the Sean Collection, with a fitted bodice and detailed beading throughout. She stood in a well-lit space, opposite the man, and looked past him. A partially hidden fan caused the bottom part of her dress to float upon the continuous stream of air. On the side of the display closest to the other display window hung a colored-pencil drawing of an open window and trees. Behind the woman, parts of the poem "The Raven" by Edgar Allan Poe were displayed for all to read.

Evelyn marveled at the textures, colors, and styles pieced together to evoke a moody, dark display. For all the sorrow and heartache reflected, the display was beautiful and evocative. It did not escape her attention how well this display fed into Halloween. Nor was she disappointed to note that, once again, all the clothes and accessories were created by well-known designers.

After running her eyes over the display for a few more minutes, Evelyn allowed a small smile to reach her lips. These designs reflected heartache and dashed dreams. She wondered whether that held true for the person who had turned out such a wonderful presentation. It was time to find out who had such vision. She would have Ira approach the boutique for a spread, including an interview with the window display designer.

Turning away, Evelyn looked around at the various people staring at the windows. A young woman wearing a knit cap, navy wool pea coat, and jeans stood off to the side and gazed at her. She seemed familiar. Thick chestnut locks fell from under the hat, while cheeks flushed a becoming red from the brisk temperature emphasized sparkling emerald eyes. Evelyn gazed at the woman for several moments, unable to turn away. The distant dinging of the boutique door as it opened and closed invaded her thoughts, and broke the spell. Firming her lips, Evelyn swept her eyes over the woman once more before returning to the car.

The storeowners might not possess much information regarding the window display designer, but that didn't matter. Evelyn would find out the truth. Soon she would know all about this mysterious designer, and she would reward such ingenuity. She had nearly forgotten what it felt like to be surprised. She found that, for once, she didn't mind not being in control.

Chapter Five

THE CROWD STANDING IN front of Lost Treasures faded out of her mind as Torry leaned against the brick wall of a neighboring building, stunned. Evelyn Allbright had just stared at her. Straight in her eyes. She felt as if the fashion icon had reached into her chest and squeezed her heart. Hard. Certainly her body believed it, judging by how fast her heart was beating. Rubbing the area absentmindedly, Torry stared after the Mercedes as it drove away. Shaking her head, she took a deep breath and exhaled, and then again. She had never experienced such a connection before. It was a little scary.

She had seen the blonde-haired beauty exit her town car and stand off to the side, gazing at her window displays, just as she had last month. Evelyn Allbright, the woman who'd attended her mom's funeral with Nana. Not that she'd known who she was at the time. Oh, sure, Nana had spoken of her, but Torry had been too upset at the funeral to connect the dots. Last month when the unforgettable woman had appeared in front of the window display, Torry had pulled on the bill of her baseball cap to hide her eyes, tugging at the collar of her Eddie Bauer coat as she'd stepped over to a nearby stoop. Not that Evelyn had noticed her. Even if she had, she wouldn't have remembered her. Torry had been on her way to pick up her paycheck so she could shop for groceries. Seeing the fashion editor glide toward the boutique had thrown her for a loop. She'd figured it was a one-time thing, as had been the entirely unanticipated shout-out in *Trending*. The woman was unpredictable. Not that Torry was complaining. With the increased visibility, sales had soared, she had sold more pieces, and the owners had been ecstatic.

When Torry had entered the store last month, the place was filled with people perusing the racks. She'd never seen it so crowded. Harold quickly followed her into the back room.

"There you are," Harold said jovially, as he swept into the small office. He stopped in front of Torry and smiled broadly. "I wish I had taken you up on your offer to design the window displays sooner, Torry. I'm sure you've noticed the influx of people. We've sold more today than in the last month."

"Really? That's wonderful, Harold! I am so glad," Torry exclaimed.

"Yup. So that responsibility is officially yours. And if business continues like this, not only will I be able to place some money aside for a props budget, but also an increase in your salary. I know you're just scraping by, and we haven't been able to give you a raise yet because, well, you don't need me to tell you." Harold clapped a hand on her shoulder. "Anyway, let's give it another month, and if the money's there, you'll get a proper bump in your pay to go with your added responsibilities."

"Thank you! I promise I'll do my best."

"I know, Torry. We're lucky to have you." Harold looked toward the door. "I'd better get back out there. Enjoy your day off. See you tomorrow."

"Okay. See you later," Torry said, as she watched him swagger through the door. As soon as the door closed, Torry spun around, exhilarated and pumping her fist in the air. "Woohoo!"

She felt that elation return to her as she watched people mill about in front of her newest display. If people continued to purchase clothes and accessories from the boutique, Torry had the potential of earning a great commission. With the salary boost, maybe she'd even be able to start saving money for the leaner months. Although the thought of cutting back her hours flitted through her mind, she quickly dismissed it. She'd rather work the same long hours and earn as much money as possible.

Torry smiled happily. Her smile broadened as she remembered seeing the small curl of lips appearing on Evelyn's face before she nodded and strode off. Still rooted to the spot, Torry blinked rapidly. She couldn't believe how one small smile had transformed the editor's regal bearing. For that moment, the intimidating businesswoman had seemed softer, more approachable, warmer. Undeniably attractive.

Torry shook herself much like a wet dog would. This was Evelyn Allbright, the woman who dismissed people's aspirations without a second thought. She'd do well to take her example by not wasting another moment thinking about her. If only she could take her own advice.

When Torry moved to New York, Nana had offered to speak to Evelyn about any job openings. Torry had refused. Although Nana reminded her that the woman had attended the funeral with her, all Torry could call forth were vague memories. She had been too distraught to really register the strong presence of the editor in chief. Today, no longer lost in her emotions, Torry had nothing to distract her from the older woman's alluring aura of power and sensuality. She took Torry's breath away. That unbuttoned French vanilla trench coat she wore had emphasized her thin waistline, as had the red belt visible underneath. A fitted, black pantsuit with an ivory shirt, unbuttoned enough to show enticing cleavage, four-inch black Louboutins with their signature red soles, and a striking statement necklace completed the ensemble. It was a good thing Evelyn hadn't recognized her. Torry knew she would have made a fool of herself.

Feeling more in control, Torry refocused on the conversations swirling around her. People stood nearby, reading parts of the poem aloud and reminiscing about when they had first read it, usually in school. Torry felt exhilarated. People really liked her work, even her pencil drawings—a necessity since she hadn't had access to all the props she'd needed. Shortly after she had moved to New York, she'd attended an open reading for Poe's most popular poems. Hearing them recited aloud had impressed upon Torry just how gifted and tortured that man had been. Such brilliance, his ability to manipulate words to reflect moods and emotions was astounding. This poem, in particular, strongly affected Torry—his despair, his melancholy, his anger, his grief. She understood the depth of these emotions, and could taste them within his words. She had felt, and at times still experienced, such emotions when thinking about the loss of her mother. And now, to a much lesser degree, she was experiencing such emotions again through her latest loss.

If only the onlookers knew the impetus for this display. Brandon had up and left her without notice, taking a job in Chicago. Although he had hinted that they might be able to try a long-distance relationship, Torry didn't see how that could work when living in the same city hadn't. He hadn't been willing to accept her long hours or her drive to do the best job she could at the small boutique. It didn't make sense. He knew what she was like, what her goals were.

When she was the editor in chief for *The Daily Free Press*, Boston University's student-run newspaper, she had easily worked thirty hours per week, and that had been in addition to a full-time course load. He knew all about that. She'd shown him the articles, and he'd claimed to be impressed. Not so much anymore. He had stopped listening, and she wasn't one to keep arguing.

That's what had drawn her to writing for the FreeP. She could prepare herself, think about how she felt and what she wanted to express. When it came to verbal sparring, however, she was an amateur trying to fight in a professional match. She'd gamely dodge and weave, trying to get her points across, but then an uppercut would land, making her too dizzy to mount a good offense. Soon, she'd find herself on her knees, shaking her head in dismay and wondering how she'd lost yet another fight. Writing had proved to be a great outlet.

What truly bothered her was that she was often shut down by others long before she could express her feelings. How she felt and what she thought, were important. She was important. Yet, she surrounded herself with people who felt that their feelings, wants, and desires were more important. Maybe his leaving was a good idea. They'd gotten to the point where he hadn't cared about what she wanted, particularly if it impinged upon his own dreams. Torry still resented his harsh words for her work ethic and the time she continued to dedicate to the boutique.

"Why do you keep working at that pitiful little Saks-wanna-be shop, Torry? Do you really believe that you'll miraculously find a way into the fashion industry?"

That hurt. "Brandon, how can you say that? I've only been working there a little over a year. It takes time to make connections, to be given more responsibility. But I can do it."

"Come on! That place is so far off the map that you'll never get anywhere. You need to work somewhere you can use all these talents you supposedly have."

"What? You...you've seen my work—"

"Oh, you mean your silly hunchback and some pictures? People don't care about the classics."

Feeling the anger well up as he ridiculed her efforts, she snapped. "Well, perhaps if you weren't such an ignorant ass and actually knew some classic literature, you'd think differently!" Seeing the shock on his face from her outburst, Torry began to backpedal. "I mean—"

"Don't bother!" He took his coat and slammed the door on his way out of her apartment. That was the last time she'd seen him.

She felt a cruel type of satisfaction remembering his shock when she had voiced such thoughts. The smirk fell off her lips just as quickly, a gust of wind making her shudder and hunch her shoulders forward. She didn't like sinking to that level. However, she was unwilling to fit the mold he had created in his mind.

She would miss having a boyfriend, even if he wasn't a very good one. He'd made her laugh. How sad that after nine months together, that's all she'd miss. They hadn't even had sex in the last couple of months. A true sign of how far apart they had grown. She had not missed his touch or yearned for his kiss. They had become strangers without her noticing.

She had changed, and he had not changed with her. She still wanted to work in a more visible position where she could leave her mark on the fashion industry, of course she did, but she understood it would have to wait while she worked hard to earn a paycheck. She needed to be patient until she created an opportunity. And, well, she had found an opening through dressing windows. She was confident that as long as she did her best, she would eventually be able to work at a more prestigious place, maybe even at a fashion magazine. She had no idea how window dressing would lead to that, but it would.

The poem resonated within Torry. It was a way for her to deal with her conflicting emotions while she became accustomed to life without a boyfriend. She also had to deal with how her relationships with their mutual friends were in transition. They blamed her for the breakup. If not for her work, if not for the opportunity to lose herself in the window designs, Torry suspected she would be pretty damn upset right about now. That's why she preferred to focus on what she could create, not destroy.

She had read recently that Evelyn was twice divorced. With two teenaged girls, Torry couldn't help but sympathize. No matter how dismissive and cruel Evelyn was reputed to be within the industry, Torry understood that how a person behaved at work could be entirely different from one's behavior with family. At any rate, Torry liked to think that the woman wasn't as evil and downright mean as others described her. She had not seemed that way at the funeral. She rubbed the back of her neck. Not that she remembered much.

A happy smile resurfaced as she watched the crowd fluctuate over the next ten minutes. It was a real ego boost, and she desperately needed to feel bolstered. Already ideas for the end of October and the next few months swam through her mind. She would start sketching them out today. Maybe, if sales remained steady, Harold would prove good on his promise by giving her that raise and a small budget for the window displays.

Finally, after her ego was sufficiently inflated and a wide smile refused to leave her face, Torry bounced into the boutique. Her eyes widened when she saw the crowd waiting patiently to be rung up. Disregarding that it was her day off, Torry pulled off her coat and stuck it under the counter as she signed in on a register. She fluffed out her bangs as she congratulated herself for having the foresight to not dress like a street urchin. "I can help you," she said, smiling at the attractive blonde lady waiting impatiently.

Reaching over, Torry took the cream-colored dress, similar to the one Torry had used for Lenore in the window display, and a beautiful, matching Tomas Maier floppy-brim straw hat. "These are beautiful," Torry said reverently, as she looked up at the woman. "Are they for you?"

"What concern is that of yours?" she asked frostily.

"Oh! I'm so sorry," Torry said softly. "I was just thinking that this dress was made for you. And the hat will look lovely with your cheekbones." She carefully folded the dress in tissue paper before placing it in a long rectangular box and the hat in a square hatbox. She finished by placing both parcels in a large bag. After ringing the purchase, Torry looked up shyly.

"Thank you, dear," the woman said, as she handed over her credit card with a small smile.

Hearing the slightly apologetic tone, Torry brightened considerably. Smiling widely, Torry returned the card quickly after glancing at the name and waited as the woman signed the receipt. "I hope you have a wonderful day, Ms. Patterson," she said sincerely when she caught the woman's eyes.

"Yes, and you." She paused a moment, gazing at Torry. "Those window displays are quite impressive. I never would have thought to enter this shop if I hadn't seen them."

"Thank you. I'm so glad you like them. I had a great time creating them," Torry gushed excitedly.

The woman's eyebrows rose dramatically. "You designed the windows?"

"Well, yes. I...," Torry paused, wondering why it was so hard to believe. "Yes."

"Where did you get the pencil drawings? They are quite remarkable."

"Wh...what?" Torry stuttered. Blinking several times, she said, "I drew them." She waved a hand awkwardly. "It's nothing, really. Just something to pull the scenes together."

The woman's eyebrows rose again. "I dare say they are not nothing. Quite far from it. I was out of town when the last display was up, but I heard that the charcoal drawing of the cathedral was brilliant. Did you draw that too?"

Nodding, Torry admitted, "Yes. It wasn't that great, though. I didn't have much time to devote to it, and I had to work from photographs I found on the web."

"I hope you kept it. Your displays are wonderful, and you should be proud of yourself. I'm sure I'll be back." The woman tucked a piece of blonde hair behind her ear and smiled at Torry before turning around to leave. Perplexed, Torry tried to make sense of the exchange but couldn't. The next customer stepped up, dropping several pieces of clothing onto the counter. Shaking her head, Torry smiled and began the process again.

Thirty-five minutes later Torry let out a sigh of relief and leaned against the wall. "Has it been like this all day?" Torry asked, glancing at Grace.

"Pretty much," she answered with a smile. "Your window magic has drawn the crowds here. I'm sure you can imagine just how excited Harold is. If we'd had any idea how talented you are at window displays, we would have had you doing them months ago."

Torry laughed. "Oh, well. I've had fun doing them. Thanks for letting me."

"Torry, you're a lifesaver!" Harold exclaimed, as he approached the register. "Thanks for helping at the register. You can come in late tomorrow."

"But I'm opening," Torry said, confused.

"Right. Well, you can take a longer lunch, then." Harold smiled. "And, as promised, you're getting a raise and a window display budget." Torry clapped her hands together, not sure which excited her more. "Now get out of here before the lull ends and we chain you to the register," he joked.

Torry retrieved her check and was out the door in time to watch another flood of customers enter the shop. Shaking her head in wonder, she practically skipped away. She wanted to deposit her check and buy some groceries. Torry was actually a pretty good cook, and she took great pleasure with trying new recipes. She knew many staples, simple dishes that she had learned from her mother, but she'd fallen into the bad habit of buying takeout lately. Perhaps she would cook a bunch of dishes this weekend and freeze them for the week.

Stepping into the bank, Torry opened the envelope to sign the check for deposit. She stared at it in shock. It was double her last paycheck, and she just knew it would keep increasing with all the exposure the shop was receiving. This would certainly make paying her bills easier. She could even splurge for that ivory Chanel dress she'd been eyeing. It was on clearance with the season change, and she knew it would look great on her. The line moved quickly, enabling her to leave the bank to complete her other errands rather quickly.

Before her last stop to buy food, Torry decided to walk through Central Park. It was a bit out of her way, but the days were becoming cooler, and she wanted to enjoy the sun while she could. She shoved her hands into her coat pockets, and wandered some of the main trails, watching people enjoy the warmth. Several children, finished with the school day, kicked a soccer ball around, laughing and shouting to each other. Torry grinned as she remembered similar days in the park near her childhood home when she had played ball with Katie and their friends for hours before their parents had returned from work. Her grin faded as she did her best not to become too sentimental. She felt loneliness steal over her and sniffled, hardly believing that she was fighting off tears.

She had finally received some recognition for all the long days working at the boutique, and she had no one to celebrate with her. No one who cared or who understood. She had no cheerleader, and she wondered why. She was a nice person, dammit! She always had supported her friends and was the first one to make a big deal when someone succeeded. Why didn't she have that? *I need to make some new friends.* Maybe now that her work was getting noticed, she'd find opportunities to meet people who held similar interests. People who understood her. Maybe she had merely outgrown her now-former friends.

How did people do it? How did they make new friends as adults? It had been so easy to meet people in college. She constantly made friends in her classes and in the dorms and at sports events and rallies and bars. Now she worked all the time. She might meet new people when they came in the boutique, but that was hardly an opportune time to start a discussion to determine whether they might want to be friends. *That will be one hundred and twenty-seven dollars, and do you happen to enjoy jazz clubs?* Torry snorted at her foolish thoughts, as she strolled over to the Bethesda fountain and sat down.

She supposed that Harold and Grace were her friends. They spent a lot of time together at the shop. They chatted, discussed what was happening in the world. They didn't get into specifics about their lives or religion or politics. That was fine with Torry, though. It was casual, amiable, and pleasant. And she was loyal to her friends.

Perhaps once she got into a new rhythm with the window dressing and work hours, she could join something like a club or recreational sport or an art class. She could get some technical training for drawing or painting. As it was now, she was a total hack. Her forehead scrunched as she thought about her strange conversation with Ms. Patterson. Her demeanor had changed when she realized that Torry was the window designer as well as the person who'd drawn the pictures, and Torry wondered why. Her mom used to encourage her, told her that she needed to listen to her heart and soul so she could express herself through her creations. Her best and most loyal supporter, her mom had fostered Torry's dreams, telling her over and over never to betray them for someone else's dreams.

"Stay true to yourself, Torry. Even if you think you want to give up drawing or writing or whatever it is you love, you will eventually resent it. And if someone asks you to do so, or if you believe you need to in order to keep that person close, it will be the worst mistake you can make. If someone cares about you, he'll never ask that of you. He'll never make you feel that you need to give parts of yourself away."

It was a conversation Torry never had forgotten. She had broken up with her boyfriend just before the summer break of her sophomore year in college. She was hurt from the failure of her first major romantic relationship, and her mother had finally gotten Torry to talk about it after weeks of avoidance. They had been seeing each other for over a semester. It was romantic and easy and comfortable. Until he began asking her where she was whenever they weren't together. Until he complained when she chose to work on her writing instead of spending time with him. She tried to compromise by inviting him over to study and by attempting to coordinate some of their meals together, but he equated study time with opportunities to distract her and meal times with opportunities to hang out with his friends. As he pushed for more of her time, Torry wondered when spending time with him had begun to feel like a chore. She contemplated dropping the stage design for the college theater production or writing for the newspaper, but she hadn't felt comfortable giving up so much for someone who refused to change his own schedule at all.

It was during that conversation Torry wondered whether her mother had regretted giving up so much for her dad, for their family. She had never dared ask, and now it was too late. Those words had stayed with her, though, and she understood now.

Since moving to New York, she'd been happiest while creating the window designs. Brandon never cared too much about her drawings. Even when she drew his profile one time, he complained that his frown was totally unrealistic. *All he'd needed to do was look in the mirror to see how accurate it was.*

Torry took solace while listening to the water pour into the bottom of the fountain. It soothed her frayed nerves. She knew it was normal to grieve the end of a relationship, even when that relationship had been practicing the pivotal death scene with as much subtlety as William Shatner quoting Shakespeare. She wished that she had expressed herself better, or found a way to illuminate how his actions had contributed to the end of their relationship. Maybe she'd send him a letter or an e-mail. Something in writing.

How did a woman like Evelyn do it? Did she even have friends? Did they stand by her as she dealt with her divorce? Or did they blame her for the failed relationship? Nana never mentioned anything about it. How were her daughters dealing with it? They were what, fifteen? Sixteen? She'd read somewhere that they were Irish twins. They must have some type of understanding of what had happened, but was that enough for them not to resent living in a broken home? Were they close to their father? Stepfather? *Why do I even care? I don't even know the woman, refused to interview with her, even though Nana kept offering to get me in the door. If only I'd spoken to her after the funeral.*

Torry had seen the woman next to Nana, chatting with others politely. Torry had failed, during that time, to find the right words, to think on her feet. She had barely spoken coherently with her grandmother, and that conversation had consisted of consoling each other. The only reason she'd been able to give a eulogy was due to the hours she'd spent writing it out, trying to make sense of her mom's death.

Well, wouldn't Evelyn be surprised to learn that Torry was working on the fringes of the fashion industry now, hoping to make her mark? Although Torry knew better than to entertain the thought that the fashion maven remembered her, she was, in truth, glad for that. Her mind still shied away from that horrible day, and she preferred that Evelyn appreciated her window designs without remembering that they'd met before. She had learned some hard truths since moving to New York, and she could only move forward, armed with such knowledge.

Two small boys competed to see who could toss a coin into the top tier of the fountain where the statue, Angel of the Waters, stood. Excited shouts abounded as they kept at it with a steady flow of pennies. They had no real shot at even reaching the fountain, but that did not seem to deter them from their fun. Looking around, Torry saw how people milled around, enjoying the day. Some, as she did, watched the boys, smiling at their antics. Torry had loved her childhood, loved playing with her sister and their friends. It was a simpler time, an innocent time. She hadn't a care in the world or any knowledge of the stresses in life. Blinking away the nostalgia, she listened to the boys as they encouraged each other. Finally, they threw their last coins and, laughing, wandered away toward the lake, pointing at the rowboats and gondolas traveling slowly across the water.

Several years ago, Torry and a few friends had visited the city over a long weekend, pooling their funds to share a motel room and standing in line for hours to buy half-off tickets to see The Phantom of the Opera. They indulged in many of the tourist traps, including renting a rowboat in Central Park. Smiling softly, Torry remembered joking and laughing for hours as they acted like total goofballs, enjoying nature and each other. She had allowed those relationships to weaken after her mom's death, and now they blamed her for her breakup with Brandon, making her question whether it was worth the effort to repair those relationships. Right now, all she had was her work.

Just before Halloween, she would change the displays again. She had a great idea in mind. And now that she had a budget, she was certain that she could produce something really eye-catching. Smiling widely, Torry knew that her life had taken a turn for the better, regardless of her lost relationships. Screw Brandon. Screw

her fair-weather friends. And screw Evelyn Allbright too. She
didn't need any of them in her life to be successful. To be happy.
She was doing just fine.

Chapter Six

"HEATHER," EVELYN CALLED JUST loudly enough to be heard. It was early evening, and she had just finished her last videoconference for the day with the editor in chief for their Italian affiliate. Tapping her fingers on her laptop as she glanced at her e-mails, Evelyn heard Heather stop in front of her desk mere moments later. Looking up, Evelyn approved of the maroon Vivienne Westwood dress with the asymmetrical hemline. "Well, it seems your taste has improved, I suppose," Evelyn groused, keeping back the smirk that wanted to make an appearance.

Heather had worked for her long enough that she knew she could trust her. She had certainly proven her loyalty and desire to please during her tenure. For that reason, Evelyn had thrown out comments every so often of which designers would best complement Heather's complexion and build. She was not surprised to see that her assistant had listened.

Evelyn glanced at the closed folder on her desk. Therein Ira had placed information he had gathered about Lost Treasures. Not much. Not much at all. "Lost Treasures should be changing their display any day now. They do it once the shop has closed for the night at ten. I want you to be present when that happens. Starting tonight, you will wait near the boutique to see who the window dresser is. I want to know what Torry Hansen looks like, his approximate age, clothes, how he works, how many are helping him. Do you understand?"

Not appreciating the face full of questions staring at her, Evelyn glowered until Heather nodded compulsively. "Since the mock-up isn't available until around the same time, I will wait for it tonight. You will have Melanie deliver it to my home, starting tomorrow. Do not disappoint me. I'll expect a detailed report the morning after the new display goes up. Leave now." Heather walked away quickly to her desk, and Evelyn nodded her approval.

Thinking of Heather's bewildered expression, Evelyn smirked. She knew she was a demanding boss. She knew she could be unreasonable at times. She knew what other people thought of her. It didn't matter, not as long as she got what she wanted, what she needed to do her job, and to do it better than any other fashion editor. She had honed her ability to see the extraordinary hidden in plain view, and she just knew that the window designer at Lost Treasures was a diamond in the rough. She simply had to know more.

Hearing Heather talking to the junior assistant, Evelyn nodded. One less thing she had to think about. She hired people to be her eyes and ears. Heather had worked hard to gain Evelyn's approval, and she had no doubt that her senior assistant would do exactly what she wanted.

Evelyn couldn't help but feel a thrill shoot through her as she wondered what Torry would create next. Moving to stand next to the bank of windows behind her desk, Evelyn took solace in the bright city lights illuminating the night sky. That silly little shop could be compared to the bright lights—impressive, incandescent, alluring. She wondered whether the window dresser was just as compelling. Didn't artists reflect their souls through their work? She shivered. If so, she could only assume that he was beautiful in every way, complex and enigmatic. So different from anyone she knew.

Sighing, Evelyn admitted, if only to herself, that she did not want to return home to an empty house. Her girls were at a sleepover. No lover waited for her return—although she still had no regrets about divorcing Bruce. Good riddance. The only one waiting for her was Sandy.

Now there was an example of unconditional love and total acceptance. All she wanted was food, some attention, and a good rub behind the ears. And when Evelyn sent her away to her pillow instead of yielding to the boxer's hopeful gaze by rubbing her tummy, she never complained. Instead, she sat with her head on her paws, keeping Evelyn company for hours, while she concentrated on her work. When Evelyn finished late at night, Sandy eagerly padded after her with a happy sonorous bark, ready to stand guard in the hall outside her bedroom. No matter how many times Evelyn ignored Sandy's pleadings for attention, conveyed through nutmeg-colored eyes, her faithful dog always greeted her excitedly. She never held expectations. She never maintained a grudge. She never acted with ulterior motives. She never failed to love.

Returning to her desk, Evelyn focused on the results of the latest photo shoot. After working steadily without any interruptions, she heard Seth from the art department enter the outer office with the latest version of the mock-up. Glancing at her cell phone, she was surprised to note how much time had passed. It was nearing nine, and she decided to go home. At least she could lounge in looser clothing and drink some wine as she reviewed the newest changes for the December edition of *Trending*. Her stomach growled. Food was a good idea too.

Evelyn gathered her belongings, glancing at her laptop before deciding to lock it up instead of taking it with her. She'd be back early tomorrow morning, and it was already late. She would not need it. Striding to the outer office, Evelyn pulled her coat on, as Melanie waited with her purse. She nodded approvingly at her assistant's choice of outerwear for her. Melanie provided her with a warmer coat than the one she had worn this morning, and it still matched her outfit.

"The girls need Halloween outfits. Something to do with that new movie that's all the rage," Evelyn murmured before leaving. She knew the junior assistant would consult with Heather to figure out what she meant, when she needed the costumes, and why her girls wanted to dress up this year. It had been years since they had gone trick-or-treating, after all. This year, though, they were invited to a costume party.

As was her habit at the end of each day, Evelyn directed Andrew to drive north on Avenue of the Americas, west on 47th, and south on Fifth so she could gaze at the small boutique's display. Several people peered at the depiction of "The Raven," their faces reflecting interest. A few customers left the store with bags hanging off their wrists. Evelyn sighed as she leaned back against the leather interior of the town car.

It was so uncommon to find inspiration incarnate. Evelyn became frustrated over her employees' lack of creativity, their inability to tap into that intangible *something* which would stand out. This window designer was obviously inspired. In turn, Evelyn felt inspired just by looking at the displays. She was reminded of why she loved fashion so much—how fashion could tell stories, convey moods, and alter perceptions.

Evelyn rarely became excited by designers nowadays. It made her job all the harder. They took shortcuts, regurgitated old collections, used the same color combinations over and over. Where were the fresh ideas, the innovation, the art? Evidently, they were embodied in a window display designer at a little-known resale shop on Fifth. Evelyn snorted delicately. How ironic.

She never had forgotten her humble beginnings. How once upon a time she had worked as a seamstress, hand-stitching gowns, spending hours meticulously attaching sequins or beads to expensive fabrics to create a certain shimmer or flattering lines.

Countless hours of sore fingers and overtired eyes had yielded an understanding of how to combine fabrics and materials to complement a figure in the best way. She had learned how much a fabric cost from different parts of the world. She had learned how to spot a signature stitch to identify the designer. She had learned how to accentuate a gown, whether it be with jewelry, shoes, or a wrap. Years, it had taken years, of watching and listening and working. Had it taken as long for Torry to master his craft?

No matter. She would approach this artist, this Torry, and find out what inspired him. She might be able to use that knowledge to spur her employees to create from the heart. And perhaps it would reignite the spark in her own.

Wishing Andrew a good evening after he pulled the town car to the curb, Evelyn entered the quiet townhouse. Hearing Sandy's short nails clicking against the hardwood floor, Evelyn placed her purse and the mock-up on a side table before leaning over slightly to pat her. "Who's a good girl?" she crooned, her voice gentle. Sandy held a tug toy in her maw, one she usually brought to the girls when she wanted to play. "Are you missing our girls?" Evelyn scratched behind Sandy's ears as the dog whimpered pitifully. "They'll be back tomorrow, sweetheart."

Removing her outerwear, Evelyn hung it in the closet and made her way to her bedroom, Sandy at her heels. "Time to get changed." Evelyn moaned with pleasure, as she removed her shoes. As fashionable as they were, walking around in five-inch heels took a toll on her aging body. She was glad that she would be receiving a massage treatment tomorrow before the girls returned home. She slipped into a maroon, cashmere pullover and loose cotton pants before sliding her feet into a pair of ballerina slippers. Humming almost silently in pleasure, she thought, *That's much better.*

"Shall we go see what there is to eat?" she asked Sandy as she walked out of her bedroom and descended the back staircase into the kitchen. She found a piece of chicken breast stuffed with spinach and feta cheese. Her personal chef worked with a nutritionist to prepare foods for her and the girls since she didn't have time during the week to cook meals and didn't want her girls eating restaurant food too often. While her dinner warmed, Evelyn took out the makings for a salad and opened a bottle of white wine. Before long, she sat at the kitchen table munching on her food as Sandy settled in a designer doggie bed near the doorway.

Evelyn rifled through the mail as she ate, enjoying the silence even as she missed her girls' presence. She opened an invitation for a showing at a well-known art gallery owned by Hillary Patterson. She'd known Hillary since before becoming *Trending*'s editor in chief. The woman had worked her way up but in the art world, first as a struggling painter, then as an art studio employee, and finally as an owner. She was a true art connoisseur, and she believed in fostering raw talent. Tapping her lower lip with her forefinger as she read the invitation, Evelyn wondered whether Hillary had happened upon Lost Treasures, yet. It might be worth following up.

The art community intersected with the fashion industry quite often, and Evelyn trusted Hillary's expertise implicitly. Opening up her calendar in her phone, she input the date of the showing. Evelyn had found some excellent fashion photographers over the years through such showings. In addition, quite a few pieces of artwork interspersed throughout her home originated from such exhibits. Just as she loved finding and championing upcoming fashion designers, she loved to support newcomers to the art scene, provided of course they had talent.

Finished with her meal, Evelyn rose to clean up the area. Taking her cue that she could leave her bed, Sandy meandered to her bowl and gobbled down her dinner. Evelyn rinsed her plates, loaded the dishwasher, and programmed it to begin the cleaning cycle. After a last wipe down of the kitchen table and counters, Evelyn looked over at Sandy. "All done?" A peppy bark answered her affirmatively, and Evelyn turned off the light before making her way over to the mock-up. She would review it in the den where she could sit before a fire and listen to some jazz.

Humming to herself, Evelyn made sure the front door was secured and the alarm system set before taking to the stairs. Stopping midstep and cocking her head to one side, Evelyn realized quite suddenly that she was in good spirits. She didn't have to think too hard to realize why. Her heart fluttered in her chest as she thought of the window designs. *He's given me hope*, Evelyn mused. *Quite odd considering the subject matter of the displays.* That didn't seem to matter, though. What did was how Evelyn felt lighter, more peaceful. Yet another reason to reward the designer for work well done. With a seldom seen smile on her lips, Evelyn ascended the rest of the steps with a spring in her step. Alluring, indeed.

***

Three days later, Evelyn strode from the elevator and handed over the reviewed mock-up to Heather as she began her litany of directives. She rounded her desk, finishing her list, and eyed her senior assistant speculatively. She looked exhausted. And her nose was red.

With a roll of her eyes Evelyn said, "What did you find out?"

Heather blanched as she straightened her stance. "The window displays were changed last night. A-Achoo-oo!" Heather grabbed a tissue and blew her nose, as Evelyn glanced at the periodicals spread across the desk. She removed her coat, placing it and her purse on a side table before she sat down. "I'm sorry. I must have caught the sniffles from standing in the rain last night."

Evelyn snipped, "Honestly, Heather, did I ask you to spew unnecessary rationalizations for spreading germs all over my office?"

"Sorry. Um, I didn't see a man decorating the windows. Just some young woman in ratty jeans, a college sweatshirt, and a baseball cap." Heather's voice dripped with disgust.

"How long did you observe?" Evelyn demanded. She was sure that Heather either had not remained long enough to see Torry's arrival or had arrived too late after the window dressing began. While her eyes remained fixed on Heather, Evelyn held out her hand to receive her coffee from the junior assistant and took a sip, humming with pleasure as the hot liquid engaged her taste buds.

"All night. I got there an hour before closing. She set up a male mannequin to stare at a picture of an old man in one window and a female running after a man in the other window. She finished around two this morning."

Evelyn glared. "You mean to tell me you watched some woman dress the windows all by herself?"

"Y...yes, Evelyn."

"No one else joined her?"

"No one. I was watching closely to see if anyone else was in the shop, but I saw no one. Also, once she finished, she was the only one to leave the place." Heather shifted nervously while gripping her fingers tightly in front of her.

Turning toward the windows, Evelyn dismissed her assistant with a wave of her hand. "How odd," she mused. Maybe Torry did the designing only and then had an assistant dress the windows. Ira had told her that they were the same person, but Evelyn supposed it was possible that the shop had hired another person to help. Tapping her lips with a finger pensively, Evelyn sighed. She had wanted to learn a bit more about the designer before approaching him directly. Well, the displays would have to do the talking for now.

A small squeak from her junior assistant as she walked toward the exit made Evelyn smirk. She ignored Heather's furious typing and annoying sniffles, not caring that she had a meeting this morning. It was more important to see the new displays. Heather could deal with the schedule. "I shall return in an hour." Evelyn swept out the door without another word.

Evelyn wondered, as she sat quietly in the back seat of the Mercedes, whether she was becoming obsessed with this window designer. She knew nothing about the man, yet she felt drawn to his designs. Just seeing the dressed windows calmed her, transformed her day into a more manageable one. Perhaps this was her way of pushing aside, for a small amount of time, all the mundane, endless disappointments that bogged her down lately—work deadlines, her empty bed, even her daughters' growing independent streaks. To most people, any of those situations would prove life changing, but to Evelyn they were just frivolous details dressed up as large life events. Or so she told herself.

Her life was changing, and, as always, she would weather such events without a crease in her ensemble. She created change. People changed because of her. She told people what materials to wear and how to prevent wrinkles and what was important and when to change. She sniffed.

Wasting no time once the car rolled up to the shop, Evelyn approached the newly designed windows. She exhaled loudly as her eyes widened with surprise. He had done it again. They were fabulous. Captivating and truly breathtaking. It did not escape her that once again Torry had not spent much money on props. It didn't matter. The clothes and accessories were showcased magnificently. Her art department could learn from his ability to work with what he had available.

Not caring about the wind whipping her hair around, Evelyn cocked her head as her eyes, protected from the wind and sun glare by her designer sunglasses, greedily captured every detail of the displays. She recognized the book immediately, *The Picture of Dorian Gray* by Oscar Wilde. The textures—velvet, corduroy, wool—reflected darkness, weightiness, gravitas. An ornate frame surrounded an older man who sneered at a mannequin of a younger man, capturing the feelings of a vain, heartless person perfectly. The window display designer had actually used another mannequin for the older man instead of a picture, an interesting technique. Both men wore expensive lounging clothes: a blood-red colored smoking jacket, caramel-colored silk shirt, and black slacks for the older man and a casual midnight-blue jacket, black silk shirt, and black pants for the younger man. Evelyn hummed with appreciation. The Lucien Pellat-Finet jackets were gorgeous and modern, matching the Ralph Lauren trousers and Forzieri shirts perfectly. One could see that the 'picture' was an older version of the younger man. He seemed sinister and cynical.

The second window showcased an upset young woman running after the same young man. Their couture—she in a modest though stylish Juicy Couture evening dress and he in a fashionable, well-cut Michael Kors suit—hinted at social inequity. He was obviously Dorian. She must be Sibyl, distraught by his rejection. The story would soon take a tragic turn for the young woman. How interesting that this presentation, like the last one, hinted at lost love.

Normally, Evelyn would question the juxtaposition of contemporary clothing with a classic tale, but somehow the window dresser made it work. He had extraordinary vision—an ability to look at life in new and exciting ways.

People milled about, many trying to guess which literary classic these designs reflected. The picture frame gave it away, of course. How could they not recognize Dorian Gray? Didn't anyone pay attention in school anymore? Even her daughters would be able to guess which book these displays represented. In fact, they would be excited to hear that a new display was up. They would make a game of guessing which parts of the book these scenes reflected. A small smile graced Evelyn's lips as she thought of them.

A gust of cold air brought her out of her musings. She gazed at the windows for several more minutes, allowing herself the luxury of studying the design layouts, the colors, the textures, and the message, before entering the boutique. It did not look horrible. Small. Yes. A bit worn. Certainly. Yet, it held a certain charm. A man stood at the register ringing up sales, while an older woman helped some customers at the back of the shop. Several people wandered around, chatting amiably as they looked at the shop's offerings. With a quick glance, Evelyn recognized many of the major labels—Chanel, Yves Saint Laurent, Valentino, Chloé, Lagerfeld. She nodded. Most pieces were last season, although she did spot a few current fashions, probably obtained from their showrooms.

Sweeping her eyes around the store once more, she noticed a young woman entering the shop, her eyes landing on Evelyn. She seemed to freeze in place before surging forward. "Do you need assistance?" she asked, as she removed a knit cap and fluffed her bangs with her fingers.

"Do you work here?" Evelyn asked, studying her closely. *Was this the woman Heather had seen dressing the windows last night?*

"Yes. Well, it's my day off, but I'm glad to help you if you need anything."

"Hmm, I would like to speak to your window designer. Is he available?" Evelyn doubted it was the man at the register. He dressed suitably, but he didn't seem to have the vision needed to create those window designs. She usually was spot-on about people. Her instincts were what had propelled her to the top of the fashion industry. She could look at people and know their capabilities long before they ever imagined them.

"Oh! Well, um, that is, I mean, if you would like to—"

Listening to the woman stumble over her words, Evelyn pressed her lips together. Normally, she would utter some snide remark to mortify the person who dared to waste her time, but she couldn't help but notice how adorable the brunette looked with her wide, emerald eyes, hands twisting together. Her nervousness filled Evelyn with a tenderness she usually felt only for her daughters. Although that wasn't quite what she felt for this stranger, if her accelerated heartbeat and sudden interest in the girl were any indication.

Evelyn found herself on the brink of smiling, as ridiculous as it was. She wanted to placate the young woman, calm her down instead of scare her to tears. It was disconcerting, to say the least. Biting down on her lower lip as she looked up through her lashes at the beautiful creature, Evelyn contemplated how to get what she wanted without verbally eviscerating the woman.

"What did you say your name is?" Evelyn asked smoothly, effectively stopping the woman's steady stream of ultimately unhelpful words.

"Wha...what? My name?"

"Hmm, yes. I—" The unwelcome intrusion of her cell phone ringing interrupted. With a roll of her eyes, she turned away and answered her phone with a terse, "Yes?"

Ira quickly told her about a problem with the shoot in a downtown art gallery that was threatening to push back production. Unacceptable. She could feel a headache forming behind her eyes. Squeezing the bridge of her nose, Evelyn wondered why it was so hard to find competent people.

Visualizing the next few hours, Evelyn huffed. "I'm on my way there now." She disconnected the call and looked at the younger woman who waited patiently. "I will have to return another time." Evelyn stared at the brunette a moment longer. Familiar. She seemed so familiar. Unfortunately, every moment spent loitering equaled thousands of dollars wasted. This would have to wait. "Hmm." Turning on her heel, she left, her mind turning to the latest potential disaster she needed to fix. Squaring her shoulders, Evelyn decided she would not settle for anything less than perfection. If a window designer with a practically nonexistent budget could reach it, so could *Trending*.

As Andrew wound his way through the midmorning traffic, Evelyn called Heather. "I am going to the Chanel shoot. Push back the run-through to five thirty, call Mark to confirm tomorrow's dinner meeting, pick up twenty skirts from Donna Karan, and confirm my fitting for tomorrow at ten." She disconnected the call and closed her eyes to center herself.

Expressive emerald eyes gazed at her earnestly and, with a gasp, Evelyn opened her eyes and blinked several times in quick succession. This would not do. *What is wrong with me?* She wouldn't normally think twice about some random person she'd just met. Yet, that girl seemed familiar. She shook her head. She didn't have time for this. She had a photo shoot to save.

Regardless of how she'd reacted to the pretty girl in the resale shop, she wasn't worth a moment more of her time. At least, that's what she kept telling herself all the way to the art gallery.

By the time she reached the location of the photo shoot, Evelyn was thoroughly disgruntled. Ira sidled up to her, handing her the photo sheets. She could see why he had called her. The lighting was all wrong, the couture was not hanging correctly on the models, and the colors looked horrible together. She contemplated scrapping the entire shoot, but the amount of money that would be wasted stopped her. The board would have a fit, and that would make her job all the harder.

"What do you suggest?" Evelyn asked, knowing that Ira would have thought of a plan.

"Well, Sabrina is standing by to alter any of the dresses if you'd like, or we can switch them out for the Magnifique line so that the colors are more complementary to the models' coloring. Otherwise, we can bring in some other models," Ira said.

Evelyn hummed as she reviewed the pictures. "The lighting is too dark. See the shadows here?" She pointed to a few photos. "Have Olivia move to the back room and set up there with more light. Have this model, this model, and this model," Evelyn said, as she pointed them out in the photographs, "wear the dresses from the Magnifique line. Their coloring will work well with those colors. Sabrina can adjust the fittings as needed."

"I'm on it." Ira hurried away.

With a sigh, Evelyn accepted a steaming cup of coffee from one of Ira's assistants and sat down in a newly vacated chair. And the day had begun so promisingly. Pushing aside any superfluous images of window displays or green-eyed girls, Evelyn hunkered down for a long day of saving what should have been a routine photo shoot.

Chapter Seven

SWIRLS OF BLUES AND golds graced the canvas, as Torry concentrated on creating the wild pool scene from *The Great Gatsby* in which the social elite let loose with debauchery and wild partying. With two weeks before the next change, Torry decided to get a head start. It didn't escape her notice that this classic, much like the other ones she'd showcased, featured unrequited love, broken hearts, and betrayal. She wanted to change that, but she knew she would continue to gravitate toward similar themes if she didn't allow herself time to grieve her own heartache. So, she allowed her emotions to choose the displays.

With the holidays fast approaching, she did feel her spirits reviving. She would travel back to Rhode Island to spend some time with her family. Her dad had sounded rather angry when Torry told him about Brandon's desertion. At first she'd feared he was upset with her, but it had become clear as their conversation continued that his ire was directed toward her ex-boyfriend. He condemned Brandon's unwillingness to stay with Torry while they tried to navigate their relationship. He told her that it was natural for her to grow and change now that she was working every day and just beginning to figure out what she wanted to do with her life. He pointed out how Brandon's actions had signified he still had a lot to learn.

She knew she still had quite a bit to learn too. Being on her own for the first time in her life was scary. She had always been surrounded by family, friends, and love interests. She'd thought that Brandon loved her. He'd said as much. And she'd allowed herself to be swept away with dreams of romance and family. When their relationship fell apart, she felt like a failure.

As she added a lighter blue to the mix, an electric-blue gaze flashed through her memory. If only they hadn't been interrupted by that phone call! What was Evelyn going to say? Of course, Torry supposed that people vied for the fashion maven's attention all the time. Torry could hardly believe that she had entered the store in the first place. This was the third time she had seen Evelyn in front of the window displays, staring at them as if they were the most fascinating presentations she had ever seen. Torry shivered at the intense look in those sharp eyes. She contemplated how it would feel to be the sole focus of such attention for more than a few moments. In a sense, she guessed she was. Well, her work was. That thought thrilled her.

Torry wondered whether she would ever have the opportunity to speak to her again. Evelyn, the woman who ruled the fashion world with her creative insight, was an inspiration. Just being in her line of sight was both exhilarating and terrifying. And, for a moment, Evelyn had stood before her, conversed with her. Perhaps she would come back as she had indicated before she'd left the boutique. Time would tell.

One thing Torry knew for certain was that Evelyn did not remember meeting her at her mom's funeral. Exhaling forcefully, Torry grinned. *Thank God for small favors.* Hearing her cell phone ring, her eyebrows drew down in confusion. She didn't receive many calls nowadays. She'd spoken to her dad and sister earlier, and she and her friends were still on a break, as far as she knew. So, that just left work. Torry saw the name Jaxine Masters flashing on the display, and her eyebrows rose in surprise.

"Hello?"

"Hi, Torry."

Torry swallowed loudly as she leaned back against the couch, unsure of what to say. "Um, hi, Jax." She waited to see what would happen next.

"Are you working tonight?" Torry looked at her drawings and shrugged.

"Not really. What's up?"

Her supposed best friend's voice sounded hesitant, nothing like she had sounded the last time they'd spoken, when Jax had all but accused Torry of driving Brandon away by ignoring him. Torry had felt shocked and hurt. They'd been friends since elementary school, long before love interests became a topic of conversation. She was supposed to have Torry's back no matter what.

"Greg and I are going out for drinks at nine. How about if we pick you up at eight thirty?" Jax asked in a rush.

"Ah, um. Tonight?" Torry stalled. She missed them, of course she missed them, but she didn't know whether she was ready to see them. Would they heap on the guilt and accusations again? If so, she didn't want to hear it anymore. Brandon was long gone. He hadn't contacted her once. At this point, she just wanted to get on with life, one without Brandon in it. "Does Greg know you're inviting me?" Torry had met Greg at college, in their sophomore American history class, and she'd loved his lighthearted, easygoing attitude.

"Torry, we miss you," Jax said in a soft voice. "Please?"

Well, that cinched it. "Okay. Sure. How fancy are we talking here? I'm just a lowly shop girl," Torry joked, relieved to hear Jax's chuckle.

"Just to Dempsey's, and the first round's on us. See you in a few."

"Okay. See you soon." Torry looked at her cell phone with a silly grin stretched across her face. Things were looking up. It was true that Jax had said some harsh words to her, but she wouldn't have called if she hadn't decided to make up and put it behind them. A few weeks ago, Torry might have told her to go to hell, but today people had praised her work, today Evelyn Allbright had walked into Lost Treasures, and today, for a few precious moments, Evelyn had focused solely on her.

Sighing happily, Torry scanned her eyes over the canvas. It was coming along. Torry added a long row of pearls to one of the revelers before calling it a day. The painting would work well with the next display. Beginning the process of cleaning her painting tools, then herself, Torry realized she couldn't wait to see her friends. Jax worked at an art gallery downtown. She had actually piqued Torry's interest in painting by dragging her to a class one summer. Although a hack at best, Torry could convey, at a very basic level, what she wished. The painting would be good enough to reflect *The Great Gatsby*, helped along by the clothed mannequins. Jax would be able to appreciate the process of designing the window displays, even if she disagreed with Torry's tendency to ignore all other aspects of her life while creating them. She'd have to ask Jax if she'd seen the article mentioning Lost Treasures in *Trending*. Torry knew that Jax hardly ever traveled uptown and wouldn't have seen any of the window displays.

Drying her hands, Torry walked into the bedroom to figure out what to wear. She tried to ignore the anxiousness she felt. The way Jax and Greg had treated her, she'd have to address it tonight. Although she wasn't looking forward to the conversation they would be sharing, Torry knew how necessary it was. Lack of communication had been one of her failings with Brandon. They'd chosen to ignore the weaknesses in their relationship until it had become too late to repair the cracks in the foundation. By the time she and Brandon had begun to argue, the cracks had become fissures, and they had not been able to get across them to each other. Torry was determined to communicate her feelings to her oldest friend, Jax. And Greg too. He had hurt her when he had not contacted her after Brandon left. She wanted to build stronger relationships with them, but they needed to realize that sometimes she would make life choices which were different than what they would choose. They needed to be able to accept that, accept her.

No matter what, Torry needed to be true to herself. She'd begun that process by moving to New York against her father's wishes. Although nothing had happened the way she'd anticipated, Torry couldn't really complain. She'd learned so much. And finally she was moving in the right direction to fulfill her aspirations. Maybe once she built up a reputation through her window display designs, she would consider letting Nana help her get in somewhere better. It was not a traditional route, but Torry was beginning to understand that she was not really the traditional sort.

This year Torry had surprised herself again and again. She had become more confident in her abilities, more willing to listen to her intuition, and more courageous while experiencing life. She had begun looking at life in new ways, and she knew that someone was waiting in the wings, someone who would see her potential, someone who would encourage her growth, her evolving perceptions, her art. Wherever she ended up, Torry was sure she would find a person who would hold her hand as they stepped boldly into the next adventure—together. She just needed to be patient and continue walking her path. When the time was right, all would fall into place, and that special someone would step up.

Glancing one more time at the painting, now propped on a chair in her bedroom, Torry felt excitement course through her. People's reactions to *The Picture of Dorian Gray* display had been better than she'd dared hope. Torry worried that she might become too dependent on the attention and that she might begin to change in ways she couldn't anticipate. Another good reason to reconcile with her friends—they would keep her humble. She didn't want to become someone who took compliments for granted. She had high expectations for herself, and she would reach every goal she set. However, in the end, she would still be Torry at the core, still the person who loved creating and wanted to reach others, to make a difference in people's lives. She certainly wouldn't become like the people in the painting—

numbed to life, caring only for the adrenalin rush that came with cavorting and extreme behavior, unhappy with all they had and wanting more. Torry would safeguard herself from such an unfulfilling lifestyle. Even if she became well known and wealthy, as unlikely as that seemed, Torry would remain thankful every day of her life for all that she had.

Looking down at herself, Torry decided to change into something with no paint stains. She pulled out a pair of designer jeans she had purchased at the shop and a warm hunter-green, cable-knit pullover. It was a safe outfit—casual but designer. Not that she expected to see anyone who would care about what she wore. She pulled a comb through her long, dark hair several times before scrutinizing her face. She looked a bit drawn, but cosmetics would hide the smudges of darkness beneath her eyes. She applied some shadow and liner to accentuate her green eyes, and lined her lips before filling them in with a glossy, fire-engine red. Pleased with her appearance, Torry stopped fussing in front of the mirror and used the rest of the time to clean up. Her small apartment had two bedrooms, a living room, and a kitchen. The furniture was old and threadbare, the bookcase overflowing with an eclectic assortment of books, and the kitchen filled with mismatched mugs and plates. Torry grimaced at what she imagined Evelyn would think of her home. So plebian and uncouth. It had never really bothered her before, but now she felt embarrassed.

Above the couch was the drawing of the Notre Dame de Paris. Tilting her head, she tried to view it as if she'd never seen it before. The details and shadows were pretty good, but she had a hard time believing that it was anything worth praising. Across the room was another drawing that showcased several gargoyles attached to the façades, watching over the city. She had enjoyed drawing them, their quirky expressions and gothic designs calling to her. They were fierce and protective. Ultimately, she had decided not to use it for the display, but she liked it enough to keep it.

The door buzzer broke through her thoughts, and Torry let her friends in, unlocking her door so they could enter once they'd climbed the three flights of stairs to her apartment. She was a bit nervous to see them. Taking a deep breath, she reminded herself that she'd done nothing wrong. Relationships changed, people changed, and sometimes no one was to blame.

"Hey, hey!" Greg said happily as he swept in, Jax behind him. He reached for Torry, delivering a bear hug. "It's so good to see you!" Torry couldn't help but giggle at his enthusiasm. She had missed him. She withstood his scrutiny as he held on to her upper arms and looked at her. "You look good!"

"Thanks." She looked over his shoulder at Jax, who shifted from foot to foot. "Hi, Jax."

"Torry," she said, some sadness attached to her name. Greg turned to the side as Jax stepped forward and pulled Torry into a tight hug. "I'm so sorry for being such a royal bitch. I've missed you," she said into Torry's neck.

Allowing the hug to continue for a few moments, Torry wondered whether she should just let it go. Everyone made mistakes, and at least Jax had come back to her. Nevertheless, Jax had hurt her. They both had. It hadn't helped that Torry had said nothing. If she didn't clear the air now, she never would.

Pulling back slowly, Torry surprised herself. "You both hurt me. I realize Brandon is your friend too, but I thought you would understand that sometimes relationships just don't make it. That doesn't mean I should have or even Brandon should have been blamed."

"We know. We messed up." Greg held both hands up, as if to fend off an attack. "We were only hearing what Brandon was saying, and we were frustrated that we didn't get to see you much. But once you guys broke up and Brandon wasn't around anymore trash talking about you, we realized that you weren't entirely at fault. You've been focusing on your job. And there was no good reason for us to be angry with you when we've been doing the same thing. I have a nine to five job, but Jax has to work nights when there's an exhibit, and even Brandon was working all sorts of crazy hours." Greg shoved his hands in his front pockets.

Jax nodded. "We're sorry for being such jerks. I'm sorry. You're my best friend. I should have listened to what you said. I know you're not great at talking about your feelings, but you tried to explain. I just didn't want to hear it. I didn't want to accept that you were changing. But you know what? We're all changing. If Brandon couldn't see what he had, then he didn't deserve you."

Torry wanted to say so many things. Yell at them for making her feel worthless and at fault. For the loneliness and misery. For having to deal with the breakup by herself. But, she didn't.

Couldn't. She hated being at odds with them. She wanted to be able to talk to them, hang out with them, grow with them. Her silence must have made them nervous, though.

"It was just…I was afraid you were shutting me out again. Like after your mother died. You wouldn't talk to me or anyone. And when you stopped defending yourself about Brandon, I figured that you were shutting down again," Jax said.

"That was different," Torry said. "I needed time to grieve, and I felt like I couldn't have fun or be happy with my mom gone. I felt guilt every time I smiled, every time I forgot for even a second that she was dead, that she'd never laugh with me again."

"We get that now, Torry, but it made us feel pretty helpless," Greg said.

"And then you moved here without us," Jax exclaimed.

"I know. I know. That was a shitty thing to do, especially after we'd talked about finding an apartment together," Torry admitted.

"Well, I guess we've evened the score with our shitty behavior," Jax said with a laugh. "But, really, I promise I won't act that way again, Torry. It's okay to change. I'm changing. Someday if he works really hard at not being a blockhead, Greg may change too."

"Hey! I resemble that remark!" Greg said with mock outrage, his eyes twinkling.

Torry laughed despite herself. "That's resent, not resemble," she chided.

"I know! I was being witty and charming."

"Keep working on it," Jax teased.

"Okay, but here's the thing," Torry said. "You both have known me long enough to know I don't like conflict or arguing or even defending myself. And maybe that's why you thought you were right. I mean, I didn't point out that we're all working hard and changing and figuring out our lives. It's easier for friends to not care about that too much, but those sorts of things can really impact a romantic relationship. Brandon and I, we were good together for a while. And then we weren't. We drifted away from each other, didn't care so much about what the other wanted or needed. You can't maintain a relationship when two people are planning different lives in their heads."

"You're right. I know what I want now is different from what I'd envisioned while I was in college," Greg agreed quietly.

"Well, I haven't really experienced that, the changing goals or the serious relationship—maybe I'm a late bloomer," Jax joked. "I let you down, Torry. I feel like the worst best friend ever. I know I have some work to do so that you'll know that you can trust me again. Just give me the chance, okay?"

Staring into earnest, dark eyes, Torry nodded. "Um, thanks. For reaching out." Torry took a big breath and let it out. "Enough of the serious stuff. Let's go get a drink!"

"Oh, yeah! That's my girl," Greg said with a smirk, as Torry grabbed her coat and purse.

"Wow!" Jax exclaimed, stopping short in front of the door. Greg looked up to see what Jax was staring at and smiled.

"That's awesome! Where'd you get it?" Greg asked.

"Oh, uh, I actually made it for a display at the boutique. It was no big deal," Torry said, shifting from foot to foot.

"No big deal? Torry, that is a big deal. It looks wicked. It's for 'The Raven,' right?" Jax said excitedly.

"Yup. I had a display up for the poem, and I needed something to tie it together."

"I wish I'd seen it," Jax murmured.

"Yeah, well, Dorian Gray is taking a turn looking tortured now," Torry joked. Chuckling, she led the way out of the apartment, her heart lighter. *That wasn't so bad.*

***

Returning from the restroom, Torry hastened to answer the ringing telephone, knowing that neither Harold nor Grace could do so at the moment. Truly, if it remained as busy as it had been lately, they would have to hire some extra help. With the holidays just around the corner, Harold was convinced it would become even busier. He was quick to attribute the influx of business to Torry, much to her chagrin. She appreciated his praise, but she found it hard to believe that her actions had influenced the shop's healthy clientele to such an extent.

"Lost Treasures. How may I help you?" Torry said into the receiver.

"Who can I talk to about the window display designer?" asked a woman with a snippy tone of voice.

"You can talk to me, I guess. How can I help you?" Torry leaned against the edge of the desk as she looked around. The office was a mess, proof of just how busy they'd been. Maybe she would clean up a bit before returning to the front of the store.

"Yes. Well. I am calling on behalf of Evelyn Allbright at *Trending*. She wants to run a spread on your window designs for the January issue. We don't have much time, so we need to schedule the shoot right away."

"Wait! What does that mean, a spread?" Torry panicked a bit.

"That means an interview, photo shoot, and article," the woman said impatiently. "I'll send Sylvia down today to meet the window designer and take some preliminary shots of the store so we'll know what we're working with. Will Torry be available?"

"Wha...today? Um, yes. Sure. What time?" Torry stuttered.

"Two o'clock. Let's schedule the interview for Thursday. Jake can go there to talk to Torry at...ten in the morning."

Torry heard the telltale clicking of the person typing. "Ten on Thursday. Okay."

"As for the photo shoot, well I suppose that depends on when the windows will be changed. Do you know?" she asked, her voice dripping sarcasm.

"Um. Yeah. Yes. Monday night...a week from today."

"What will it be? I'll need to tell the photographer," the demanding woman asked.

"*The Great Gatsby*. I—"

"Right. I'll tell the photographer. Hopefully, he'll be able to work with that. I still have to find out when he's available, but let's tentatively plan for next week."

"What—" Torry pulled the earpiece away from her and stared mutely. The woman had hung up. "Shit." Bewildered, Torry quickly found Harold to tell him what was happening.

"That's great, Torry! *Trending*. Oh, my God! Grace, we'll have to hire more help. Geez, do you know what this type of exposure will do for us, Torry? Just that little article they published has doubled our sales." Harold ran a hand over his scalp as he turned back to Grace, excitedly continuing to chatter as Torry looked around the shop with new eyes.

They didn't have much time. She began to straighten the racks, pulling out the better pieces to display more blatantly. It didn't help that they were still so busy. She constantly was stopped to help customers, as she did her best to tidy up the shop. Looking up when she heard her name mentioned, Torry saw a slim, pixie-haired blonde making her way toward her.

"You're Torry?"

"Yes." Torry picked up a blouse that had slipped off a hanger and placed it back as the older woman stuck out her hand and smiled.

"I'm Sylvia. I was sent to take some photos of the store, of you, and of the current displays as well as gather some information. Is now a good time?"

Torry shook the woman's hand and smiled brightly. "Sure."

"You are awfully young. How old are you?" Sylvia asked, as she stared at Torry.

Shifting nervously, Torry looked around before refocusing on Sylvia. "I'm twenty-five."

Sylvia nodded. "How long have you worked here?" she asked, as she began to unpack her cameras.

"A little over a year," Torry answered.

"And you're the window dresser?"

"Yes."

"Who designs the displays?" Sylvia asked, while attaching the lens.

"I do that too. We…it's just a small shop. A couple of months ago, the owners agreed to let me give it a try, so I decided to show some of the great classics. Every couple of weeks I change the displays. Next week I'm changing it to *The Great Gatsby*." Torry petered off at the incredulous look on the woman's face.

"Wait. You are the window designer and the window dresser? You create all the displays?"

"Y…yes. I, it's just me." Torry gave a little wave before realizing how dorky she looked. She swiftly lowered her hand and grasped it tightly with her other one behind her back. Sylvia's smile eased her nervousness, though, and she couldn't help but smile back.

"Well," she said, while studying Torry closely. "That's phenomenal, Torry. If you don't mind, I'll just wander about a bit and take some pictures. I'll come find you after I've gotten some photos. Okay?"

"Oh, sure. Of course. Go, go wander." She waved her hands toward the front of the shop. Torry's eyes widened at the smirk on Sylvia's face. *Geez, I sound so stupid.* Nodding, Torry turned away and pretended to straighten some more racks. Giving up, she approached the registers where Grace rang up a customer. Deciding to shrug off her unease, Torry smiled brightly at the next person in line and assisted her with her purchases.

About twenty minutes later, Torry looked up when she heard the sound of a camera clicking. Sylvia took several pictures of her before lowering the camera. "Do you have a few minutes to talk to me about the displays?"

Torry noted the new tone of respect Sylvia's voice reflected and smiled widely. "Of course." Moving away from the registers, Torry walked purposefully toward the window displays. "What do you want to know?" she asked, as she reached the front of the store.

"I was wondering how long you will continue with the classic books theme?" Sylvia asked, as they stopped next to the window displays.

"At least until the new year. There are so many books to choose from, you know? And I already have some more in mind. Then, we'll see." Torry reached in and tilted the corner of the frame slightly before gazing around to make sure everything else in the displays were positioned properly.

"Where did you earn a retail merchandising degree for window display design?"

"Oh! No. I don't have one of those. Is that what it's called?" Torry chuckled self-consciously. "I used to do some set design in college, and my mom taught me all about fabrics. I just try to make the designs interesting enough for people to come inside. Half the battle of a sale is getting a customer through the door." Torry gave Sylvia a pained smile. She was totally blowing it. She sounded stupid and unsophisticated.

"Then you're a natural," Sylvia said. She took several pictures of the window displays, including a few with Torry in them before packing up her equipment. "Well, when you're interviewed you'll be asked much more in-depth questions. My job is to give them a framework, so to speak. It was great meeting you, Torry." They shook hands once more, and Sylvia left.

Releasing a breath, Torry grinned. That hadn't been so bad. Surely the interview would be relatively painless too. Hopefully, the added exposure would boost sales, and Torry could continue to focus on creating displays that touched others' hearts.

"Do you work here?" a woman asked politely.

Turning around, Torry saw a dark-haired woman close to her age with two skirts and three blouses. "Yes. How can I help you?"

"I'd like to try these on."

"This way, please." Torry held out a hand toward her left, where the dressing rooms were located. "My name is Torry. If you need me to find anything for you, please let me know."

"Thank you."

Torry opened the door with her key and removed a few articles left by an earlier customer. "All set." She kept herself busy by straightening up some displays near the dressing room in case she needed to retrieve any other pieces for the woman.

"How does this look?" Torry heard. Turning around quickly, she studied the woman before her critically. She wore a pale-blue silk blouse with three-quarter sleeves paired with a mahogany-colored maxi skirt.

"The skirt is a bit too long, but the blouse looks good with it. You'll either want to hem the skirt or wear shoes or boots with higher heels." Torry hoped she wasn't insulting the woman. "I'd also suggest a statement piece, such as long, chunky jewelry, a scarf, or a sash around the waist. Something colorful. One moment." Torry strode to the back of the store and picked a few long and short Hermes silk scarves and some beautiful costume jewelry. "See if you like any of these," she said once she returned to the customer, handing over the accessories.

"Thank you."

The customer tried the jewelry first, and Torry noted that it pulled the look together well. She tried the scarves around her neck and at the waist, and Torry breathed a sigh of relief when she saw that most looked great. She could see the customer thinking as she stared at herself in the full-length mirror. Torry remained quiet, allowing the brunette to determine what she liked best.

"You know, I really like what you gave me. So much that I simply cannot pick just one." The woman handed two scarves and one of the necklaces to Torry. "I'll take those with this outfit. Just let me try the other ones."

"Sure." Inside Torry was doing a little jig. Accessories tended to be marked up much more than clothes. She would earn a pretty penny from this transaction. Ten minutes later, Torry rang up the woman's purchases: one skirt, two blouses, four scarves, and one necklace. "If you need anything else, please feel free to contact me," Torry said, as she handed over the merchandise with a smile.

"Thank you. You know, you'd be a great personal shopper. I may have to come back to steal you from this place."

"Oh, ha, that's really nice of you to say. It was my pleasure to help you. Have a great rest of your day." Torry crossed the store to return the nonpurchased items to their rightful places, shaking her head as a smile remained firmly in place. With a spring in her step, she strolled toward the registers. Who knew what would happen next? She certainly had not foreseen all this publicity for her little designs. Feeling gratitude flow through her, she smiled fully at an older gentleman, as she took the clothes he handed her to ring up on the cash register. She could hardly believe how the displays, her way of communicating, were attracting so much attention.

Trending. Evelyn Allbright. Lost Treasures. January issue. Wow!

Chapter Eight

IRA SWEPT INTO EVELYN'S office, a folder nestled under his arm. "Good morning, Evelyn. I have the results of the photo shoot. You are going to love them. Torry is extremely photogenic. And the new display, did you see it, yet? Marvelous."

Quirking an eyebrow in amusement, Evelyn took the folder and opened it, spreading the pictures over her desk. Her eyes lit up as she gazed at the photos of the new window designs. One of the female mannequins was dressed in an Oscar de la Renta, silver fringe dress that stopped midthigh. A matching wrap and headband completed the look. A male was dressed in a smart, black Burberry tuxedo with a white bowtie, an elegant cane in his hand. Behind them, a large painting of revelers near and in a pool gave context to the scene.

The other display reflected casual wear. The woman wore a layered, translucent, cream-colored lace Valentino dress with a Hermes scarf wrapped loosely around her neck and a large, off-the-face floppy hat over dark hair. A long string of white pearls and dangling clip-on earrings complemented the ensemble perfectly. The man wore a sand-colored, single-breasted, two-button Signoria lightweight suit by Gucci with a pale-blue, pinstriped shirt and gold tie. A plaid beanie sat jauntily on his blonde locks.

Evelyn smiled. "These are quite good." High praise. She rarely gave it, but the displays were wonderful. The photographer, an up-and-comer much like Torry, had captured the essence of the displays, illuminating them in such a way as to emphasize the clothes.

Staring at the painting in the background, Evelyn tilted her head. It was also quite good. The painter had reflected equal parts giddiness and desperation in the revelers' facial expressions. "Who's the painter?" Evelyn questioned, while pointing at the photo.

Ira looked down and shrugged. "I don't know. I don't remember reading about it in the interview or in the write-up, either." He reached for the folder and withdrew the documents.

"Hmm. Did you meet Torry?" she asked, as she continued to study the photos.

"Yes. We really hit it off. In fact, we're meeting for drinks tonight. She has such interesting ideas—"

"She?" Evelyn interjected as she looked up quickly.

"Yes. Oh. Torry is short for Victoria. This is her." Ira reached across and pulled a picture off the desk, handing it to her.

Studying the picture, Evelyn gasped. "She's just a baby!"

Ira laughed. "With those curves, she's no baby." The humor apparent in his eyes caused Evelyn's lips to curl with amusement. "She attended Boston University and earned a degree in English with a minor in journalism, all with honors, of course. She was accepted to Harvard Law School but chose to move here to pursue her dream of design. After several months, she gave up trying to get a job as a stagehand on Broadway or as a designer at a magazine and began working at Lost Treasures."

"And the window display designs? Where do they come into play?" Evelyn studied more of the photos containing Torry.

"She grew up with an appreciation for fashion, thanks to her mother. While in college, a friend convinced her to join stage crew. She learned set design there and fell in love with the creative aspects of it. After working for the boutique for about nine months, Torry began to pester the owners about letting her decorate the windows. And the rest is history." Ira waved his hand with a flourish.

"Hmm, so drinks. Are we *experimenting*, Ira?" Evelyn asked lightly. He had never showed an interest for the fairer sex, but such a dark-haired beauty could certainly make a person question one's sexuality. When no answer was forthcoming, she looked up from the photographs with a quirked eyebrow.

"I don't know. Are we, Evelyn?" Ira drawled as he waggled his eyebrows and smirked.

Feeling heat suffuse her face, Evelyn scowled. "Don't be absurd. Until a few moments ago, I thought she was a he." Evelyn tapped at one of the photographs, deciding she would use it for the first page of the spread.

"Evelyn."

She looked at Ira, caught by the gentle tone of voice and earnestness in his expression.

"You've been captivated by Torry's work ever since she came on the scene a couple of months ago. And after spending the last few days with her, I can tell you that she's something special. You two should meet."

Pensively, Evelyn tapped at her chin. Ira was one of the few people who knew she was attracted to women. She was attracted to men too. After all, she'd married twice. And she had loved both men. As well as others. Yet, she could not deny that she also had found herself drawn to some women over the years. Evelyn chose not to think about her proclivities too much. When the pull was present, she chose whether or not to pursue those feelings. Just because the window dresser was a woman, well, that did not have to be a stumbling block. Not if the attraction proved mutual.

"Yes. We should. Invite her to the Winter Ball. Send her the blood-red strapless Armani Prive gown with the matching Blahniks on the pretext of thanking her for agreeing to the interview. After all, she set up the location for the shoot."

"The one with the onyx and black crystal dragon brooch on the back? Ah, very subtle, I must say," Ira said with a smirk.

Evelyn stared at the photo of the young designer while pursing her lips slightly. "I've met her before. I entered the boutique a few weeks ago, and she offered to assist me. I was called away to that disastrous Chanel shoot in that art gallery before she gave me her name. She seemed familiar to me even then. Hmm."

"Well, I don't believe she's been in the business long. I could find out…"

"No, no. Bring her to me at the ball. I will speak to her then." Evelyn waved a hand negligently while continuing to stare at the pictures of the beautiful brunette. She did not bother to look up at Ira's soft-spoken farewell. Yes, she would get to know this woman. If nothing else, Evelyn would determine what it was about this window designer that caused her heart to race each time she saw one of her presentations.

Suddenly needing to see it for herself, Evelyn called out to Heather, "Please call my car for me." Gliding toward the exit, she accepted her belongings from the junior assistant with a nod of thanks. She would see the displays up close before succumbing to several more hours of tedious decisions, decisions only she could make. She needed to feel rejuvenated. Torry's creativity would surely do the trick.

***

In front of a lit vanity mirror, Evelyn sighed softly. Downstairs, the main ballroom was filled with people waiting for her to make her grand entrance to the Winter Ball. Ira was entertaining Torry, introducing her to some of the movers and shakers of the fashion industry, while Evelyn finished preparing for their own meeting. She was unsure what to expect, and that made her feel unsettled.

To think Torry was a girl—a woman. A very attractive woman with mesmerizing liquid eyes and a smile illuminating everything around her. And that was reflected merely through the candid photographs taken of her at that little resale shop. No doubt, she would be even more stunning in person. Evelyn was scrambling to reorient her feelings for the window designer. Maybe she shouldn't have allowed herself to become so invested in the person. After all, they hadn't even met, and yet Evelyn's mind was buzzing with thoughts of future collaborations, ways to incorporate Torry's vision with her ideas for future magazine layouts.

Staring into her own light-blue eyes through the mirror, Evelyn willed herself to calm down. She would meet Torry, invite her back for a nightcap, and offer her a job at *Trending*. It would be a dream come true for the window designer, and Evelyn would have countless opportunities to observe her, guide her, and befriend her. Not that she necessarily wanted to be friends with the woman. Business acquaintances, certainly. She intended to help Torry along, just as she had countless other professionals who had crossed her path and shown promise. No reason existed for her to feel anxious. She had merely built up this meeting too much, imagined it too many times.

Seeing the time, Evelyn rose, walking purposefully to the full-length mirror to look at herself critically. She wore a beautifully tailored, strapless, ebony Valentino gown with matching four-inch Jimmy Choo heels. Her hair and makeup looked immaculate, the jewelry minimal. She was ready. Nodding to herself, she left her suite and made her way to the grand ballroom's sweeping staircase. She waited a moment as she straightened her spine, lifted her chin, and breathed calmly, hearing the noise level lower significantly as others noticed her. The thrill of having everyone's eyes directed upward to where she stood rippled through her, and she slowly descended the stairs as her eyes methodically roamed across the hall over those in attendance.

As her foot touched the floor of the ballroom, she caught Ira's gaze. He nodded faintly before turning toward an exquisite woman to his left. She gasped, realizing that his companion was none other than Torry. Even as her heart palpitated wildly, she glided toward the middle of the room, Heather tailing her wordlessly. Soon, Ira stood before her with two glasses of champagne in hand.

"You look lovely, Evelyn," Ira said, as he leaned in to deliver air kisses to both cheeks.

"Thank you. This tuxedo is quite flattering on you, Ira," Evelyn said, allowing some warmth to permeate her words. His smile widened. He handed her a flute and touched it gently with his own in a silent toast. They both sipped.

"Torry's doing great. I pulled her into an interview with *NY1 News* and introduced her to the world while mentioning the spread in the all-important January issue and how she's a rising star. The reporter asked several questions about the boutique before I shut it down in my charming way. I didn't want her to give away all of her secrets. Then, who would need to read *Trending*?" he chuckled.

"Indeed." Evelyn turned slightly so that she could watch Torry mingle without having to stare directly. It would not do to be caught watching the beautiful woman. She had an image to maintain, and having eyes only for Torry would cause quite a stir. "She seems to be enjoying herself," she said quietly, as she watched Torry laugh with several others.

"Evelyn, it is wonderful to see you again," said an older and conservatively dressed woman by way of greeting, ending Evelyn's conversation with Ira. It was time to go to work. These events were never merely about mingling and having fun. Oh, no. They were more about networking and ferreting out who might be beneficial to her or to the magazine, whether it be through talent, beauty, or money. Regretfully, Evelyn realized she could not continue to watch Torry. Turning to the woman, Evelyn pasted a slightly insincere smile on her face. This woman and her husband, Phyllis and George MacAllister, were huge benefactors for one of the charities where Evelyn sat on the board. Although not directly beneficial to the magazine, they were still worthy of her time. As a bonus, they were not entirely boring.

Forty-five minutes later, Evelyn was ready to leave the crowded affair. She flicked her eyes to Ira, who nodded with a smile and said softly, "I'll go get her."

"You are dismissed," Evelyn said to her assistant. "I will expect to see you at work no later than eight; weekend apparel is acceptable." She was giving her an extra hour to sleep in, rather magnanimous of her, and permission to wear jeans to work—

designer, of course. She knew Heather was exhausted, having worked a fifteen-hour day. She waved off Heather's thankfulness as her eyes cut through the crowd, searching for Ira and Torry. She quivered, anticipation filling her as she focused on the beautiful young woman.

The noise of the crowd dimmed as their gazes connected. Evelyn noticed how Torry clasped her hands together tightly and she smiled a bit timidly. Heather gasped, but Evelyn ignored it, too mesmerized by the look in Torry's eyes. She studied Torry carefully, slowly raking her eyes down Torry's body before raising them once more to capture widened emerald eyes. Evelyn struggled to maintain a polite expression as a ball of heat settled low in her stomach.

"Evelyn, please allow me introduce you to Torry Hansen, the window display designer at Lost Treasures," Ira said with a formal air.

Evelyn leaned forward, her hands reaching for Torry's forearms, and air-kissed both sides of her face. She smelled heavenly, and Evelyn's eyelids fluttered before she pulled back and reluctantly released her. "It is a pleasure to finally meet you, Torry. Is that your full name?" Evelyn asked, knowing the answer already.

"Uh, oh. No. It's Victoria, but everyone calls me Torry. Except my grandmother. So, yeah. Um," she answered awkwardly.

It was endearing, her nervousness. Victoria was a beautiful name, certainly more fitting than that silly nickname. Perhaps she would use it, unless the younger woman objected. "Victoria, may I call you Victoria?" Evelyn began, noting the affirmative nod. "I trust you are enjoying yourself tonight?" Evelyn kept her demeanor polite, doing her best to not reveal her amusement. She found the woman to be slightly dorky and entirely too adorable, and she struggled not to smile. Add her appearance—exquisite, sexy, and sophisticated—and the mixture was quite enticing.

"Oh, yes. This is wonderful. I have met so many people who love colors and textures like I do. I had no idea. Thank you for inviting me. And for this gown," Victoria added as she indicated the red sheath encasing her curves.

"It was made for you," Evelyn pronounced, her voice throatier than she had intended as her eyes once more burned every inch of Victoria's body. Oh, yes, she was not merely a girl. Not with those curves. "I was about to leave. Would you care to join me for a nightcap?"

"Yes. I'd love to," she answered quickly.

Evelyn nodded before turning to whisper to Ira, "You were right. That gown showcases her assets quite appealingly."

He smirked before turning to kiss Victoria's cheek. "Drinks on Thursday?"

"That sounds great, Ira."

"I'll text you the details." Leaning closer, Ira whispered, "Don't let her scare you, Torry. Just be yourself. Good luck."

Pretending not to hear Ira's comments to Victoria, Evelyn drawled, "Shall we?" Without waiting for an answer, she moved toward the staircase. She could feel Victoria's eyes on her, and she directed herself sternly to keep gliding smoothly. Of course, she was used to people watching her every move. Normally, she had no problem ignoring such admirers. This young woman, though, affected her. Once they reached the top of the staircase, Evelyn walked through a set of doors and toward the elevator banks, feeling Victoria's presence every step of the way.

Evelyn entered the elevator and eyed Victoria briefly as they stood next to each other. She could see that Victoria was extremely nervous. It was silly, really. It wasn't like Evelyn had propositioned her or was taking her to the hotel suite to enjoy a night of debauchery. This was just a nightcap, a chance to talk. A careful introduction. Normal. Innocent. Disappointingly so.

Evelyn busied herself with opening the champagne, while Victoria gazed around the presidential suite in awe. Evelyn bit gently on her lower lip to stop herself from smiling. The young woman was obviously impressed by the opulence spread out before her. She doubted Victoria had ever seen such a room before. Evelyn watched as the attractive woman walked over to the sofa and sat on the edge—legs together, hands to her sides, back straight—then crossed to her and offered her a glass of champagne.

"Thank you," Victoria said meekly. Evelyn settled herself on the sofa and left a decorous amount of space between them.

"You seem familiar to me. Have we met before?"

"Oh, uh, we met at the boutique," Victoria answered quickly. Too quickly.

Waving her hand at Victoria as if to swat away the suggestion, Evelyn's dissatisfaction showed on her face. "I realize that, but I felt even then that I knew you."

"Well, I did see you outside the store a few times. Maybe you recognized me from that?" Victoria asked hopefully.

Evelyn could tell that the woman was hiding something. She wanted to know, though, and she would find out. "No, no. Somewhere else." She trained her eyes on Victoria and demanded, "Where?"

Not able to sidestep the question any longer, Victoria sighed. "At my mother's funeral. You attended with my grandmother, Cynthia Smythe, over three years ago." She looked away as she ran a finger over the rim of her glass distractedly.

"She was here tonight," Evelyn said. "She had mentioned that you were in New York but that you wouldn't accept any help from her."

"That's true," Victoria agreed, a pained look flittering over her visage. "She was surprised to see me here tonight. You see, after Mom died, I pushed everyone away, including my family and friends. And I pushed aside my dreams. I realized, though, that avoiding anything that reminded me of my mom wouldn't bring her back. So, I got the job at Lost Treasures. It's been a struggle, but I'm happy being immersed in the fabrics and colors and designs Mom loved so much. It doesn't hurt so much anymore."

"I remember you now. I remember the eulogy you gave. I would have helped you if I'd been asked," Evelyn mused and tilted her head. "You wear couture well, and you obviously have talent and drive."

"Thank you. That means so much."

"You created this opportunity for yourself." Evelyn drank the remainder of her champagne before rising to refill it. She brought the bottle over and topped off the young woman's drink.

"Thank you," Victoria murmured. "It all worked out. I mean, I would have missed the opportunity to design the boutique's windows if I had used Nana's connections, and I would never know whether I was good enough to make my way into design."

"Hmm." Evelyn looked at Victoria probingly. "How is it that you are designing window displays at a small boutique instead of at a large department store?" Evelyn sipped from her glass.

"I only asked Harold and Grace a few months ago for the opportunity to dress their windows. They were nice enough to allow me to play, and people seem to like it. I'm just so grateful that I get to express myself in this way."

"You do understand that you will soon be fielding offers for employment from places such as Saks and Macy's, don't you?"

Victoria shook her head as if the idea was preposterous. "Oh, I doubt it. We're just a small shop. I'm surprised it's gotten as much notice as it has. Actually, I have you to thank. I really appreciate the shop being mentioned in *Trending* and now the article for January's issue." She shook her head again. "It's incredible."

"You can do quite well for yourself. The larger stores will provide you with a better salary and more visibility. With your talent, you could rise to the top quickly. You could branch out into a neighboring industry if you preferred. You could design sets at theaters, fashion shows, photo shoots. Or," Evelyn paused and shot a look that carried the weight of her intent, "you could come work in the art department at *Trending*." Evelyn watched closely as Victoria processed her words. Normally, she would not offer a position to a virtual unknown, but Evelyn knew that the woman was special. Design was in the young woman's genes.

"Oh, I couldn't leave Lost Treasures. Their business has just picked up. I couldn't do that to them. Plus, I have the freedom to do whatever I want there. I doubt I'd have such autonomy anywhere else." Victoria sat stiffly, wringing her hands together, a guilty look on her face as she rationalized why she wouldn't entertain the notion of accepting a job elsewhere. "They've been so good to me. Leaving them would be like betraying them just to get ahead."

"Victoria, don't be naïve. They expect you to leave. Talent like yours is not meant to stagnate in a little resale shop." Evelyn's gaze pinned Victoria to her seat. "Come work for me. I can guarantee that you will learn so much more. We can mold you, train you. Or go somewhere else. Just go somewhere."

"But Harold and Grace, they're my friends. I won't turn my back on them."

Evelyn could hardly believe what she was hearing. Friends? How absurd. "Don't be ridiculous, Victoria. They aren't your friends. They are your employers. People who are nice and amiable until you do something they do not like. Do not mistake pleasantness for affection. Your loyalty is sweet but misguided."

"They like me," she sputtered. "They care about me. You're wrong." The young woman's face twisted with outrage and righteous anger on behalf of her employers, much to Evelyn's dismay.

"Like you? Please. Victoria, they don't know anything about you—your family, your friends, your education, your hometown. They knew nothing when we made inquiries because they don't care. You need to look out for your own interests. It is clear they are only looking out for theirs."

Victoria stood up abruptly, and Evelyn's eyebrows flew up in surprise. This was not going well. At all. Evelyn wondered why the truth was making the younger woman so upset.

"I...I have to go. Thank you for the nightcap." She placed the glass down on a side table, her hand shaking. "Good night." She hurried to the door.

"Victoria," Evelyn called out with dismay, not quite believing that she was leaving. "Torry," she tried again. No one had ever cut short a meeting with her, not in all her years in the fashion industry.

"Bye." Victoria gave a little wave and left.

Evelyn stared at the door as if expecting Victoria to reenter with a sheepish apology. Pressing her lips together, she sighed, thoroughly miffed. Squeezing the bridge of her nose she muttered, "Well, that went swimmingly. Ira will be so impressed." *And I can just imagine how Cynthia will feel once she finds out about this conversation.*

Evelyn grimaced as she sipped her champagne. Cynthia had become a good friend since her daughter's funeral. They met monthly for lunch, and Evelyn trusted her implicitly. She wondered whether Cynthia knew that her granddaughter was the window designer Evelyn had brought up in conversations during their last couple of meals. She found it hard to believe that Cynthia would have kept this from her. What would she have gained?

She allowed her mind to sift through her options, scrambling to find some way to reach out to Victoria. It all came down to not giving up. She would be persistent, wear her down with offers that the young woman would be a fool to refuse. *Like working for Trending*, her mind unhelpfully reminded her. She obviously did not understand the ways of the world. Of course, that was part of her charm, and no doubt what colored her perceptions and produced such inventive designs. She was so refreshingly open. All Evelyn needed to do was look into the young woman's eyes to know what she was feeling. No artifice or guile. It was rare to find someone within the industry who was so unspoiled. Evelyn felt protective toward Victoria. And who will protect her from you? She shook off the unwanted thought.

Tomorrow, she would find her tomorrow and repair any damage she had unintentionally wrought tonight. They both needed to sleep, but Evelyn would seek her out in the morning. With that comforting thought, Evelyn walked into the bedroom suite. All was not lost. Not by any means. She would just have to be more patient and remember that Victoria was different, very different.

Early the next morning, Evelyn stepped out of the Mercedes after directing Andrew to wait. She had dreamt of running after Victoria but losing her in the crowd. Then, she had become the one chased, although she had not been able to determine who was after her. She approached Lost Treasures, her eyes fastened on the window display. It was early, too early for the resale shop to be open. A small crowd stood close to the store, several pointing and cocking their heads. Evelyn searched for the subject of their interest, understanding that they were not merely appreciating the reflection of two scenes from *The Great Gatsby*.

Expelling a breath in surprise, Evelyn walked closer to the boutique. In the window display Evelyn could see Victoria sprawled across a plush sofa with the back of her hand resting over her eyes, asleep. Thanks to her formal wear and upswept hairdo, she seemed to fit into the scene of frantic revelry perfectly. Evelyn listened to the people nearest her position as they speculated on whether Victoria was an extremely lifelike mannequin or a real person. They concluded she couldn't be a real person since no one would be part of a display when the store was closed. They must be tourists, Evelyn mused.

Obviously, Victoria needed to be awakened. Evelyn walked back to the car and summoned Andrew. "Bang on the window to rouse the girl from her nap." Evelyn watched as he knocked on the store window several times. Victoria stirred, stretching like a cat before opening her eyes. When she did look around, she sat up straight, shocked to find she was a part of the display. She stood up quickly and smoothed down her dress self-consciously, her eyes sweeping across the gathered individuals.

When Victoria's eyes connected with hers, Evelyn felt her breath catch. The unfocused, hazy look in her eyes hinted at an unadulterated sensuality which called to Evelyn. Her eye color was mesmerizing. *Are they forest green? No, too dark. Perhaps fern green or shamrock.* Such thoughts caused Evelyn to pause for a moment. Seeing Victoria so unguarded, so soft and vulnerable was extremely compelling. Evelyn wanted to pull the young woman into her arms, but she was unsure whether her desire stemmed from wanting to protect her or kiss her. She acknowledged that it was probably both. After a few moments of silent contemplation, Evelyn indicated with a sharp jerk of her head that Victoria should open the door.

"Evelyn! What are you doing here?"

"Preventing you from making a fool out of yourself any longer, so it would seem. Really, Victoria, sleeping in the display?" Evelyn rolled her eyes. "I will give you a ride home."

"Wha...no, Evelyn. That's not necessary." Victoria lowered her face and looked up at her through lowered lashes.

Evelyn felt as if she had just been sucker-punched in the stomach. She pressed her lips together, angered by her inability to control her libidinous reactions. "No, no, that wasn't a question," she said firmly as she waved a finger from side to side. "Stop wasting my time. Let's go." She turned away and strode to the car, knowing Victoria would follow her.

After a few minutes of tense silence, while Evelyn alternately cursed herself and the other woman for this undeniable attraction, she made a decision. "I wish to purchase the painting that is part of the present display."

"Oh, um, that's really kind of you, but I just painted it to help people recognize the book." Victoria shook her head. "Don't waste your money."

Evelyn tilted her head. "You painted it?" She watched Victoria blush and look away.

"Yes. I needed something to tie the scene together. So you see, it's not worth anything." She shrugged self-consciously.

Evelyn tried to control herself from staring at the younger woman incredulously. It was a struggle, even after years of keeping tight control over her emotions. Does Victoria really believe she cannot paint? What an odd creature. And why would she refuse payment? "Not worth anything? Are you saying that I have no taste?" Evelyn asked slowly. She nearly smiled as a look of panic flitted across Victoria's face.

"Of course not! Everyone knows that it's your ability to recognize beauty that drives the fashion industry."

"Quite right. I believe that your painting is very good. I take it you have never sold your work before." Evelyn waited for the woman to shake her head. "And I suppose you have no formal training for such a medium, as you do not for window display designs?" Victoria confirmed her educated guess with more shakes of the head. Evelyn was astounded by the raw talent Victoria possessed. To be able to guide her, mold her, develop her skills—Evelyn felt dizzy with the potential Victoria had not yet tapped. Evelyn nodded once. "How much do you want for it?"

"I don't want your money. If you really want it, I'll gift it to you once I change the current display."

"That's absurd. If you'd rather, I will have an art dealer come to the store to determine a fair price," Evelyn said, huffing in frustration.

"No. Perhaps for future works, but I will give you this one," Victoria said resolutely. Evelyn stared at the younger woman, noting her chin jutted out defiantly, her body held stiffly, and her eyes shining brightly.

Evelyn decided not to push the issue. She would find a different way to recompense Victoria. She found it rather intriguing how woman did not cave in to her demands. Very intriguing.

"As you wish. I do want it, but if the only way you will deliver it is by gifting it to me, that is your choice. However, perhaps you might think about why you are so quick to deny your talents and dismiss the accolades you so richly deserve." Seeing they had arrived at Victoria's apartment, Evelyn took a deep breath and asked, "Does that little shop allow you to leave for lunch?"

"Um, yes?" Victoria replied. Evelyn nearly smirked at her obvious confusion.

"I will pick you up on Wednesday. My assistant shall contact you with the details." Evelyn turned her gaze out the window and did not glance away as Victoria exited the car. She studied the way the woman hurried up the stairs, fumbling with her keys briefly before entering the building. Evelyn did not attempt to hold back her chuckle, feeling more alive than she had in a long time. Warmth filled her, and she sighed as she firmly pushed aside any thoughts of what that might suggest. Hearing a polite clearing of a throat, she glowered at Andrew through the rearview mirror, not liking how he had caught her watching. Firming her lips,

Evelyn growled, "Did you forget the way to *Trending*?" She didn't bother listening to his response.

Chapter Nine

TORRY WANDERED AROUND HER shadowed apartment aimlessly. She was too perplexed to settle down even though she really needed some sleep. A candle flickered, and Torry shivered, rubbing her arms with brusque motions. She walked over to retrieve the afghan from the back of the couch. Torry remembered sitting next to her mom for hours, watching her crochet, as they talked about the colors and how it would look once it was finished. Torry wasn't able to visualize the design at the time, but it came out just as her mother had promised, the blues and greens, the black and white interwoven and connected into a beautiful pattern. Skating her fingers over the yarn, Torry smiled, sadness twisting her lips. Warmer, Torry moved to the window to stare out onto the empty street, focusing on nothing, nothing but the enigmatic editor.

For the last four days, thoughts of Evelyn had intruded on her peace of mind. Every time she lay in bed and closed her eyes, images of Evelyn interrupted her rest. Torry had so many questions when it came to the bewildering woman, but the most prominent question, the one that kept echoing in Torry's mind, was why did Evelyn show up at the boutique the morning after the gala, after she'd left the editor so abruptly? She had felt like a fool, awakening to a crowd of curious, amused faces. Torry groaned. It was all so embarrassing.

Having been so upset with what Evelyn had said to her, Torry sought solace through her designs. She let herself into the boutique, not bothering to switch on the lights, locked the door, and stumbled to the window displays. Those designs coincided perfectly with the ambiance of the event Torry had left—the rich, the famous, the elite, all schmoozing and pretending that they were happy when nothing could be further from the truth. They were on display, looking around to make sure others were watching them as they smiled and laughed and struck poses meant to impress everyone. Of course, no one noticed since they all were too busy acting the same way.

Torry just didn't get it. Evelyn had indicated that she should want that too. But Evelyn was missing the point entirely. Torry wanted to create, to touch hearts and souls. She didn't care about becoming famous and earning a better salary. Sure she liked money, but she didn't want to accept a job offer just for that. It wasn't a good enough reason to desert her friends, and no matter what Evelyn said, Harold and Grace were her friends. They did care. If they didn't know much about Torry's background, that was due to her reticence to share the intimate details of her life, not their lack of questions. Just because she didn't truly remember them ever asking about herself.

It made her wonder whether it was possible for the elite to have money and power without losing their souls. According to *The Great Gatsby*, the answer was no. Had Evelyn lost her soul? Did she even care about her colleagues? She had the power to dash a person's dreams or make anyone feel unworthy of breathing the same air with a supercilious look or elegant sneer. From all she'd heard about Evelyn, she was the Queen of Mean, the Dragon of Fashion, respected in the industry but feared. No one wanted to cross her. Maybe she hadn't cultivated friendships, believing it easier to retain her power and reputation for excellence by not sharing herself.

I'm not like that. I could never be like that. Sighing, Torry rubbed her head. Evelyn was friends with Nana, though. When Torry had bumped into her grandmother at the gala, it had become clear that they were closer than mere industry acquaintances.

"Victoria! What are you doing here?"

"Nana! I had no idea you'd be here. Ms. Allbright invited me. She saw the displays I created for my work at Lost Treasures—"

"That's where you work? Evelyn hasn't stopped talking about those window displays for months. Why didn't you tell me?"

The way she spoke indicated that she was hurt, causing Torry to wince. She never wanted to upset her grandmother. "I'm so sorry, Nana. You know how much I love you. I just wanted to make it on my own. I wanted you to be proud of me."

"Oh, child, I am." Her nana pulled Torry into a quick hug. "Now, no tearing up. It will ruin your makeup. Come over this weekend, and you can tell me all about it then."

"Okay," Torry agreed, smiling broadly. "I'm so glad you're not upset. That would be unbearable."

"How could I be upset? You're making a name for yourself, and you've done it on your own. I couldn't be prouder."

"Thank you, Nana."

Soon after Ira had joined them, chatting with her grandmother for a moment before whisking Torry away to meet Evelyn. That weekend Torry had learned that the two had maintained a friendship over the years and met regularly.

Evelyn had made an indelible impression on Torry at the funeral. During that time, even submerged by grief, Torry had recognized how powerful the woman was. Torry had always lived her life without planning ahead—walking through doors as they opened, traveling the paths that appeared under her feet. It wasn't until she had arrived in New York that she began to comprehend just how naïve and unformed her dreams of making a difference were. She realized that she couldn't expect anyone to take her seriously if she couldn't advocate for herself. She couldn't continue floating along in life as she had. No one was going to just give her a chance. She needed to create her future. With that in mind, she'd refused everyone's help to mold her future and taken responsibility for her life.

Returning to her bedroom, Torry lay down in the dark and closed her eyes. Immediately she visualized Evelyn's impenetrable blue eyes focused on her, a small smile on her face. With a gasp, she opened her eyes. During that moment when she had approached Evelyn for a proper introduction at the ball, those piercing eyes had captured her and the noise of the crowd had dimmed into indistinguishable background noise.

After a few moments, Torry sighed and gave in, allowing her eyes to slide shut once more. She allowed herself to mentally focus on Evelyn's face, her shoulder-length blonde tresses, her perfect cheekbones, and her swanlike neck. Evelyn was gorgeous, mysterious, and powerful. Torry had recognized all these attributes upon their first unforgettable meeting, even though she'd had no idea that Evelyn was the editor in chief of *Trending* until her grandmother had told her about a week after the funeral.

The way Evelyn carried herself, the way she spoke, the way she tilted her distinguished head, all let others know, even those as obtuse as Torry, that she was someone important. And when she had followed Evelyn back to her suite for a nightcap, she had quite suddenly realized what an attractive woman she was. She'd followed docilely, enthralled by Evelyn's graceful movements, her defined back muscles, and her fabulous backside. Torry had reminded herself strictly not to appear too obvious. She was quite sure Evelyn would not have appreciated being ogled so blatantly in such a crowded room. The woman was stunning, though, and

Torry was certain that others had lost that battle of will and fallen under the regal woman's charms.

The entire night had been like nothing Torry could have imagined. Excitement chased its way through Torry when she first laid eyes on the Ritz-Carlton. People in evening wear streamed through the entrance of the famous hotel, and she found it hard to believe that she was attending an event at such a luxurious locale. Nana had invited her to such events in the past, but Torry never attended. She hadn't felt worthy.

As she walked past the paparazzi, she tried not to blink too much in response to the camera flashes. She didn't understand why they were taking pictures of her, a nobody. Regardless, Torry tried to keep a smile fixed on her face. She felt relieved when Ira called her over, although she certainly did not expect to be pulled into an interview. Once he escorted her into the venue, her thoughts turned to Evelyn.

"Is she here?" Torry was suddenly very nervous as she glanced around. They entered the main hall, weaving through the crowded room.

"Not yet. She likes to make a grand entrance. She'll come down that staircase." Ira pointed across the hall to a set of sweeping, circular marble stairs. "Let's get some bubbly in the meantime."

Clutching the crystal tightly, Torry chatted politely with each person Ira introduced to her. As time passed, she relaxed. It wasn't so bad. It was just like any other party, only the people were better dressed, more famous, more affluent, and more important. Taking a sip of the champagne, Torry stiffened as she felt the air change. Looking around for the reason why, she noticed how everyone turned toward the staircase with a sense of expectation.

"Here comes the Queen of Fashion," Ira announced softly.

She did not disappoint. Evelyn's bearing alone broadcast her importance—the noble tilt of her head, the flawless, alabaster skin, the sway of her hips, and the gleam in her sharp eyes. Torry was captivated. She watched as Evelyn took her time descending the wide staircase, her keen eyes sweeping over the mass of admirers. Once she reached the bottom of the stairs, Evelyn glided toward the center of the room, a young woman trailing behind her.

Torry let out a gush of air. She hadn't even realized that she'd been holding it.

"She has that effect on people," Ira chuckled. Torry smiled ruefully. "Well, I should go check in with her. I'll catch up with you in a little bit."

Torry nodded, her eyes still attached to the elegant woman. Soon, though, she was drawn into another conversation. Time passed as she met several more people. They seemed genuinely interested in talking to her. It was a surreal experience for Torry. She was surrounded by people who loved fashion, loved the materials that were used to create the wonderful gowns and suits worn by the elite.

Consequently, Torry felt inspired. She wanted to rush back home to sketch some of the ideas flowing through her mind. One gown she saw reminded her of the ballroom scene in *My Fair Lady*, while the cut on a distinguished man's tuxedo whispered *Jane Eyre* into her ear. She thrived on the energy buzzing throughout the ballroom. It had made her feel more alive than she had ever experienced.

Scrunching her brows, Torry frowned as she allowed the memory of last Friday night's gala to fade into the darkness. If only Evelyn weren't so ruthless. Torry had no doubt that the woman hadn't meant to hurt her feelings when she declared that Harold and Grace were merely her employers, not her friends. Obviously, Evelyn had been applying her own work experience to Torry's situation. It gave her the insight that Evelyn probably was not friends with any of her subordinates except perhaps Ira, but the jury was still out on that one. She doubted that Evelyn was very nice to her employees, at least not during business hours. Was she different outside of work? Did she associate with them on a personal level? It was all so confusing. Torry shook her head. *How lonely.*

From what Torry knew, Evelyn worked long hours, tirelessly striving to keep *Trending* at the top of the fashion industry. With whom did she share her triumphs? When did she relax? Did she ever laugh or joke? Did Evelyn's relationships break down due to her unwillingness to slow down, to share, to prioritize her significant other before her job? Was Evelyn even happy?

Torry certainly didn't want to end up like that! What was the point of being successful if she had no one next to her? Who would celebrate her triumphs with her? Who would support her when her spirits flagged? Who would let her know when she was too wrapped up in her work to enjoy life? What was the use of being so successful if she didn't have the time to enjoy it? Not that she had a certain someone with whom she could share her current or future successes. And there was the prickly point that Brandon had left her because she had been so wrapped up in her own work. But that would change as she became more established, Torry was sure. Torry had to admit it was true that she was happiest while creating. Was that how Evelyn felt while she was piecing together the next *Trending* issue?

Ira had told Torry to not let Evelyn scare her. He seemed to know Evelyn well. If that was his advice, maybe she needed to give Evelyn the benefit of the doubt. Evelyn was fierce and scary, but it was possible that she was different in her personal life. That just left one question, did Evelyn consider her—Torry—work? Was she merely attempting to shape her, to woo her to *Trending*? Although, she had urged her to work at a department store if she preferred or to branch out into a neighboring industry. Her thoughts stalled as she stared ahead blankly, barely making out the colored-pencil drawing of the open window and trees she drew for "The Raven" display. She liked having it in her bedroom, since she had no actual window in the room. The colors lifted her spirits. Not that she could see the colors at the moment. Sighing, she closed her eyes once more, allowing her mind to continue obsessing over Evelyn's motives.

Well, if her plan was to get Torry to leave Lost Treasures, Evelyn was destined to fail. She loved working at the shop. They allowed her to decorate the windows in any way she wished. She didn't need permission to implement her designs. They trusted her, believed in her, liked her. She had a great relationship with Harold and Grace. If they did not talk outside of the store—well, that meant nothing. They were all extremely busy. Evelyn just didn't understand because she chose to treat her employees as dispensable, nameless bodies. *Another reason why I could never work for her.*

Nodding her head definitively, Torry made her decision. She would go to lunch with Evelyn, but she would make it clear that she had no intention of leaving the boutique. Evelyn would simply have to respect her choice.

***

Picking up her visitor's pass at the front desk, Torry nervously entered the elevator. She was surprised by the invitation to shadow Evelyn for the day at *Trending*, particularly after the disastrous lunch they had shared last week. Evelyn had offered her a position at *Trending,* again, and Torry had politely, but firmly, refused to leave Lost Treasures. She simply would not do that to Harold and Grace.

Ira had urged her at least to take the opportunity to see what happened at the top magazine on a typical day. Although Torry hadn't changed her mind about leaving Lost Treasures, she was curious to see what Evelyn did. Of course, she wanted to explore the art department too. Ira had even promised a tour of the famed *Closet*, where a wide selection of clothes, accessories, shoes, and outwear were stored and used for fashion shoots.

Stepping out of the elevator, Torry made her way to the receptionist and gave her name. A few moments later, a blonde-haired, stick-like woman approached her. She recognized her from the ball as one of Evelyn's assistants.

"I'm Heather, Evelyn's first assistant. She's waiting for you. Follow me." Torry hurried to keep up with the speed walker while looking around curiously. Lots of glass and white walls surrounded her—modern, sleek, airy.

People hurried through the halls, all intent on some destination. No one smiled, no one chatted, no one joked. Torry felt her eyebrows rise in surprise. What kind of work environment was this? She stopped short when Heather suddenly turned to her. "Wait here."

She watched Heather enter another office and heard her named mentioned. Evelyn must be in there. As if to bear out her supposition, a mellifluous voice massaged her full name, drawing her forward as surely as a siren's song would a hapless sailor. No one called her by her full name except Nana and Evelyn. She kind of liked it. A lot. The way she rolled the syllables on her tongue like a fine wine and stalled on the last syllable gave her shivers. She could practically see Evelyn's mouth when she finished uttering her name, lips parted and tongue peeking out.

Torry felt her heartbeat pick up speed as she crossed the threshold to Evelyn's office and enjoyed her first glimpse of the fashion icon. She looked exquisite in a Prada crinkle chiffon blouse and matching tweed-and-lace trumpet skirt in blues and grays. Torry stood just inside the door, captured by how Evelyn's blue eyes darkened. Specks of light reflected off them in a way that compelled Torry to look more deeply, as if she were watching the sky change at dusk.

A cleared throat redirected her gaze toward a quirked eyebrow and defined smirk. Torry blushed furiously, knowing she had been caught gazing like some lovesick teenager. "Evelyn," she said a bit too breathlessly. "Good morning. Thank you for inviting me." Noting how the woman's smirk widened, Torry jutted her chin out while clasping her hands tightly behind her back. When their eyes reconnected, the air between them vibrated.

"Good morning, Victoria," Evelyn drawled.

As she watched, Evelyn's smirk softened into a small smile. When Evelyn finally broke their gaze to run her eyes over Torry's outfit, Torry took a shuddering breath. She hoped the draped vermillion stretch-silk Zac Posen dress and black Jimmy Choo shoes were acceptable. The gleam in Evelyn's eyes and the definitive nod indicated they were. Torry beamed at the woman, so glad to be with her.

With one last visual caress shot her way, Evelyn leaned back in her chair and indicated that Torry should also sit. "A typical day at *Trending* consists of run-throughs of pieces I am considering showcasing in the next issue, previews of upcoming fashion lines, photo shoots, and meetings. Add on countless telephone calls, e-mails, and all those people who clamor for my time while I attempt to pull together the best fashion magazine possible before the impending print deadline, and you will begin to understand what it is I do. Working in this industry is a labor of love and no place for the faint of heart."

Noise at the door stopped Evelyn. She waved them forward, and a crowd of people swarmed the room, carrying accessories and pushing a rolling rack of clothes. Ira entered last, and after shooting a smile Torry's way, he began directing the others on how best to set up the couture.

"Hmm," Evelyn stepped purposefully toward some cocktail dresses and held one up. "Ira, what do you think of this dress?"

"Oh, gorgeous. The lines across here," Ira ran a finger over the bodice, "and the fringe at the bottom hint at a certain playfulness indicative of spring. Add those strappy sandals and that hat, and voila!" he said, while twirling his hand upward.

"Not bad," Evelyn murmured. "What else do we have?"

Watching the run-through, Torry gained an appreciation for Evelyn's discerning eye. The way she pulled together textures, colors, and fabrics stimulated Torry's imagination. Evelyn used combinations Torry never would have imagined to convey a richness, sensuality, and playfulness perfect for the end of winter.

Everyone practically fell all over themselves trying to please the editor. Even Ira pandered to her, quickly agreeing with every word she uttered. Torry couldn't imagine wielding such power every day. She wondered whether Evelyn acted the same way in her personal interactions and whether she expected others to react just as obsequiously. She certainly hadn't seemed happy when Torry had refused her offer of employment both times. But that wasn't personal.

Once the run-through ended, Torry sat silently, a bit dazed by what she had witnessed.

"Do you have questions?" Evelyn asked, pulling Torry from her swirling thoughts.

"Um, well, are run-throughs always like that?" Torry wondered whether *Trending* employees ever dared to offer their own ideas. If so, were they well-received, or did Evelyn shoot them down if she hadn't thought of the idea beforehand or had a different vision? Evelyn hadn't really acted in a harsh way, just brusquely. Maybe Evelyn didn't act as cruelly as others had represented over the years.

"No. This one ran surprisingly smoothly." Evelyn seemed extremely pleased. "What you saw was how every run-through should proceed. Unfortunately, my time is often wasted with shortsighted people and their regurgitated ideas. Fashion is all about creativity and uniqueness. We must introduce ideas that no one has seen before, visions others have not anticipated but will accept wholeheartedly. That is why we remain the top magazine in the fashion industry."

Torry found herself nodding her agreement. She felt like a newly initiated acolyte to the Goddess of Fashion. In her element, Evelyn exuded power. She seemed bigger than life and oh so sexy. The types of clothes at her disposal, her ability to make or break an upcoming fashion line, the sycophants surrounding her every day, it was clear that Evelyn thrived on them. It was all so different. Torry created by herself, using whatever clothing was on hand and her ingenuity. Torry knew that if she had access to the most fashionable clothes and props, she could create unforgettable displays.

Evelyn stood up, rounded the desk, and walked into the outer office. Torry stared after the mysterious woman, wondering what she was supposed to do.

"Victoria, come along. Stop dawdling." Torry jumped up to follow, grabbing her belongings. As soon as Evelyn saw her, she strode out the door, and Torry followed, hot on her Prada heels.

Once they exited the building, Torry saw Ira standing next to a black town car. "Victoria will ride with me to the preview," Evelyn said, as she handed him a folder. He nodded and winked at Torry before ducking in to the other car's interior.

Inside the showroom, Torry sat next to Evelyn on a low couch, while Ira sat in a chair on Evelyn's right side. Several members of the art and design department sat behind them. Before they entered the loft, Ira had pulled Torry aside to educate her on Evelyn's way of communicating her approval or rejection of clothes.

"She tends not to say much. Instead, she prefers to study every aspect of the clothes, their colors and textures, how they drape and flow. If she likes what she sees, her eyes will light up, and she'll smile. Have you seen her smile? Really smile? It's like a supernova."

Torry stared at Ira, intrigued and aghast, seeking a smirk or some indication that he was yanking her chain. Nope, he was absolutely serious. She nodded her understanding.

While watching the preview, Torry kept sneaking looks at Evelyn to witness her reactions. A blank look. Tilted head. Uh, oh. She watched as Evelyn pressed her lips together. The designer's voice faltered mid-description about what Torry viewed as a hideous dress. He wrapped up the preview quickly, and they left.

"That was an utter waste of time," Evelyn said, as they made their way to the cars. "Ira, deal with it. Come along, Victoria."

Torry and Ira exchanged looks before she hurried to the driver's side and slipped through the open door into the back seat. "Andrew, drive us to Pastis." She gazed at Torry speculatively. "Why do you suppose I felt that line was so horrendous, Victoria?"

Nervous about providing the wrong reason, Torry swallowed convulsively. "Well, I know why I didn't care for it," she started hesitantly. "The fabric looked like plastic—thin and shiny, reminiscent of a trash bag. And the lines of that last dress were too severe. The asymmetrical cut did nothing for the chaotic design of the dress. And that bow on the second dress…" Torry shuddered as the dress flashed before her eyes. "He'd be better off ditching the bows and sticking with traditional hemlines." While Torry talked, she stared at her hands, which she held tightly in her lap. She looked up through lowered lashes to see Evelyn's reaction.

Evelyn stared at her in surprise, pleasure flittering across her face before a small smile took over. "Perhaps I should have you speak to him instead of Ira. You are exactly right. It's a shame, really," Evelyn sighed as she looked out the window. "I've had such high hopes for him." Torry watched her shake her head, disheveling blonde locks just enough so that a few strands fell over her left eye. Torry's fingers twitched with the urge to move them away. She tightened her grip on her fingers.

The car pulled to the side of the street before Torry could formulate a reply. They entered the restaurant quickly, and the hostess immediately seated them. She looked around, noting several celebrities nearby. When she looked at the menu, she blanched. Everything cost so much! Fourteen dollars for an appetizer salad? She was used to spending four dollars for a large piece of pizza and a soda. Talk about different worlds. "Do you…do you eat here often?"

"Yes. Their food is quite acceptable. The steak is always perfectly prepared." Evelyn looked up from the menu, her eyes dissecting Torry. "I assume you have not eaten here before."

"No. I haven't had the opportunity."

"Hmm. Well, you cannot order a substandard dish here. I trust you will enjoy the food." Evelyn closed the menu and placed it beside her plate. A waiter arrived before Torry could follow suit. Evelyn ordered a steak, while Torry stuck with her tried and true safety dish, a Caesar salad.

The salad was excellent, although small. The chef had arranged some romaine lettuce with four chunky croutons and a large, thin slab of parmesan cheese. Torry had requested no anchovies, and she idly wondered how the chef would have artistically arranged them on the plate. A circle of creamy Caesar dressing around the plate was surrounded by halved cherry tomatoes. It nearly looked too pretty to eat. Trying not to gobble the pleasing display too quickly, Torry wondered what was on the agenda for the afternoon. She couldn't wait to see the Closet. She had heard how vast it was. Torry knew that she would probably end up drooling while facing the myriad fabrics, designs, and colors.

"Victoria, we have a photo shoot scheduled for next week with Al Spencer which you might be interested to see. It will give you a better idea of what happens at one. I will have Ira provide you with the details."

"Oh, thank you, Evelyn. I'd love to see what happens in a photo shoot. I love his work. He takes such wonderful photos." Torry eyed Evelyn thoughtfully as she took a sip of her water. "Why are you allowing me such access? I'd been led to believe that all of this, the run-throughs, the previews, the photo shoots, are typically confidential so that none of your competitors can steal your ideas."

"Are you planning to reveal the details to my competition? Or use them yourself for your next display?" Evelyn asked, eyebrows raised.

"Of course not! I would never do—"

"Exactly," Evelyn interrupted with a smirk. "I know you wouldn't."

That stopped Torry. But it did not answer her question. She stared at Evelyn, wondering how she could get a straight answer. "But why?"

"Is it so hard to believe that I want to help you? You have a creative spark that most do not possess in this business, a type of innocence and genuine love of design, unsullied by desires or greed. I can help you. You are not meant to remain tucked away in a small resale shop." Evelyn had leaned forward while talking, and Torry could easily see how earnest she was.

Torry didn't know how to respond. It seemed too good to be true. However, she still didn't feel right accepting Evelyn's help when she had no intention of working for her. She didn't want to waste Evelyn's time.

"Evelyn, I am flattered and grateful. But I don't feel right quitting Lost Treasures. They've been good to me. I don't want to waste your time or lead you to believe that I'm ready to work at *Trending*. It's a good chance I never will be." Torry sighed, saddened by the thought that she might not get the chance to spend more time with Evelyn. This day had opened her eyes to possibilities. Not to mention, the woman was brilliant. She could learn so much from her.

A hand covering hers caused Torry to look into a penetrating stare. "You have made it perfectly clear, Victoria, that you are not ready to leave that little shop. Nevertheless, I will not allow you to waste your talent. Not only are you able to design windows that emphasize the clothes in the best ways possible, but you're also a very good painter. I am willing to bet you can write well too. Cynthia mentioned you wrote for your college newspaper."

Astounded, Torry nodded her head dumbly. Evelyn's warm hand felt like it was burning her soul.

"Now that I'm thinking about it, Cynthia said that you were the editor in chief of Boston University's student-run paper, correct?" Evelyn continued, not letting go of Torry's hand.

"Yes. I haven't written anything for a while, but I was thinking of writing about the window designs and seeing whether I could get the article published," Torry offered, distracted by Evelyn's thumb rubbing gently over the back of her hand.

"When it's ready, send it to me. I'd like to see it." Once Torry nodded, Evelyn let go of her hand and sat back. Evelyn continued to stare at her. "Tell me a bit about yourself, Victoria. I know so little."

"Oh, well, I'm not that interesting. I grew up in Newport, and I couldn't wait to go away to college. Attending BU was a wonderful experience. It opened my eyes to possibilities, new ways of viewing life. By the time I graduated, I was full of hopes and dreams, and I was convinced I could do anything." Torry grimaced at her naiveté.

"We had a photo shoot in Newport about four years ago. The mansions are gorgeous. Have you visited them?"

"Oh. Yeah. That's where I lived. Not in the mansions." She giggled nervously. "In Newport, though. It's actually quite a small community. A good one, I mean, I learned to sail and play tennis, and the school had some great teachers. And I visited all the mansions growing up. I loved exploring them."

"Yes, they are lovely." Evelyn sipped from her glass, her clear eyes urging Torry to continue.

"Well, you know the rest, pretty much. I came here and couldn't get a job doing what I wanted. So I got the job at Lost Treasures."

"Did you come here by yourself?"

"Yes. Well, not really. Some of my college friends moved here around the same time, and I knew I could contact Nana for anything. Asking her for help, though, would have felt like I'd given up on myself."

"No one else?"

"Like, you mean…no. I was with someone, but we broke up recently. He didn't like all the hours I devoted to the boutique, so he left me. He obviously couldn't get far enough away since he moved to Chicago," Torry said bitterly. She took a sip of water, keeping her eyes down. "And to add insult to injury, my friends sided with him. I went out with them recently, but it's not the same. I still feel hurt by their actions and it will take time for me to trust them again."

"And your family remains in Rhode Island?"

Torry took a minute before answering. She wondered why she was revealing so much. She mentally shrugged. For some reason she trusted Evelyn. "Yes. Of course they were opposed to my coming to New York. I had a hard time adjusting to my mom's death. I even took a year off from college to get my head on straight. But, I was determined to come here after I graduated. When they found out Brandon had left me, my father urged me to return home. Truth be told, he hasn't stopped hounding me. It's like he doesn't trust me to do what I've set out to do. If he had his way, I'd write for the local paper or, better yet, go to law school. He's always wanted me to join his law firm. Work with him."

Evelyn hummed before sipping some water, a pensive look on her face. "Cynthia mentioned that your relationship began once you entered college. Did you learn about fashion through her?"

"No. It was my mom." Torry felt her eyes well up. "She…she's the one who taught me all about colors and fabrics. We'd spend entire afternoons poring over designs and gowns and colors and materials. If only she could see me now." Torry shook her head.

"I'm sorry, Victoria." Evelyn's hand once again covered Torry's in a sign of comfort.

A silence blanketed them as Torry tried to regain her composure. Once she did, she shot a watery smile at Evelyn. "Thanks."

Evelyn squeezed her hand and let go. "You said they were opposed to your coming to New York. Are you talking about your sister?"

"Yes, my father and my older sister, Katie. But I wanted to try. After Brandon left and they urged me to return, I thought about why I wanted to remain here. The answer was simple. I came here for a reason, and I intend to reach my goals. I refuse to give up. I don't want to go back with my tail tucked between my legs. I don't want to wonder whether I could have succeeded. I don't want to give up." Torry stopped talking when she glanced up and read the emotions on Evelyn's face of compassion, admiration, and approval.

"You will go far, Victoria. You have a mind of your own and the drive to succeed."

Torry grinned at the praise, letting it settle over her like a warm blanket. If she had learned anything since Evelyn took an interest in her work, it was that the woman did not hand out compliments freely.

"Um, if you don't mind my asking, I'd like to know about your daughters. I mean, aren't they teenagers now? That must be so hard, working so much and trying to spend time with them..." Torry trailed off, not sure whether she had crossed a line.

"Jennifer is sixteen, and Julie is fifteen. They are vivacious and intelligent. I have no doubt you'd get along with them. They have enjoyed your displays. They make a game of guessing which scenes the displays reflect from the literature you've chosen for your designs." Evelyn smiled softly.

"Oh! I'd love to meet them some time. Maybe they can give me some suggestions for future scenes. I have some ideas, but I usually wait until a few days before changing the display to commit to a design." Torry wondered at the look Evelyn had on her face. Contemplative? She wasn't sure.

"Yes. I'm sure they would love to meet you. When do you intend to change the display?" Evelyn sipped from her glass before signaling to their server for the check.

"Thursday night. I have just about everything ready." Torry became excited as her thoughts turned to her plans for the window design. She really hoped Evelyn would like it.

"Are you working on Saturday?" Evelyn asked, as she slid a credit card into the billfold and handed it back to the server.

"Yes, but only until six. Harold wants to rearrange the clothes, so he's closing." Torry jumped up as Evelyn rose gracefully from the table. "Thank you for lunch, Evelyn."

"You're very welcome. The girls and I will come to the store at six on Saturday. That way they can take a closer look at the displays and talk to you about them over dinner."

Torry ran around the car to slide into the back seat. Realizing that Evelyn had just invited her to dinner with her children, Torry smiled brightly. "That sounds like fun. I look forward to it." Knowing she was going to spend time with Evelyn again so soon made her feel exhilarated. All those stories about how unfeeling and cold she was—that was all just a bunch of crap. Evelyn had treated her with respect and warmth the entire day. Sure, Evelyn was condescending and sharp-tongued at work, but she had to be. Torry had witnessed how others perceived her as extremely intimidating, but this Evelyn, the private Evelyn, was alluring and attractive. Torry felt privileged to be the recipient of such treatment. She certainly wouldn't take it for granted.

Lost in the genuine smile Evelyn directed her way, Torry felt a wave of heat spread throughout her body, settling below her belly button. After several seconds, Evelyn cleared her throat and looked away.

"This afternoon I have a meeting with the new CEO of Magellan-Weeks Publications. While I attend, you will tour the Closet with Ira, and then head over to where next week's photo shoot will occur. Currently, they are prepping the area for the shoot. Feel free to ask Ira any questions."

Torry nodded her understanding. "Okay. Thanks." They exited the car and walked toward the elevator banks silently. The tension between them pulsed relentlessly. Torry felt like pulling on her collar, she was so hot. Once the elevator doors opened, Torry received a glare from Heather before the woman delivered several messages to Evelyn and proceeded to jot down the editor's responses. Halfway back to her office, Evelyn stopped and turned to Torry.

"Ira's office is that way." Evelyn waved a hand down a side hallway. "I am planning to join you at the shoot location this afternoon, but if I do not make it, I will see you on Saturday."

"Okay. Thank you for today, Evelyn. I really appreciate you letting me tag along." *I loved staring at you, listening to you, feeling your hand on top of mine, just being near you*, she wanted to add but did not dare. "Bye." Torry began to deliver a dorky wave before getting it under control and turning away. She made her way to Ira's office and knocked on the glass door before entering.

"Well, well, if it isn't the belle of the ball. Have a seat, Torry." Ira finished marking a sheet of negatives before placing the red pencil on the table. "Ready to see the Closet?"

"Are you kidding? I've been looking forward to it all day."

"Right. I'm sure you were bored out of your mind all morning," he drawled. Torry blushed. She certainly had not been bored.

Smirking, Ira moved toward the door. "This way."

When they entered the Closet, Torry gasped. Row upon row of clothing and accessories were neatly arranged. It was overwhelming and fabulous and oh so wonderful. Torry's eyes jumped everywhere, not knowing where to focus. "Oh, my God. Ira, this is, this is…I never could have imagined what this is!" Torry touched a gown with reverent fingers, allowing the fabric to slide over her palm. Decadent, the slinky satin screamed sensuality and seduction.

"I felt the same way when I saw it for the first time. That was years and years ago, before you ever laid eyes on your first pair of Jimmy Choos." Ira winked at her and walked slowly down the center aisle. "This way, dear. Let me reveal the mysteries of the Closet."

For the next hour, Ira explained the design of the Closet, allowing Torry to explore the orderly sections as she asked question after question. "It just blows my mind, Ira. How do you ever get any work done? I'd just want to revel in all this beauty every single minute," she gushed.

Chuckling, Ira said, "Believe me, I spend as much time as possible in here." He looked at his watch. "Unfortunately, we need to get going to the photo shoot location."

Sadness washed over her at the thought of leaving so soon. A hand on her shoulder brought her eyes to Ira's smiling face.

"Don't worry, Torry. I'm sure you'll get to see the Closet again."

Torry smiled in response, cheered by the thought. Besides, she really was looking forward to seeing how a fashion photo shoot was created. "Lead the way." After receiving a squeeze on the shoulder, she followed Ira, knowing that the rest of the afternoon would expand her perspective in ways she could never anticipate.

Chapter Ten

"SWEETHEARTS, ARE YOU READY to go?" Evelyn asked, poking her head into Jennifer's room. As usual, she sat on the bed reading, while Julie typed on her computer.

"Yup."

"Yes."

Julie quickly signed off and stood as Jennifer placed a bookmark between the pages and set the book aside. They followed Evelyn down the stairs and to the closet for their coats. It was cold out, just a week before Thanksgiving. The days were shorter and, for some unfathomable reason, her employees seemed to become less productive with the sun setting earlier and earlier each afternoon. It was absurd, really. The work was always waiting, regardless of whether the sun shone as bright as Victoria's smile. Evelyn's heart thumped pleasantly at the thought of seeing her again. She hoped her girls would behave.

Evelyn shook her head. Victoria was so naïve it was comical. Her loyalty was admirable but certainly misplaced. In some ways, Evelyn found the younger woman refreshing. No subterfuge or artifice. Victoria's words and behavior were as fascinating as her luminous emerald eyes.

It had occurred to Evelyn, when they were eating lunch at Pastis, that she might be approaching this the wrong way. Obviously, Victoria's decisions were ruled by her heart. It was that thought which had caused her to ask Victoria personal questions. Normally, she would keep such meetings focused purely on business. It was clear, however, that her normal way of operating was not working. Victoria was unique, refreshing and truly incomparable. The old rules did not apply. If she wanted to help Victoria, she needed to create a connection, one that transcended the workplace. And last week's lunch meeting had reinforced her theory.

Smiling slightly, Evelyn realized that she wanted to find out more about Victoria. To spend more time with her. She could clothe it any way she liked, but Evelyn had to admit, at least to herself, that this was not just business. It was personal.

To everyone else, it would seem as if she were nurturing another business relationship. Unlike all those she had guided over the years, knowing they would remain loyal to her for her efforts, Evelyn knew she would receive much more through any interactions with Victoria. Already, she could feel the excitement, the spark, the flow of creativity transforming her perspective and elevating her mood. Spending time with Victoria certainly proved to be no hardship. What she had already learned merely whetted her appetite.

"You didn't tell us what book she based the displays on, Mom," Julie said, as they drove to the boutique. Evelyn had chosen to drive her Roadster. She did not get to drive often, mostly transported by one of the work cars for business events. This was personal, though, even if Victoria did not quite realize it yet. Even if Evelyn was just realizing it herself.

"You're right, dear. I want you two to guess, as you have with the other displays." Evelyn slowed the car for a light.

"What if we get it wrong, though? I don't want to sound stupid," Jennifer chimed in.

Evelyn looked through her rearview mirror to catch her daughter's eye.

"You'll guess correctly. Victoria is very good at what she does. You'll recognize the scenes, of that I have no doubt." Evelyn hummed under her breath. The newest designs were as captivating and thought-provoking as the others had been. Evelyn took such pleasure in viewing Victoria's work. And yesterday afternoon, Victoria had delivered the painting from the last display. Evelyn had been out of the building, unfortunately, but Heather confirmed it was Victoria who brought the painting to *Trending*. Evelyn knew just where to place it, and it looked beautiful in her home.

"You've seen it?" Julie asked with excitement. "Give us a hint, then."

"Oh yes, Mom, just a hint. Have we read the book before? Is there a movie based on it, or a play? What time period is it from?" Jennifer peppered her with questions, leaning toward the front of the car.

"Well, if I remember correctly, you read the story this past summer, and Julie read it last year. Over time, many have adapted it for film and television. That's all you'll get out of me. I expect both of you will recognize it," Evelyn said, as she double-parked. "Be careful getting out. We won't stay long, so take a good look at the displays."

The girls hurried to the large display windows, exclaiming over the presentations. Although a cold wind pulled at their coats, they seemed impervious as they stared at the two scenes representing

Jane Eyre. The first window was easy to recognize. Jane watched Rochester as he walked sightlessly nearby. He wore a stylish, black Tom Ford suit with a slate-colored vest, off-white silk shirt underneath, and a black, gray, and red patterned tie. He carried a walking stick, and his eyes looked unfocused, his mouth open, and head tilted upward, as if concentrating on the sounds around him. Jane stood watching, resplendent in her slate-blue, Stella McCartney fitted coat over a matching ankle-length, heavy wool dress and stylish, dark-gray, Chanel boots which reached her knees. A bonnet was attached with a matching ribbon that tied under the mannequin's chin.

The other display was much more symbolic. Jane wore a fiery-red Christian Dior gown, the fabric resplendent with its waves of gradient color, while an older gentleman, Evelyn guessed he represented St. John, was dressed in a simple, yet elegant, light-gray Gucci suit. He held a frosted glass filled with liquid as he looked on, a sad smile on his face. Jane was walking away from St. John toward a painting of a large manor in flames—Thornfield. Fire and ice, passion and repression, Evelyn's breath caught in her throat. Certainly, Victoria was fire to Evelyn's ice. Evelyn wanted to break free from her self-made prison. She used to be passionate in all aspects of her life. Over the years, though, she had learned to control her emotions, to diffuse them, until the sparks eventually had extinguished. Until Victoria entered her life and reignited that passion. Now Evelyn felt her spirit burning brightly, and she did not want to go back to a passionless existence. She would not.

As if summoned by her thoughts, Victoria walked out the door and smiled widely as she buttoned up her coat. She quickly donned thick wool gloves and made her way to Evelyn's side. "Hi," she greeted Evelyn.

Amused and charmed by Victoria's exuberance and clear excitement, Evelyn nodded as her lips turned upward. "Victoria. I believe my girls approve of your latest designs." She tilted her head toward Jennifer and Julie, who stood talking animatedly, waving their arms and pointing at the displays.

"That's great. Do you, um, what do you think?" Her eyes skittered away nervously, only to return with a look of hope glistening through them.

"You have yet to disappoint me," Evelyn answered softly. She stared into Victoria's animated face, jolted by the realization that her own reply made her happy. She was so used to ripping people apart in order to get what she wanted, what the magazine needed. Although she could sweet talk when necessary, she hardly ever meant the words she used as a tool to further her goals. Now, though, she wanted nothing more than to elicit, again and again, the sparkling eyes and wide smile currently directed her way, and not just to create leverage for convincing Victoria to join *Trending*. Evelyn felt her heart thump with the realization that she cared for Victoria.

"What is it, Evelyn?" Victoria asked, as she stepped closer and laid a glove-clad hand on her forearm. Evelyn looked down at the hand and back into slightly panicked eyes. Feeling Victoria's hand starting to slide away, Evelyn placed her own on top of it, effectively keeping it in place.

"I find myself continually surprised by your visions and your ability to execute them as well as you do with so little means at your disposal," Evelyn said, her eyes running over the windows once more. She wanted to say something much different, something along the lines of *I find you exhilarating. My thoughts keep returning to you again and again. I want to kiss you. May I kiss you?* Evelyn realized she was staring at parted lips, the condensation she saw with each exhale at odds with how hot she felt at the moment. *Who's the fire, and who's the ice?*

Returning her gaze to Victoria's questioning eyes, she cocked her head pensively. She saw open eyes, eyes that began to darken the longer they stood staring silently at each other, eyes that expressed a desire recognized by Evelyn's body even before her mind could translate it. Evelyn felt her nipples tighten in response, and a telltale wetness made itself known between her suddenly weakened legs. Victoria's hand trembled slightly under her own. Evelyn squeezed it reassuringly, wanting her to accept the attraction coursing between them.

Evelyn's mind flashed to the conversation she had shared with Ira the day after her first lunch meeting with Victoria. Ira had brought her the latest proofs for the Testino shoot before broaching the subject.

"How was your lunch?" he asked casually.

Evelyn flicked her eyes at Ira suspiciously. He stood looking at Testino's photos as if he'd just inquired about the weather, an innocent look on his face. She knew better.

"Not as successful as I had hoped," Evelyn sighed.

"No?" Ira said mildly, raising an eyebrow.

"No," Evelyn agreed, her voice flat. "For such an intelligent, creative woman, she is quite the innocent when it comes to the business world. No doubt her heart will be broken when she realizes that people do not care about her, just about what she can do for them."

"I care about her. I find her charming and quite remarkable. And I think you feel the same way." Ira stared into her eyes, challenging her to deny what he'd said. Evelyn pursed her lips, not happy that he could read her so well.

"If no one watches out for her, her talents will be wasted and that spark will be extinguished. When is the last time we found someone with such raw talent? Yet she refuses to consider working for us or joining one of the larger department stores. It's ridiculous. She is ridiculous," Evelyn groused as she pinched the bridge of her nose between thumb and forefinger. When she looked up, she noted the speculative look in Ira's eyes. "What?"

"Why not invite her here to see the inner workings of *Trending*? It may be that she has no idea what we do. If she sees the grander scale, the endless supply of clothes at her disposal, the way a photo shoot is prepared and executed, and you in your element, then she might change her mind."

"Hmm."

Evelyn had not found fault with his suggestion, and she was grateful that they had implemented the idea. Victoria had seen inside Evelyn's world, and Evelyn had learned more about her. What Evelyn realized, though, was that her efforts to spend time with Victoria were no longer about the golden opportunity she'd missed when Victoria first moved to the city. It was silly, of course. Cynthia had mentioned her over the last year, even going so far as to voice her desire to help Victoria break in to their industry. Evelyn just hadn't listened closely enough, hadn't remembered the girl who'd delivered a poignant eulogy.

Since their lives had intersected once more, Evelyn was determined not to repeat the mistake. She refused to allow Victoria to slip away so easily again. That oversight mortified her. She had missed an opportunity not only to introduce raw talent to the fashion industry, but also to nurture it, nurture her. Even worse, though, she had lost a year of getting to know this woman who was easily turning her life upside down with her broad smiles, bright eyes, nimble mind, and sensitive nature.

Surprisingly, Evelyn found that she wanted that chaos in her life, wanted Victoria in her life. If Victoria continued to refuse employment through Evelyn, then she would have to find another way to connect with her. Based on the way her body responded to the green-eyed beauty, her heart had chosen the route.

"Mom! Can we go? Oh, is this the window designer?" Jennifer said.

Julie looped her arm through Jennifer's and smiled at Victoria. "Hi. I'm Julie. This is Jennifer. We love your displays."

Victoria squeezed Evelyn's arm before withdrawing her hand and turning her attention toward Evelyn's daughters. "Hi. I'm Torry. I'm glad you like the displays. I've been looking forward to talking to you about them." She transferred her gaze from Julie to Jennifer, including them both in the conversation.

"Torry? Mom, I thought you said her name is Victoria," Jennifer said, turning her head to look at Evelyn directly with a question in her eyes.

"Well, your mom likes to call me by my given name, which is fine. She can call me whatever she wants," she muttered to the girls, who erupted in laughter. "But everyone else calls me Torry." She flashed a brilliant smile, and the girls smiled back.

"Shall we go? We can discuss the displays while warming ourselves in front of a cozy fire." Evelyn turned and led the way to her car. She was tempted to drive home, arrange for food to be delivered, and claim the kiss that she desperately desired. Of course, she would not. Shaking her head minutely, Evelyn chastised herself. What was she doing, lusting after this woman? It was ridiculous, humiliating really. Victoria was closer in age to her daughters than to her. The most she could hope for was to build a friendship. Anything else was merely the product of fanciful daydreams.

Lost in such thoughts, her mind arguing against her heart, Evelyn remained quiet, while the girls peppered Victoria with questions. Most answers Evelyn already knew. She pulled into a parking garage near the restaurant, and after turning off the engine, glanced at Victoria. Caught in a warm gaze, Evelyn took a deep breath and exhaled with a small smile. She jerked her head toward the car door and exited without a word.

Those ridiculous desires were once again swirling through her, settling low in her stomach, causing her body to tremble with anticipation. Everything took on a peculiar sharpness: the dirty, concrete floor they walked on, the clicking of her heels against it, the laughter of her daughters, and the warmth of Victoria's body walking closely next to hers. It was as if her perceptions had shifted once she realized, truly realized, how her feelings had developed. Ira had hinted at the possibility, but Evelyn hadn't taken him seriously.

Without slowing down, Evelyn strode into Per Se and nodded at the maître d'. He grabbed some menus and led them to a table close to the roaring fire, but not so close as to cause them to feel uncomfortably warm. The nearby windows showcased a fabulous view. Evelyn watched as Victoria's eyes traveled around the room before settling on her. Her shy smile was captivating.

"This is wonderful, Evelyn. Thank you for inviting me." Victoria took off her outerwear and handed it to the waiting maître d', as did Evelyn, Jennifer, and Julie.

"You're going to love the food here, Torry. They have the best chef's menu," Jennifer said.

"Oh, I'm sure I will," Victoria replied.

"I was not sure what types of food you prefer," Evelyn said, wanting to ask outright but not wishing to make Victoria uncomfortable. She assumed that the woman was not used to dining in three-star Michelin restaurants. In truth, although she limited how often her girls ate out, Evelyn had no choice but to eat in restaurants nearly every day. She worked with a nutritionist to curtail any damage the restaurant food she consumed might cause her body. She was sure no one was aware of how strict she was with her diet.

"I like American, Italian, seafood, Chinese. I heard Thai was good. And French. I'm open to trying new things," Victoria answered.

Raising an eyebrow, Evelyn smiled slowly, not realizing until she saw a flush crawl up Victoria's neck how provocative her expression might be. Flirting, Evelyn? Really? Not that she had any control over her reactions, or so it seemed. "Hmm. Well, I'll keep that in mind," Evelyn drawled, mentally slapping herself when she heard how low her voice sounded.

"Have you tried Japanese? Mom likes sushi, but I think it tastes weird," Jennifer said, making a face.

"No, I haven't tried sushi, but I wouldn't mind taking a taste," Victoria said softly.

Evelyn bit her bottom lip, gazing at Victoria through her lashes as her mind flashed on an image of her hand-feeding sushi to the beautiful woman, fingers gently nestled between those moist, luscious lips. "We'll have to rectify that at some point," Evelyn said, unfortunately with a rather throaty voice. Clearing her throat, Evelyn looked away and drank some of her water. She needed to get herself under control.

"So, the displays are for *Jane Eyre*, right?" Jennifer asked. Evelyn was never so glad for a change in topic.

"Yes, you're right. Did you recognize the scenes?" Victoria asked, a twinkle in her eyes.

"One was when Jane left the pastor to return to Rochester," Julie said.

"He was a minister," Jennifer said.

"I don't think it said that. It said he was going to be a missionary." Julie looked at Victoria. "Isn't that right, Torry?"

"I think the book called him a clergyman. He was going to India to be a missionary, and he asked Jane to marry him and go with him. What else did you get from that design?"

"She represents fire and was walking toward the fire. We talked about symbolism in school. And also Rochester's house burned down. She was traveling toward that, too, toward her passion." Jennifer preened at Evelyn's approving smile.

Her daughters were so intelligent. They consistently excelled in school. In fact, Evelyn often worried that they were not always mentally stimulated. Perhaps she was overreacting, but it seemed as if they were apathetic to just about everything. Thankfully, Victoria's displays had helped them to become interested in books again. Now they sat fully engaged as they commented on the other display, the one representing Jane's realization that Rochester was blind.

With the arrival of the nine courses in their meal came exclamations of how tasty and aesthetically pleasing each dish was. Victoria's shining eyes and careful attention while tasting each offering warmed Evelyn as if she were the chef seeking approval. The girls knew that eating here was a special treat, and they barely held back from gobbling down the food, attempting to maintain a modicum of manners. Evelyn had a hard time not smiling at their obvious enjoyment of the meal.

That was another revelation. Evelyn felt the urge to smile more and more often. In the past she had felt tired and sucked dry by the end of each work day. Lately, she felt rejuvenated and vibrant. It did not take a genius to deduce why.

"What do you like to do outside of school? I mean, do you play sports or like to read or draw?"

"We both play the piano, but I like basketball and soccer too," Julie said.

"I like to read more than she does, and I write mysteries," Jennifer said proudly.

Evelyn sat listening, wondering when she last had asked these questions. She couldn't remember. Often her daughters would natter away about what they were doing while she worked, but she had never attended a sports event where Julie had played, nor had she read anything Jennifer had written.

"And she draws really good. I mean she draws well. She draws people," Julie added as she patted Jennifer's shoulder.

"I like to draw too," Victoria said eagerly. "I'm not very good. I mean, I've never had formal training or anything, but I like doing it."

"Really, Victoria. You speak as if you have no talent," Evelyn chided. She looked toward her daughters. "You remember the painting that was in *The Great Gatsby* display, the one I brought home last night?" At their nod, Evelyn continued. "Victoria painted it."

"You did? Really?" Jennifer asked, her eyes wide. "No way! You're talented. Mom hung it in the drawing room."

Tilting her head in a pose Evelyn often adopted, Julie studied Victoria. "You're really different. I mean, you're interesting. And you don't treat us like little kids or try to impress us so we'll like you. You're just you." Julie shrugged her shoulders.

"Uh, thanks. I like spending time with you. All of you." Victoria swept her eyes around the table, settling on each girl briefly before connecting with Evelyn's eyes.

Evelyn felt that pulsing energy flowing between them once more, so strong she thought for a fleeting moment that she felt herself leaning toward Victoria. Evelyn blinked and wet her suddenly dry lips as she pulled back. "We will simply have to do this again," Evelyn murmured.

"Yeah. And maybe I can see some of your drawings," Jennifer said excitedly.

Julie elbowed her sister. "I want to see them too."

"Girls. I am sure Victoria would be amenable to showing them to both of you if you ask nicely," Evelyn said, smiling at how quickly they were bonding with Victoria. This was a welcome surprise. "She might even allow me to see them," she added with a smile, capturing shining eyes and raising an eyebrow in question. Receiving a small nod and a charming, shy smile, Evelyn smirked.

"Torry, you'll show them to both of us, won't you? Maybe you can give me some tips. I'll show you what I've done," Jennifer said.

"Well, I don't know that I would be much help," Victoria hedged, "but I'd love to see your drawings. The next time we get together, I'll bring my sketchbook over. And maybe both of you can give me some ideas for future displays."

"Okay. What are you going to do next?" Jennifer asked.

"I have some thoughts," Victoria said mysteriously, a sweet smile covering her face.

"Do you like sports, Torry?" Julie asked, clearly wanting to connect with her in some way. Evelyn's heart warmed even more.

"Well, I jog as much as possible, and I used to play basketball and tennis, although I haven't in a while. With the colder weather, I'm not sure how much running I'll be doing. It's not like I'm a die-hard jogger or anything," she added with a chuckle.

"Maybe you can come to my school one afternoon and shoot hoops with me. I bet Mom can get permission for you, right, Mom?" Julie turned her head toward Evelyn for confirmation.

"If Victoria can find the time and is able to join you, I am sure I can arrange for a visitor's pass," she answered. Of course she would do whatever she could to make her girls happy.

As they finished their dinner, Victoria answered more questions about her work and family while asking questions about them. Although normally very private, Evelyn welcomed the interest and shared more of herself than she normally would.

"So, you aren't going home for Thanksgiving?" Jennifer asked.

"No. I decided to save my money and go back for Christmas. It's not a big deal. I'll watch the Macy's parade and have a turkey sandwich," Victoria said with a sad smile.

Both girls looked at Evelyn with pleading eyes. She understood what they wanted. Evelyn found she liked the idea very much. "Victoria, it is unnecessary for you to be alone. We usually watch the parade at a friend's house before returning home to eat. Why don't you join us?"

"Yeah, Torry. We can stand on the balcony and watch the parade. It's way better than standing in the crowd or watching it on TV. Come with us," Julie implored.

"You'll have fun with us. And you can bring your sketchbook," Jennifer added.

"And we can play Wii," Julie said.

"It will be great," Jennifer said.

Evelyn watched as Victoria's face broke into a smile at her girls' enthusiasm. She saw the question in the woman's eyes and smiled. "You are welcome to join us, Victoria." As Victoria's beautiful face beamed happiness, her toothy smile and expressive eyes communicated to Evelyn just how much she wanted to spend the day with them. Evelyn couldn't help but smile back.

As Evelyn drove toward Victoria's apartment, she felt saddened by the thought that she would not see the younger woman for three days. Evelyn took solace knowing she would see her at the photo shoot, and on Thanksgiving, soon enough. Pulling up in front of her apartment, Evelyn parked the car and watched her passenger as she unbuckled her seatbelt. She was amused by how nervous Victoria looked.

"Well, um, thank you for dinner. I had a great time." Victoria turned to look toward the back where the girls sat.

"Bye, Torry. See you on Thanksgiving. Don't forget your drawings," Jennifer said.

"Bye, Torry. Maybe we can play basketball this week. I'll have Mom contact you about it," Julie said.

"Julie, you can contact her directly too. Isn't that right, Victoria?" Evelyn said, knowing the answer even as she watched her nod her consent.

"Okay. Give me your e-mail address or your number so I can text you," Julie said enthusiastically.

Victoria took out a small notepad from her purse and wrote on it before ripping the page out and handing it to Julie. "There's my number and e-mail address. You can use either." She turned toward Evelyn and said softly, as she placed a hand over Evelyn's where it rested on the stick shift, "Thank you, Evelyn. I'll see you soon."

Just managing to nod, Evelyn could have sworn that Victoria's hand remained on hers throughout the drive home. Regardless of how improper her feelings were, regardless of their age difference and disparate social standings, she couldn't deny Victoria's hold over her. Evelyn wondered whether it was a good idea to spend more time with her. She felt her chest tighten at the thought of not seeing her again. For better or worse, her heart was invested. She could only hope that Victoria would allow this tenuous connection to strengthen.

For once in her life, Evelyn decided she would allow herself to explore this attraction without fearing how it might affect her reputation. The girls obviously liked spending time with Victoria, and Evelyn could not deny her desire to become closer to her. She smiled softly. Perhaps she was allowing herself to become too wrapped up in the excitement of a new relationship when they had not even discussed the possibility, but Evelyn had learned from her past failed relationships. She would not make the same mistakes.

For some unfathomable reason, she had been given another chance at happiness. She'd be a fool to shy away from the obvious bond they shared. Decision made, Evelyn kissed her girls goodnight and picked up the latest mock-up to review. She would make sure she spent more time with Victoria so that they could get to know one another. Whether they became friends or more, Evelyn would keep Victoria in her life. She liked how she felt around the younger woman. And if Victoria's reactions were any indication, she liked being around Evelyn too.

Chapter Eleven

LEAVING HER APARTMENT WEARILY, Torry pulled her heavy winter jacket closer and carefully walked on the black ice coating the sidewalk to the waiting town car. It had snowed yesterday, blanketing New York with several inches. Unfortunately, the temperature had proceeded to drop to the teens overnight, creating treacherous walking conditions. Torry wondered whether this weather was a warning that more of the same would occur. It wasn't even officially winter, yet. Walking around the city, while trying to keep warm and remain on her feet, was not a fun activity.

Not that she had to walk anywhere today. She was hitching a ride to the *Trending* photo shoot in an impressive black Lincoln, courtesy of one Evelyn Allbright. She smirked before feeling it fade as she fell back into thoughts that had plagued her for several days. She could get used to such luxury. Too used to it. The chauffeur-driven cars, the expensive, tasty meals, the couture, and the limitless materials at her disposal if only she agreed to work for Evelyn were all so enticing. Torry kept reminding herself that this was not what she wanted. Well, she did want it, but she did not want to trade in her ideas of what she believed would be best for her. If she accepted these perks, took them for granted, what would be next? Would she wake up one day and be unable to recognize who she'd become?

Although Evelyn had told her that she would be able to rise quickly within the company as she honed her skills, Torry didn't see how that would be possible. She would be forced to obtain permission for every action she took, every dollar she spent, every idea she created. Where would her freedom, her autonomy, her authenticity be? Her ideas would become diluted, colorless, ordinary. Torry sighed. It was a perplexing problem since she knew Evelyn strived to showcase originality. Maybe she wasn't experienced enough to understand the process. Maybe she should listen to Evelyn, trust her. Maybe she was afraid of being held accountable.

Hurrying inside the New York Public Library at Fifth and 42nd, Torry walked over to where Ira had decided the photos should be taken. As she strolled through the Rose Main Reading Room, Torry felt awed by the endless shelves of books just waiting to be read. Tilting her head, she gazed at the restored ceilings, loving how they gave the room a grandiose atmosphere.

"Good morning, Ira," Torry said brightly, as she joined him and another man.

"Oh, good, you're here. Torry, this is Al Spencer, our photographer," Ira said.

"It's a pleasure to meet you, Torry. Even before I saw your fabulous window displays, I had heard about them. I am honored to have you here," the photographer said.

"We're having some problems with the designing of the shots. When we came here last week, the sun was shining through much differently. Turns out this lighting won't work. We still want to use this room, but we won't be able to use the shots we originally planned for here."

"Have you thought about using Astor Hall for some of the photos? It is majestic and timeless, a great backdrop for vivid, bold colors," Torry said. She studied the sketches for the photo shoot. Noting the interested looks on Ira's and Al's faces, she continued. "The staircase is particularly magnificent. It would showcase these gowns," she said, pointing to several pictures of gorgeous Atelier Versace evening gowns in dark greens, deep reds, and midnight blues.

Looking around her once more, she asked, "Which clothes were you planning to shoot for this room?" She listened attentively as Al explained his vision for the morning's activities. Looking through the portfolio of designs to be used, she stopped at a set of photos. "How about these dresses? They'd be complemented by the bookshelves and tables, don't you think?"

The men stared at the photos before they looked around the hall. Ira smiled widely, and Al nodded his head. "Excuse me, Torry," Al said before walking away, pointing toward some bookcases as he directed his assistants to set up over there.

"You are a breath of fresh air, Torry," Ira said. "Wouldn't you agree, Evelyn?" he said, as he turned to the side, revealing the editor leaning against a table, her penetrating gaze causing a flash of heat to race through Torry's body.

"Good morning, Evelyn," she said hesitantly, wondering whether the woman would be angry that she'd pretty much inserted herself into the planning of the photo shoot. She hadn't meant to, but the ideas were flowing, and she wanted to help. She watched as Evelyn pushed off the table with her hip before slowly approaching them.

"Victoria," she said in greeting. "What other ideas have you provided?" She continued to stare at Torry, who felt frozen to the spot.

"She gave us a great idea for the Versace gowns. We are going to set up in Astor Hall, particularly on the staircase," Ira said.

Evelyn nodded her approval but did not turn away from Torry. "Do you have any other ideas?" she asked softly.

"Ye...yes. I was thinking that the walls of the McGraw Rotunda might be the perfect backdrop for some of the Salvatore Ferragamo pantsuits." Noting the encouraging look Evelyn gave her, she pointed toward the Bottega Veneta photos. "And these black, lambskin jackets paired with those Alexander Wang embroidered turtlenecks would look great in front of the paneled walls in the Periodical Room." She tried not to fidget, while Evelyn's eyes searched hers for several moments. She lost her breath when Evelyn directed a full smile her way. She couldn't help but smile in return.

Once Evelyn turned away to implement her ideas, she took a deep breath, just stopping herself from grabbing at the table like some Victorian heroine. Talk about dramatic. She felt a bit unsteady, but she wouldn't allow herself to pass out just because Evelyn had smiled at her.

The morning flew by as she watched the inner workings of the photo shoot, often contributing her ideas when asked. She was pretty surprised by how often Al requested her thoughts. Evelyn did not say much, but she remained close to her as the hours passed. During a rare moment while Evelyn took a call, Ira sidled up.

"You are doing a wonderful job, Torry. Your ideas have saved the shoot. Don't think no one realizes that," Ira said, as he watched the models shifting into different poses at Al's direction.

"Oh, Ira, I'm just, you know, I see the colors and the textures, and I just know that they would look wonderful together," Torry said, self-conscious at the undeserving praise directed her way.

"Hmm. You do realize, don't you, that it is highly unusual for Evelyn to remain at a photo shoot this long? Particularly when we have used the photographer before." He looked pointedly at her, as if to tell her that she was the reason for the exception.

Before she could formulate a reply, Evelyn rejoined them.

"Victoria, come along."

Torry raised her eyebrows as she looked at Ira and then at Evelyn's retreating back. Ira made a shooing motion and smiled. With a shrug, she hurried to catch up, grabbing her coat and purse as she followed Evelyn out the door and into the waiting car.

Evelyn took her to lunch at a nearby deli, surprising Torry. Starved, she ordered a pastrami sandwich, while Evelyn ordered a hearty salad. As they ate, Evelyn asked her question after question about the shoot, what she had seen that had impressed her or confused her, and why she had paired certain fabrics and colors with particular rooms.

They also talked about Thanksgiving, Evelyn providing more details of their usual activities. It was one of the few times during the year when she did not work. According to Evelyn, the pace was decadently slow. She spent the entire weekend with her daughters, usually indulging them by participating in activities they wished to do. Torry felt a twinge of envy at the thought of having Evelyn's undivided attention for so long.

Once they were back in the car, Evelyn announced, "I am sorry to say that I have meetings this afternoon which will prevent me from returning to the shoot with you."

Torry tried not to show how disappointed she felt. "That's okay. I'm glad you were able to be there this morning. And thank you for lunch."

The car pulled up in front of the library, signaling that Torry must leave. She felt bereft, even as she admitted to herself just how silly she was since she would see the woman in two days for Thanksgiving. Their gazes locked as Evelyn reached over and covered Torry's hand with her own.

All day Evelyn had terrorized her employees, pushing them to be better and to produce their best, while Torry had watched. During that time, Evelyn had maintained a calm, cool demeanor. Even during lunch, although Evelyn's interest in their conversation had seemed genuine, she'd treated Torry with a formality that bespoke a business relationship. Yet now, during these last few moments before Evelyn had to leave, she held Torry captive through look and touch. Torry was mesmerized by the soft gaze, glimpsing the woman behind the business mask. Warmth shone through darkened blue eyes, reaching into her soul. She felt naked and vulnerable, and she was sure Evelyn could read the emotions welling up so suddenly, so strongly.

"We will pick you up at seven thirty on Thursday morning for the parade. Dress warmly. You are welcome to stay over Thursday night. We have several guest rooms," Evelyn said softly before leaning forward and resting her smooth cheek against the side of Torry's face. Her eyes closed. The sensations were overwhelming to Torry, as the familiar fragrance of Evelyn's perfume embraced her. Her breathing hitched, as she inhaled deeply of the heady mixture.

"O...okay," she whispered, feeling Evelyn shiver before pulling back slightly. When their eyes reconnected, Torry gasped, feeling her body tremble in response to the look she saw in those stormy eyes. She watched while Evelyn's mouth opened slightly to sip air. When she exhaled, her breath caressed Torry's face. Slowly, turning her hand to tangle their fingers together, she whispered reverently, "Evelyn." An elegant hand touched her cheek, finding its way to the nape of her neck where a gentle pressure was exerted.

Torry leaned forward to brush her lips against a welcoming mouth. Once, twice, three times she grazed her lips gently across, hardly touching Evelyn's dark lips. Hearing a small moan, she obligingly pressed more firmly, loving the feel of their lips moving in concert. Parting her lips a bit, she groaned when she felt Evelyn's tongue swipe gently in between, just touching her tongue in greeting. She breathed through her nose as they slowly, so slowly rubbed their tongues together, the friction delicious, provocative, and promising.

When they parted, Torry opened her eyes to find a tender look directed her way. She touched her lips with her fingertips, hardly believing what they had just shared. Biting her lower lip shyly, not knowing what to say, she smiled tremulously. She felt Evelyn squeeze her hand before letting go.

"I'm sorry, but I really must go," Evelyn said, her voice slightly hoarse, regret hanging between them.

Nodding her understanding, she opened the car door, got out, and leaned back in. "Bye," she whispered before closing the door.

The rest of the afternoon flew by, her head in the clouds as she replayed the kiss again and again. Ira patiently explained the process, why at times the photos were subpar or the set did not showcase the fabrics sufficiently, why they had chosen these clothes and accessories and that location and photographer. She began to understand how much planning was required for a spread, but still she had questions, so many questions.

At the end of the day, as they were breaking down the last set, Al said to her, "You really helped me today. I'll make sure you receive some compensation, if not from *Trending* then from me. And I was wondering, would you be willing to help me with some upcoming shoots?"

"I...yes, I'd love to," she squeaked, amazed that he wanted to work with her. "Thank you," she added sincerely.

"Great! Give me your contact information. I'll call you once I have the details in front of me." She quickly complied while trying not to allow a silly grin to overtake her face. Once he walked away, she shook her head in amazement.

Sighing, her thoughts turned toward work. She'd have to figure something out so she could work at the photo shoots. She didn't think Harold and Grace would give her a hard time. Business was booming. She had a feeling they'd be hiring someone soon, which would cut into the number of hours she was allowed to work. At least if she wasn't working so much there, she could freelance. And it wouldn't be working for Evelyn directly, even if some of the photo shoots happened to be for *Trending*.

After that shared kiss, Torry was even more certain that she shouldn't work for Evelyn. It would be too complicated. However their relationship evolved, and Torry really hoped it would include more kisses, she never wanted to question Evelyn's motivations.

Until this afternoon, Torry hadn't seriously considered leaving Lost Treasures. She still felt terribly conflicted. The last thing she wanted to do was leave her friends in the lurch. Nor had she imagined how it would be possible to move on from the place that had provided her with a way to express herself. However, the photo shoot had opened her eyes. Maybe she could consult with a few photographers for their photo shoots or even with a few designers for their fashion shows. In addition, Macys, Bloomingdale's, and Saks had offered her window designing positions. So had Lord & Taylor, Nordstrom, Gianni Versace, Bergdorf Goodman, and Louis Vuitton. In just over a year, Torry had redefined her career aspirations and was blazing a trail in an industry she thought she had left at her mother's grave. All due to her talent.

Torry became more excited as ideas formulated. The possibilities were endless. Now that her name was becoming known, she might be able to form a niche in the fashion industry while maintaining her independence. She could manage her autonomy while creating in several forums. Smiling at the thought, Torry decided to really think about her future tonight.

First though, she wanted to stop by the boutique to see what type of winter coats were in stock for her next display idea. Walking through the door, Torry was surprised to see a woman behind the counter laughing as she rang up a customer. She seemed to be around Torry's age, maybe a little younger, with long red hair and light eyes. Torry looked around the boutique and spied Harold next to one of the *Jane Eyre* window displays, conversing with a man who stared greedily at the painting of the burning Thornfield estate.

Not quite understanding why she felt a heaviness steal over her, Torry walked over to a rack of coats near the front and turned away so her back was to the men, pretending to be browsing as she listened to their conversation. She couldn't help but believe they were talking about her work. With that rationalization, she steeled herself to listen without feeling guilty.

"So, your window designer, Torry Hansen, painted this and the other painting?" asked the man.

"Oh, yeah. And she did all the drawings. Torry has great talent. She does a great job," Harold answered. Torry felt pride flow through her, happy to hear her boss say such complimentary words about her.

"I called a few weeks ago about the pool scene painting. I spoke to a man. Was it you?"

"Oh, no. It must have been one of my employees," Harold said jovially. "I hope you weren't waiting for a call back or anything."

"Actually, I was. I had left a message asking for the painter to return my call. Is Torry around now?"

"No, she has the night off. I'm sure I can answer your questions, though," Harold said.

"Do you think she would consider showing her work in a gallery?"

"Um, well, I could present an offer to her on your behalf. You know, she's young. I wouldn't want her to enter such an arrangement without reviewing the terms on her behalf. I'm sure you understand," Harold said.

"Right. Well, here's my card. I own an art gallery in SoHo. Please give it to her and ask her to call me. I'd like to sit down with her and take a look at her portfolio."

"Sure. Sure. I just, you know, perhaps we could reach an agreement where I can just deliver the paintings each month after she has finished using them. She just throws them away. You can pay me a delivery fee, if you know what I mean, and everyone will be happy."

She froze, stunned by what Harold was suggesting. He was basically trying to sell her paintings and keep all the money for himself. How dare he! Torry turned quickly and moved toward the men, feeling anger flush her cheeks.

"I'm going to give you the opportunity to explain what sounds to me like your underhanded attempt to sell my work without my permission," she said in a low voice.

"Torry! When did you get here?" Harold took a step backward.

"Just in time, it seems." She turned to the other man. "Hello. I'm Torry Hansen." She held out her hand and shook his firmly as he smiled a greeting. "I'm so sorry for any confusion. I never got your message."

"I am sorry to hear that." The man shot a suspicious look at Harold. "Clive Ludsky. I'd like to sit down with you to discuss your paintings and drawings. I had an interesting conversation with a mutual friend last month. He believes you to be extremely talented, and I'm inclined to agree."

"Thank you. That is very kind of you to say. How about tomorrow morning?"

"Torry, you're working tomorrow," Harold interjected.

"No. No, I'm not." She held Harold's gaze firmly, letting him see just how angry and hurt she felt.

"Right. I forgot that you were taking tomorrow off," he said quickly. Of course, that wasn't true, but he was capitulating, probably hoping she would calm down.

"And Friday," she clarified before turning back to Clive. She didn't care if the day after Thanksgiving was the busiest shopping day of the year. She needed some time away from the boutique to deal with this betrayal.

"Tomorrow, then. Does ten o'clock suit you?"

"That sounds perfect," she answered with a smile. They said their goodbyes and a loaded silence descended upon Torry and Harold.

She looked at her boss as her mind worked furiously. "I am going to take some time off while I think about what just happened," she said, surprised that her voice sounded so calm.

"Torry, it's not what you think."

"No? You didn't conveniently forget to tell me that he called and left a message for me? You weren't just trying to make a deal with him where you'd be paid for delivering my paintings without my permission? You weren't throwing away an opportunity for me to be rewarded for my talent so that you could profit instead?" She stood with her arms folded tightly over her chest, indignation stealing over her once more. He had no right to cavalierly throw away her chance to show her work and to be compensated for it.

"It, it sounds worse than it is, Torry. I figured you wouldn't do anything with the paintings, so why not give them to the guy—"

"Stop." She held out a hand for emphasis. "Don't lie to me. I thought you were my friend. I've received so many offers to leave here, and I've refused every time because I was loyal to you. I'm such a fool. You don't care about me at all."

"I do!"

"No. You only care about how many hours I can work and how much money I can make for you." Torry stared hard at him. "You'd better hope I decide not to tell Evelyn. I have no doubt she would take great pleasure in destroying you on my behalf," she said, as she turned away. "I'm leaving." She exited the store quickly, not wanting him to see the tears building in her eyes.

Torry traveled home as if in a trance. Unlike earlier when she felt dazed by the kiss she and Evelyn shared, now her mind stuttered over the events in the shop. Sighing as she sat down on her well-worn sofa, she realized that she had quite a bit to think about. She'd received several offers, precisely as Evelyn had predicted, and new offers kept streaming in. She had never given them much thought until today. Now, though, her perspective had changed rather dramatically. With the new possibilities of working for fashion photographers and designers, she could freelance with them and create window designs at any of those stores.

Evelyn had been correct. Torry felt foolish, naïve, and stupid. Her thoughts kept returning to Harold's duplicity. How could he do that? How could he trade in her loyalty, all she had done for the boutique, for a quick buck? She sighed loudly. Evelyn would insist that she leave Lost Treasures. Torry was inclined to agree.

What will I do if I quit? Working with Al was a start. And maybe something would come of tomorrow's meeting with Clive. She still didn't think her works were good enough to show in a gallery, but she would just have to trust his judgment. As for the department stores, she wondered whether she might be able to arrange to become a consultant of sorts. She could do freelance work for them, and that way she wouldn't be limited to one store. Maybe she'd bring it up with Evelyn and see what she thought.

Hearing her cell phone ring, Torry answered, "Hello?"

"Damn, girl! Why didn't you tell me you started painting again?"

"Hey, Jax." She leaned back, resting her head on the sofa's back cushion. "You knew. You saw some of them."

"I saw some drawings, but I thought that's all you were doing. Torry, your name is everywhere in the art world. My boss was talking about your window displays with an art dealer, and I overheard him saying that he was interested in showing your art," Jax said excitedly.

"Really? It's all so weird. I'm meeting with some guy, Clive Ludsky, tomorrow. He wants to show my work too. And I worked with Al Spencer on a photo shoot today for a layout that will be featured in *Trending*. He asked me to work with him on some upcoming photo shoots. It's like all of a sudden I'm able to create in all these different ways." She smiled. "I love it."

"Well, just don't forget the little people," Jax joked.

"I would never do that. I'd never desert my friends." She could hear the bitterness in her voice. She was thinking not just about Harold's duplicity but also about how Jax and Greg had acted when Brandon left. She was sure Jax understood her tone.

"Yeah. I know, Torry," Jax said softly. "So," she said in a louder voice, "when are you going home?"

"Oh. I, um, I'm staying in town. I decided to spend Christmas with the family instead." Torry sat forward, gripping the phone tightly.

"Are you spending it with your grandmother, then?"

"No. She's going to Newport without me. Amazing what a few years can do, huh?"

"Yeah. How'd that happen?"

"After Mom's death, she and Dad had a long talk. They decided to bury the hatchet for Mom's sake. I can't say they're the best of friends, but it's not too bad."

"That's amazing. Too bad this didn't happen before the accident."

Torry agreed with the sentiment. So many things might have been different. Neither spoke for a few moments, allowing the silence to say what they could not.

"Do you want to come over, then? I'm cooking a small turkey with all the fixings," Jax said.

"That's really nice of you, but I've made other plans." Torry squeezed her eyes closed and pulled her shoulders up toward her ears.

"Doing what?" Jax asked in surprise.

"I, uh, I'm spending it with Evelyn and her daughters." Torry held her breath.

"Evelyn Allbright? Editor in chief of *Trending*? The Grande Dame of Fashion? How did that happen?" Jax squealed.

"You know *Trending* did a spread on Lost Treasures, which will be in January's magazine. We just, we've been spending some time together." She exhaled with relief and shrugged even though she knew Jax couldn't see her. "I like spending time with her."

"Torry...are you? It sounds like you...." Jax trailed off, and the line became silent for a few loaded moments. "Are you...dating her?" she asked slowly.

"Dating? No," Torry exclaimed.

"Because the way you talk about her, your tone of voice makes me think that maybe you are."

"We're not dating." Torry forced a laugh. "We live in different worlds. She's taken me under her wing, for some unknown reason, and I'm grateful. That's all it is, though." She inwardly cursed at the clear wistfulness in her voice. She was sure Jax could hear it.

"Oh, my God! You want it to be more! Wow, Torry! This is huge," Jax nearly shouted and then practically whispered, "How does she treat you?"

Torry stifled a chuckle. She could just imagine Jax looking over her shoulder to make sure no one was listening. Torry smiled affectionately. "She's wonderful. You know, she has her public persona, the way she has to act at work to get things accomplished. She isn't like that in private, though. You should see her with her girls, Jax. She's a different person. And she's been so nice to me." She took a deep breath and exhaled. "I'm being careful. I mean I refused her job offer. Several times. I don't want that between us. I have to admit that she fascinates me."

"Girl, are you listening to yourself? You are a lost cause. Just be careful, all right?"

"Yeah. Hey, while I have you on the phone, I don't suppose you're free tonight?"

"Why? You sound suspicious."

Laughing, Torry said, "Don't be so dramatic. I have to get a portfolio together for tomorrow's meeting, and the last time I created one was with you in college. Will you help me?"

"Sure, but you're feeding me," Jax sighed.

"Absolutely. Pizza or Chinese food?"

"Chinese. And don't be stingy on the eggrolls. I'll see you in a bit."

"You're the best," Torry crowed.

"Yeah, yeah."

She sat for a few minutes thinking about their conversation. How could she be so arrogant as to believe Evelyn returned her feelings? Just because they were attracted to each other, it didn't mean that Evelyn was willing to enter into a relationship with her. The ringing of the phone once more interrupted her spinning thoughts. "Hello?"

"Torry, it's Julie. Want to play basketball tomorrow afternoon? You can come back home to have dinner with us afterward," she gushed excitedly.

"Sure. That sounds like fun," she agreed, smiling at the thought.

"What? Okay," Julie said, her voice muffled. "Torry, Mom says you can sleep over tomorrow and we can go straight to the parade the next morning. Isn't that cool?"

"Uh, yeah. That's really nice of her," she said, dazed. Evelyn had invited her to stay in her home Thanksgiving night already. And now she was inviting her to stay over tomorrow night too. That must be a good sign, right? Evelyn wouldn't casually extend such invitations if she didn't have feelings for her. Would she? Torry doubted it. The woman was so private that she couldn't help but believe that she would never let her get so close if she only thought of Torry as a business connection. "What time and where?"

"Dalton at two. We have a half day because of the holiday, but I'm going to lunch with some friends," Julie said. "Oh, and Jennifer wants me to remind you to bring your drawings."

"I will. Sounds good. See you tomorrow." Torry twirled around after they hung up. The thought of spending time with the Allbright women raised her spirits significantly. It looked like her life was moving forward whether she was ready or not. Obviously, Evelyn's reentering her life was serving as a catalyst for all these changes. She still couldn't figure out why she was in Evelyn's life, though.

Shaking off her insecurities, Torry decided to jot down some ideas on possible designs that had popped into her mind while at the photo shoot. They wouldn't fit with the classic books motif she'd been using at Lost Treasures, but maybe she could use them in the future. As for what she would do about the boutique, she decided not to think about it anymore that night. She would meet with Clive tomorrow, and then she would review her options.

One stray thought made her smile. She had stood up for herself, said exactly what she wanted to without feeling as if she had missed her chance to express her feelings. Unlike in the past when faced with the unexpected, she hadn't spent the time since leaving the shop berating herself for all the things she should have said but hadn't been fast enough to think of or courageous enough to voice. She hadn't stuttered or dismissed her feelings for fear of rocking the boat or engaging in an argument. It was quite an accomplishment, this new way of expressing herself. She was growing a backbone, and it felt good to be heard. Really good.

Chapter Twelve

HEARING THE DOOR OPEN, a frisson of anticipation raced down Evelyn's spine. She heard Jennifer yell out, "Torry's here!" as she gazed at her reflection in the bathroom mirror once more. Although she hadn't anticipated seeing Victoria again before Thanksgiving, events had conspired to grant her the opportunity to spend more time with her just a day after the photo shoot, after that delicious kiss. How she was supposed to act unaffected around the younger woman while they were in the company of her daughters was her present quandary. What she wanted to do was pull Victoria into her bedroom and kiss her while on a bed, with no interruptions, and no clothing.

She was not used to feeling so out of control. Although exhilarating, it was also unnerving. Her only saving grace was that she was certain Victoria felt the pull just as strongly. Moving through her bedroom to the door, she took a deep breath and coached herself not to appear too excited. It was unseemly for a woman her age. She slowed her steps as she descended the stairs, hearing a flurry of movements and a door opening. They must be removing their coats.

Turning into the foyer, Evelyn saw Victoria dressed in sweatpants and a t-shirt. An extremely tight t-shirt that left no question that the woman was fit. And desirable. And a bit chilled. Evelyn swallowed, her mouth suddenly dry. She heard the tail end of the conversation as she forced herself to move forward.

"...I'm sure you can take a shower before we eat. I'll show you where you'll be sleeping," Julie said, as she closed the closet door.

"Okay. Great," Victoria said. Evelyn watched them turn toward her.

"Hi, Mom," Julie said. "I'm going to show Torry around so she can get cleaned up." At Evelyn's nod, Julie moved toward the staircase. Evelyn wasn't watching her daughter, though. She trained her eyes on Victoria and moved closer.

"Hi," Torry said softly.

"Hello, Victoria," Evelyn murmured, stopping before her. Evelyn rested her eyes briefly on glistening lips and smiled when she heard a small gasp. It reassured her, knowing that she could affect Victoria with just a look. She wanted to kiss her. She was going to kiss her.

Moving forward, Evelyn changed course at the last moment when she heard Julie call Victoria's name. Instead, she kissed

Victoria's soft cheek and whispered, "I want to kiss you," pulling back just enough to see her face. Evelyn loved the flush that crawled over Victoria's neck and face as the younger woman's respiration picked up. Staring for another moment, she stepped back and turned to the side so Victoria could pass.

She smirked as the woman stalled in front of her. Julie's insistence that Victoria hurry up finally stirred her into action. Before following Julie, however, she stepped into Evelyn's space. "I fully expect you to claim that kiss once we are alone," she whispered boldly while delivering a smoldering look.

Shivering with anticipation, Evelyn's lips quirked upward, as she turned to watch Victoria walk toward the staircase with her overnight bag. This woman kept her on her toes. She liked it.

Evelyn retired to her office to finish up her work obligations. She wanted to be able to concentrate on her family without the magazine getting in the way. She wanted to focus on Victoria, on how she made her feel, on the wonderful activities she wanted to share with her. A knock on the door made Evelyn look up. She noted that nearly an hour had passed since she had begun her work. She looked down once more, happy to find that she was nearly finished. "Yes?"

Victoria poked her head in. "Sorry to interrupt. I just wanted to let you know that dinner will be ready in ten minutes," she said with a smile.

"Very well. I am nearly done." Evelyn looked down once more and furrowed her brows when she saw an error on the page. She began writing down the correction and barely heard the door shut. After making a few more revisions, Evelyn closed the mock-up, satisfied with how it was shaping up. She sent a text to Heather to arrange for it to be picked up and returned to the art department. Although Evelyn was taking the rest of the week off, a skeleton crew would be working on Friday and Saturday. Smiling with satisfaction, she looked toward the closed door. Now that her work was done, she could enjoy the rest of the holiday week.

Evelyn entered the dining room to find her daughters and Victoria already seated, as their chef placed the dishes on the table. Victoria beamed at Evelyn, eliciting a smile. Evelyn sat down at the head of the table and took a sip of water before addressing the cook. "Thank you, Sherry. You may go. Enjoy your weekend, and have a good holiday," Evelyn said with a nod. Once Sherry left the room, Evelyn picked up her cutlery to signal they could begin their meals.

"I hope you found a way to occupy your time while I attended to some work demands," Evelyn said, as she focused on her guest. Victoria looked delectable in a white, Derek Lam jersey dress. The neckline emphasized her defined collarbones and hinted at cleavage, drawing Evelyn's eyes toward breasts she wanted to taste. With the drape of the deep cowlneck bodice, Victoria could not be wearing a bra. She wanted to find out. Desperately.

"Can we, Mom?" Jennifer asked.

Crinkling her eyebrows in confusion, Evelyn realized she had missed the conversation. In fact, she had woolgathered for most of the meal. She had no idea what her daughter was asking her to do. She looked at Victoria, who sported a knowing look on her face.

"What do you say, Evelyn? Can we watch the new Star Trek movie?" Victoria asked sweetly.

Evelyn nodded as she attempted to rein in her desires. It seemed she would not be alone with Victoria any time soon. She had to hand it to her. Victoria was purposefully provoking her. If Evelyn could tamp down on her feelings long enough, she might be able to turn the tables. Yes, two could play this game. "That sounds delightful. Girls, why don't you set it up? Victoria and I will clear the table." Evelyn watched as Victoria swallowed convulsively, suddenly less sure of herself. Evelyn kept her eyes on the woman while her daughters took their plates and left the room.

"Victoria, I do not believe I have complimented you on your attire. Allow me to rectify such an oversight." Evelyn stood up and approached her quarry. Victoria stood just as Evelyn reached her. Evelyn extended a finger and traced along the neckline lightly, just teasing the skin with her fingernail. "You look delicious," she said in a low voice. She could feel the tremors underneath her finger, see them running throughout Victoria's body.

"I do?" she asked breathlessly.

"Mmm. I bet you taste delicious too," Evelyn said, as she wrapped an arm around Victoria's waist and pulled her closer. Quickly discarding her plan to toy with Victoria, she claimed the kiss she'd desired to experience again since the day before.

Hungrily, Evelyn pressed herself flush against Victoria's supple body, her hand weaving through luscious locks as she consumed kiss after kiss, each fueling the fire raging through her. The realization that she might climax just from the passion exploding between them drove her to pull away suddenly. She was so aroused, her body pulsated with need. Opening her eyes, she watched Victoria take several deep breaths to calm down. That same hazy look she had seen while watching Victoria wake up at the boutique presently graced her lovely features. Along with that, though, desire burned brightly in those darkened eyes.

"As much as I'd love to continue this, my daughters are waiting for us," Evelyn said apologetically. The crestfallen look in Victoria's eyes gave her no choice but to pull the younger woman back into her arms. She held her tightly, running her hands over defined back muscles soothingly. "If I'm moving too quickly, I'm counting on you to tell me. I won't think less of you," she said softly. "There is something about you that draws me in and makes me lose my restraint."

"You aren't rushing me. Far from it. There's nowhere else I'd rather be than right here." Victoria turned her head and delivered hot kisses to Evelyn's neck.

Sucking in a breath as her body responded to several gentle nibbles, she pushed aside any thoughts of joining her daughters and turned her head to capture Victoria's full lips again. She just couldn't resist.

When Victoria moaned into her mouth and thrust her pelvis forward, Evelyn felt the first tremors of an orgasm building. Although she had not anticipated that her first time with Victoria would play out this way, she could do nothing but continue to move against her, groaning when she opened her lips wider to welcome more of Victoria's tongue into her mouth.

She was lost. Her body shuddered as she gave in and wrapped her hands around a luscious bottom, kneading as she took control of the kiss. If she was going to have an orgasm while fully clothed in her dining room after merely ten minutes of deep kissing, she was going to make damn sure Victoria was right there with her. Feeling Victoria's lower body jerking against hers, she guided her into a rhythm, shifting her leg between Victoria's long ones as she sucked on her tongue. She pressed into Victoria's hot center with her thigh and pulled her forward, feeling her jolt hard. Victoria ripped her mouth away, tucking her head into Evelyn's neck as she released, her erotic groan causing Evelyn to clench. Evelyn heard her name exhaled and experienced her own climax, pulling the woman as close as she could while they continued to move against each other. Exhaling, Evelyn closed her eyes and leaned heavily against Victoria while aftershocks rocked her body for long moments.

They remained locked in a tight embrace, while their breathing slowed down, Victoria delivering short, sweet kisses on her neck and collarbone. It amazed Evelyn how strong this encounter felt, how profound her reactions to this woman were. She couldn't wait to explore Victoria's body again, this time without the hindrance of clothing. Smiling, she loosened her hold. She noticed how bashful Victoria seemed and chuckled. "Victoria, surely you're not feeling shy now, are you?" Evelyn raised her eyebrows. "It's a little late for that, wouldn't you agree?" she teased.

"No. That's not it. It's just, how am I supposed to sit next to you while Jennifer and Julie are in the same room without climbing on your lap? I want more," she whispered intensely.

Evelyn felt her heart skip a beat as her eyes widened in surprise. "Perhaps, if you keep in mind that you'll be sharing my bed tonight, it will encourage you to restrain yourself," Evelyn offered with a smile.

"Hmm, I don't know. That just makes me want to take you to bed now," Victoria answered with a smile of her own.

"Don't tempt me. The girls would be extremely disappointed." She delivered a lingering kiss and stepped away from Victoria, running a hand through her hair before picking up some plates. "There's a bathroom down the hallway on the right," Evelyn said, waving a hand in the general direction. She raked her gaze over Victoria's body, remembering quite clearly how good it had felt moving against her. With effort, she turned away.

While Victoria freshened up, Evelyn placed all the dinnerware into the dishwasher quickly, knowing the girls would be wondering where they were. Once Victoria returned, Evelyn took her turn to make herself more presentable. It would not do to have the girls guess what had delayed them.

Before they climbed the stairs, Evelyn leaned in and delivered a slow, gentle kiss. "I had no idea I would lose control so quickly. That hasn't happened to me before." It was a hard truth to disclose. She felt vulnerable.

"Me either. I've never responded that way to anyone's touch." Victoria traced a line down Evelyn's cheek with her finger. "You have taken over my thoughts. I can't get enough of you."

"You say that now, but soon enough you'll become bored," Evelyn said flippantly as she turned away. Victoria's hand on her shoulder stopped her progress.

"No, Evelyn. You're wrong. If anything, it's more likely that you'll become tired of me. Only time will prove to you that I'm telling you the truth. That you become more and more fascinating to me each time we are together. I'm willing to wait around to prove it to you."

How could she refuse what Victoria was offering? Turning toward her, Evelyn cupped her cheek, reveling in the softness. "I am also willing."

Victoria's smile was tinged with relief. How could she think Evelyn didn't want to spend more time with her? She took Victoria's hand and pulled gently. They walked up the stairs and to the entertainment room with fingers tangled.

Before they reached the door, Evelyn stopped. "It's obvious that my daughters like you, but I would rather they become more used to your presence before exhibiting any behavior that might lead them to conclude we've embarked on a romantic relationship." She looked at Victoria apologetically. "I won't keep this from them for too long, I promise, but the last divorce hit them hard. When people realize that I'm not only with someone new but with a woman, a beautiful, younger woman," she shrugged. "I doubt we will enjoy much privacy."

"I understand. I don't want to make your life more difficult. If we need to keep this a secret, then we will. For as long as you need." Victoria squeezed Evelyn's hand and let go.

Evelyn cupped Victoria's beautiful face once more. "Please don't think that I am embarrassed to be seen with you. I'm not. It's just...my girls. The papers will say anything to make a profit, and it's so unfair to my girls."

Victoria gazed at Evelyn with a sweet expression. "Don't worry. As long as we can keep our hands off each other in public, no one will think twice about our being seen together, particularly since my work seems to be pulling me into your sphere."

Raising her eyebrows, Evelyn muttered, "That is easier said than done." She dropped her hands and turned toward the entertainment room. Victoria's laughter followed her as surely as her luscious body, causing Evelyn to smile as she stepped over the threshold. "Is the movie ready?" she asked, settling in her favorite chair, tucking one leg under her.

"Yup," Julie said, her eyes traveling between Victoria and Evelyn.

Victoria sat on the lounge, the farthest piece of furniture from Evelyn, much to her amusement. Evidently, Victoria was taking no chances. Running her eyes over the woman, she felt her pulse quicken. That dress left little to the imagination, yet hid far too much from Evelyn's greedy eyes. Her fingers itched to touch every inch, and she would once they retired for the evening. She could feel herself becoming wet once more, her body readying for more lovemaking.

She truly hoped the movie was good; otherwise, she didn't think she'd be able to derail her thoughts. Shifting to a more comfortable position, Evelyn said, "Jennifer, will you be a dear and retrieve a bottle of water for me?" She watched as her daughter hopped up and crossed the room to the full bar. A small refrigerator was always stocked with water, juice, and soda.

"Torry, do you want one?" Jennifer asked. She grabbed another bottle at Victoria's nod.

"Thank you," Evelyn said once she received the bottle, twisting the top open quickly and nearly gulping half of it. She was so hot. When she finished, she glanced up to see Victoria watching her closely. She knew.

Irritated, Evelyn barked out, "I thought we were going to watch a movie, not sit in silence. Julie, any time you would like to begin, please do. You know how I feel about dillydallying." A moment later the movie began and Evelyn felt remorse blanket her. She should not take out her sexual frustration on her daughters. Honestly, she was acting like a schoolgirl in the throes of her first love affair, all googly-eyed, hot, and bothered. It was pathetic, but she just couldn't seem to control her responses, and that made her all the more frustrated.

Taking some deep breaths while pretending nothing was amiss, Evelyn attempted to settle herself. She would have Victoria in her arms in a few short hours. Then she would feast on that lovely body, every inch. Feeling calmer, Evelyn glanced over at Victoria and promptly wished she had not. Victoria stared at her through lowered eyelashes, lips parted, one hand gripping the sofa arm, the other a tight fist. Good Lord! Evelyn ripped her gaze away, afraid one of them would act inappropriately. Not daring to look that way again, she trained her eyes on the television. After a while, Evelyn's body lost its tension as she was swept up in the story.

By the time the movie ended, Evelyn felt much more in control. She turned to her daughters. "Did you enjoy it?"

"It was great, Mom. Thanks for getting us a copy," Julie exclaimed. Of course it was not yet available to the general public.

"You are quite welcome, dear."

"I liked it too, Mom. Thanks," Jennifer said with a smile. Evelyn smiled back.

"All right. Time for bed. Go wash up, and I will be there in a few minutes to say good night."

"Thanks for playing basketball with me, Torry. I really had fun," Julie said, as she got up.

"Me too. We'll have to do it again soon," Victoria replied.

"And tomorrow, can we see your sketches, Torry?" Jennifer asked.

"Absolutely. I can't wait to see yours. Good night, guys."

"Night," they both answered before leaving the room.

Silence reigned, as Evelyn finally allowed herself the pleasure of staring at the younger woman. Victoria stared right back, passion darkening her eyes so much that Evelyn could hardly see the irises. Suddenly they were both striding toward each other, meeting in the middle of the room, their lips meshing in a heated kiss. Evelyn groaned as pleasure coursed through her. Victoria's hands framed her face as her tongue invaded Evelyn's mouth, plunging forth again and again. Evelyn's hands clamped onto strong shoulders to keep herself from sinking to the floor in a pool of lust and heat.

"If you don't take me to your bed right now, Evelyn, I will strip you where we stand, consequences be damned. I need you," Victoria said heatedly.

"Come along," Evelyn said, desire clearly present in her raspy voice.

Evelyn led the way quickly, practically feeling Victoria's heated breath on the back of her neck. When they reached the third-floor landing, she stopped short. Hot hands grabbed her shoulders. Evelyn turned her head slightly. "I have to say good night to my girls. My room is on the next floor to the right. I will be there soon." Victoria's hands dropped away as Evelyn turned into Julie's room.

"Good night, dear. We'll leave here no later than eight, so be ready." She leaned over to deliver a kiss to her daughter's cheek.

"I'll be ready. Good night," she responded.

Evelyn approached the door. When her hand was on the doorjamb she heard, "Mom?" She turned with a raised eyebrow, waiting to hear why her daughter had stopped her. "I really like Torry. I hope we can spend more time with her."

Evelyn smiled as she nodded. Yes, she had every intention of making sure Victoria became a fixture in their lives. "I have no doubt that we will. Good night." Evelyn walked through the door and headed toward Jennifer's bedroom next door.

"Good night, dear. Make sure you set your alarm. We will be leaving by eight." She kissed Jennifer's cheek. As she turned, Jennifer also stopped her.

"Mom. Are you and Torry…are you friends?"

Evelyn's eyebrows rose at the emphasis added to the last word. "Yes, we are friends," she replied slowly while studying her daughter's face. She knew Jennifer was leading up to more. Always the more sensitive child, Evelyn had realized years ago that the girl's instincts were usually accurate.

"Good friends?" she persisted.

"What are you getting at?" Evelyn asked, as she sat on the edge of the bed.

"I, we really like Torry. And we think you do too. She's different. We can tell she really likes you. And since you started talking about her, you seem happier. So, it's okay. I mean, as long as you share her sometimes. Okay?" Jennifer looked at her hopefully.

"Okay," Evelyn answered, touched that both her daughters were giving their blessings in their own unique ways to her budding romance with Victoria. Not having to hide her feelings while in her own home would help lessen the burden of secrecy they would have to carry during the ensuing months. Although she wanted to spare Victoria and her children from the media frenzy, she wondered whether it was necessary. She smiled at Jennifer before rising. "Good night," she said softly before leaving the room.

As she ascended the stairs her thoughts focused on who was waiting in her room, hopefully naked. Then again, having the privilege of peeling off that dress certainly held its own appeal. Opening the door, she saw that neither was the case. Victoria sat on the edge of the bed in a black satin negligée. Immediately, Evelyn could imagine gifting La Perla lingerie to this woman. Her mouth watered as she locked the bedroom door and feasted her eyes on Victoria's delectable body.

"It seems," she drawled, as she crossed the room, "that my daughters approve of you. In fact, they both expressed their hope that they would be seeing much more of you."

"They said that?" Victoria's face lit up, revealing her pleasure.

"They did." Evelyn smiled as she leaned forward to claim a kiss. "I am going to freshen up. I won't be long." Knowing Victoria was watching her, Evelyn emphasized the sway of her hips as she exited to the bathroom suite. Normally when sharing her first night with a new lover, she would keep her makeup on, even touching it up in the wee hours of the morning so that she would look her best when they awoke. Evelyn felt no compulsion to mask the natural progression of age as evidenced by the fine lines on her face. Even the finest beauty products could only slow down aging to some extent. She knew on a very elemental level, however, that she need not hide herself from Victoria.

Evelyn reentered the bedroom wearing navy silk lingerie and saw Victoria gazing at photographs that graced a small bookcase. Several were of her daughters, a few had her with them, and one old black and white photograph was of Evelyn's parents. When Victoria looked at her, she could see curiosity burning brightly, but it morphed into desire rather quickly.

"You look amazing," Victoria said huskily, as her eyes caressed Evelyn's body.

"I could say the same to you," Evelyn answered. Without hesitation she pulled Victoria to her and covered her mouth with a scorching kiss. Her hands began the lovely task of mapping out Victoria's body even as she guided her toward the bed. Soon, she had Victoria splayed out before her, chest heaving and body flushed.

Lying to the side of Victoria, Evelyn ran a hand down her arm, landing on a hip before changing direction. Hardly touching, Evelyn skimmed her fingers between breasts she fully intended to taste. "You are beautiful, Victoria," she whispered, as she slid a finger under one of the spaghetti straps and lowered it, repeating the process for the other one. Now that she had time, calmness settled over her. Although the passion was present, accompanied by need and desire, she did not feel the desperateness she had experienced in the dining room.

Insistent hands pulled her forward. Victoria kissed her, such deep kisses that Evelyn felt herself swooning. She was not surprised when Victoria broke the kiss to pull off her negligée and then Evelyn's lingerie with swift, sure motions. Evelyn shifted, hovering over Victoria for a sweet moment while their eyes connected, before lowering herself into a welcoming embrace. She groaned at the indescribable feeling of Victoria's breasts pressing against her own.

A full breast beckoned Evelyn's mouth closer. Her lips surrounded the stiffened peak, as her tongue snaked out to taste it. Exquisite. Addictive. Victoria's whimpers spurred her to suck harder, to lash out at the bud stronger and faster with the tip of her tongue. She moved her hand to massage the other breast, as she continued her loving assault. They fell into a rhythm that threatened to sweep Evelyn away. If she could just hold on a little longer.

Evelyn switched breasts once she was satisfied with the hard, swollen bud in her mouth. She continued to knead the newly abandoned one with her hand, loving how Victoria thrust her chest upward, as if begging for more. Leaning fully on her, Evelyn's other hand traveled down a shaking body, reaching between toned legs and gently stroking along the crease. A strangled groan, so low it sounded as if it had been pulled from Victoria's toes, electrified Evelyn. She felt a surge of wetness rush through her, bathing the flexing leg beneath her, as she moved her fingers in no particular pattern, brushing across Victoria's engorged clitoris every so often. With each pass of her fingers Victoria shuddered harder, her body filled with tension. Evelyn did her best to push Victoria's passion higher.

The power Evelyn felt as she guided Victoria toward orgasm astounded her. Victoria was so giving, so raw, so open that Evelyn simply could not get enough. Pulling her mouth away from those luscious breasts, Evelyn rested her forehead against Victoria's and stared into eyes filled with emotion.

"Victoria," she moaned, as she felt Victoria's body straining to reach its completion. While they maintained their gaze, Victoria came undone. The mesmerizing vision before her caused Evelyn's sex to clench rhythmically. She'd never seen anything so beautiful in her life. She rocked slowly against Victoria, doing her best to ignore her own body's needs, if only for a few more minutes.

Evelyn lifted her body, repositioning herself to knead their centers together. *God! This feels so good.* Picking up the pace, Evelyn braced her hands on either side of Victoria's shoulders, listening to the mewls and whimpers Victoria voiced. Evelyn knew she wouldn't be able to stave off her climax for much longer.

"I want you to come with me," Victoria gasped, passionate eyes burning into Evelyn. With those words, Evelyn felt her body race toward orgasm. She picked up the pace so that their bodies pushed against each other addictively. When her orgasm hit, Evelyn froze in place for a joyous moment, throat muscles working as she let loose a guttural groan that seemed to be ripped from her very soul.

Moving with a more pronounced roll of the hips instead of the sharp, short jerking of a few moments ago, Evelyn enjoyed the aftershocks sparking through her body. She could feel a deeper, more profound orgasm calling to her. Reveling in the physical sensations driving her to claim Victoria once more, Evelyn shifted again and began circling Victoria's opening with her fingers as she looked into glazed eyes.

"Yes, Evelyn. Please. Don't stop," Victoria encouraged, her voice ragged. Evelyn wasted no time entering the woman with two fingers and rubbing firmly with each thrust. Victoria's moans and whimpers drove Evelyn crazy, spurring her to slide herself over Victoria's leg again and again. The surprise of feeling fingers enter her caused Evelyn to shout Victoria's name. Heat rolled through Evelyn at the added stimulus, and a light sheen of perspiration covered her as she sank onto Victoria's magical fingers while thrusting her own fingers into Victoria at a steady pace. She crooked her fingers to rub strongly with each stroke, grinning fiercely at the sounds ripped from Victoria's throat. Evelyn's movements became frenetic, another orgasm overtaking her, when Victoria climaxed with a shout. Evelyn called out to Victoria, her voice so primitive that it was nearly unrecognizable, loving how Victoria kept pace. She felt Victoria's body clinging forcefully to her fingers as they gyrated together, the pulsing and passion and slickness nearly overwhelming Evelyn.

She wanted to do so much more. She had hardly even begun to explore, and she wanted to become intimately familiar with every inch of Victoria. Her traitorous body, however, was insisting that she rest. She vaguely registered that Victoria was stroking her back slowly, soothingly. With a sigh, Evelyn snuggled into the crook of Victoria's neck and murmured, "I'm not through with you. I haven't even begun to do what I intend to do." She felt a soft kiss on the crown of her head.

"Well then, we'll just have to continue after we've restored our energy with some sleep."

Sleep sounded good, nearly as good as the steady thrumming of Victoria's heartbeat beneath her ear. She withdrew her fingers slowly, not wishing to cause discomfort, and cupped the area possessively. Soon, although Evelyn did not wish it, she would give in to her lethargy, submitting to the dictates of her well-sated body. She knew she would sleep well, at peace with the world while held by the woman who'd captured her heart.

Chapter Thirteen

STARING AT THE ROARING fire as the wood snapped, Torry sighed with contentment. It was hard to believe that she was sitting in Evelyn's home after a long, pleasurable day spent with three females she was quickly growing to love. Without much struggle, she had fallen willingly under their charms.

Today had been a day of firsts. The first day she ever attended the Macy's Thanksgiving Day Parade. The first day she played Wii. The first day she awakened to Evelyn's loving ministrations. Torry shook her head, amazed. The woman was insatiable. It was hard to believe that Evelyn found her so irresistible. Not that she was complaining. She loved every moment she found herself the recipient of heated gazes and passionate touches.

Of course, Evelyn had acted appropriately while they were at her friend's house watching the parade and while with the girls, but whenever they were alone, even for just a few moments, it was as if a veil was lifted, revealing a woman barely able to control her desires. She felt powerful knowing she could affect Evelyn to such an extent.

She looked up when she heard the telltale clacking of heels on the hallway floor. Evelyn entered the room bearing glasses of wine. She handed one to Torry with a slight curl of her lips before taking a seat next to her on the couch.

"Thank you," Torry said, while keeping her eyes on Evelyn.

After settling herself and taking a sip of her wine, Evelyn tilted her head, gazing at Torry for several moments. "What is troubling you, darling?" she asked softly.

Smiling ruefully at how easily Evelyn could read her, Torry stalled by sipping from her glass as she attempted to marshal her thoughts. "It's work. After the photo shoot on Tuesday, I stopped by the boutique to begin planning the next display." Torry glanced at Evelyn. She sat listening attentively, her face pensive. "When I got there, I noticed that they had hired another person, which is fine," Torry was quick to assert. "I've been making enough money since starting the displays that I no longer have to work as many hours. But the problem is, I mean, what I discovered..." Torry took another sip. In some ways she was afraid to say it, since then she would have to make some tough decisions, decisions that would change the direction of her life.

Torry startled when Evelyn laid a warm hand on her knee. "Tell me, Victoria. You must know I will do everything in my power to support you."

Torry nodded slowly. "When I got there, I saw Harold speaking to a man near the display. Something seemed off, so I got close enough to hear without revealing my presence. Harold was trying to strike a deal where he would deliver my paintings, once I changed them out, and get paid for them. Without my knowledge or consent." Torry picked at invisible lint on her pant leg. She did not look up, not wanting to see Evelyn's reaction just yet.

"When I realized what was happening, I confronted them. The man turned out to be Clive Ludsky. I actually met with him yesterday, before I joined Julie to play basketball. He wants to showcase my work at his gallery in January. That combined with the work Al Spencer has offered will help me to support myself if I decide to leave Lost Treasures, but," Torry shrugged, "if it weren't for Harold, I wouldn't have all these opportunities now. He gave me the chance to design the windows, not knowing whether I could do a good job. I guess I'm having trouble walking away, even though he betrayed me."

Finally she looked up and froze, surprised to see the fire evident in Evelyn's eyes. "Evelyn?"

Evelyn seemed to shake herself from her thoughts, a calm look settling over her features. "I'm glad Clive approached you. Ira had mentioned his interest a few weeks ago. Nor am I surprised that Al asked you to work with him. You're able to write your own ticket now. You can freelance with designers, photographers, and department stores while showing your work at various art galleries, if you so wish."

Evelyn's words of praise warmed Torry. "Thank you, Evelyn. That means so much coming from you. I hope, I hope you understand why I can't work for you directly."

Evelyn waved a hand as she placed her glass of wine to the side. "You will be working for me indirectly, Victoria. Our paths cannot help but cross in this industry, particularly with the trajectory you're traveling. I am well aware, though, that given the change in our relationship, it would not be prudent for you to be my employee."

Torry nodded. "Exactly. It would cause complications between us that I'd rather avoid." She smiled, feeling shy suddenly. "I knew when I saw you a few months ago that my life would change. And it did. You've altered my perspective to such an extent that I was able to achieve my career aspirations. Just like that." Torry snapped her fingers for emphasis. She noticed the questioning look on Evelyn's face.

"I realized that I had distanced myself from what I most loved in some futile attempt to escape the grief I felt over my mom's death. I felt guilty and angry, and I pushed away what she loved most—fashion—as a result." She looked into Evelyn's eyes, even as she felt the tears building. "When I finally decided to embrace my love for design, for colors, and textures, and fabrics, I refused my grandmother's help, and by extension, your help. Meeting you again, it shook me awake. You showed me the possibilities. You believed in me before I did. I've finally embraced the part of my life that I had experienced with my mom." She put her wine glass down, swiped at the tears, and produced a watery smile. "And my life started to get better."

"So, you're saying that it's better that you don't work for me because I acted as some type of catalyst in your life?"

"Well, yes. I mean, look at what happened when you entered my life again." Torry spread her hands wide. "You've turned my life upside down. I mean, you brought attention to what I was doing at the boutique and propelled my career forward by several years, opening up avenues to me that someone of my age and experience normally would not have." Torry reached over to take Evelyn's warm hand in hers. "More importantly, somehow, for some inexplicable reason, you opened your heart to me. And I am so grateful, Evelyn."

"You really have no idea, do you, Victoria?" Evelyn leaned over to deliver a tender kiss. "I knew the first time I saw your window displays that you were special. You embody a pure, unsullied creative spark that I have rarely seen in this business. I was drawn to that. Intrigued."

Feeling long fingers stroke her cheek, Torry closed her eyes. She felt sweet breath on her lips just before Evelyn kissed her. Slowly they shifted positions so that Torry was supine with Evelyn resting on her. "Victoria, I would have settled for building a friendship with you if that was all you were willing to share with me. I knew that I wanted you in my life in some capacity." Torry arched as Evelyn delivered open-mouthed kisses down her throat, while a hand found its way under her sweater, driving Torry crazy as she felt sensual shapes delicately drawn over her ribcage.

"I am not a woman who questions her decisions. If I did, I would not be where I am today. That said, I am intelligent enough to not make the same mistake twice. You reentering my life was not an accident. It was a second chance. Although I am certain that if I had helped you last year, you would have changed me in some fundamental way. It's also likely that you would not be in my arms right now."

Torry shook her head, ready to deny Evelyn's words. They were meant to be together. It just hadn't been the right time last year. A finger against Torry's lips stopped her from expressing her thoughts.

"Shhh. We will never know, Victoria. It doesn't matter. Last year you were a diamond in the rough. I didn't take the time to really look at you, and I lost you. Cynthia and I had discussed you several times, but for whatever reason, I didn't do anything with that information. You came back to me, though, and I am not about to lose you again."

Torry sighed as they kissed, swept away by Evelyn's fervor. Feeling Evelyn pull away, Torry opened her eyes in question. "Why have I opened my heart to you?" Evelyn whispered, her voice laden with some indefinable emotion. Torry lost her breath, captivated by the intense look in her eyes. "I know I can trust you with it. That is a priceless gift to me. And you have inspired me. I can imagine days filled with passion, creativity, and heart. All because of you, because of who you are."

As Torry gazed into clear blue eyes, she could see the truth of Evelyn's words. She was blessed, truly blessed. Not able to resist, she framed Evelyn's face with her hands and pulled the woman forward for another kiss. Languid, bottomless kisses, Torry loved this sensation of being immersed in Evelyn, surrounded by her. She could feel Evelyn's curves sinking into her as their tongues glided together, one of Evelyn's hands curving around the back of her neck, while the other hand rested on her hip.

"Come to bed, darling," Evelyn murmured against Torry's lips.

Unable to suppress a moan, she felt her desire for Evelyn rising to the forefront once more. She felt the loss keenly when Evelyn rose gracefully and extended a hand to help her off the couch. Torry smiled as they stood close together, allowing the tension to build before they turned toward the stairs and ascended, hand in hand.

***

After thinking it over during the holiday weekend, Torry decided to return to Lost Treasures to design and dress the windows one more time before ending her tenure there. She entered the store slowly after watching the crowds outside peering at the *Jane Eyre* displays.

"Torry! Let's go in the back room to talk for a bit," Harold said, waving her forward.

She took off her jacket and hung it up, attempting to control her emotions. A surge of anger had swept through her when she had first spotted Harold. She was sure no one would blame her for walking right back out. Taking a few deep breaths to calm herself, Torry turned toward Harold.

"You wanted to speak with me?" Torry asked politely.

"Yes. I wanted to apologize. Listen, Torry. We really appreciate all you've done for us. I never meant to hurt you. What I did was stupid and selfish. I hope you'll stay with us," Harold said, his expression a study in earnestness.

Torry didn't believe any of it. She shook her head. "Harold, I am giving you one week's notice. I'll work this week and set up a new window display, but that's it. You have someone else working the floor now, and I'm sure there are plenty of people who would love to decorate your windows, particularly since your shop has received so much publicity." Because of me and because of Evelyn, Torry did not say.

"Is there anything I can do to change your mind?" Harold asked, clearly crestfallen. "I can up your commission percentage and pay you separately for your work on the displays."

Eyeing the man pensively, Torry thought about it. She and Evelyn had discussed how much Torry could demand for her work with designers, photographers, and department stores. Torry was keen to do freelance designs. Evelyn had also coached her with the prices she could attach to her paintings and drawings that Clive planned to showcase in his gallery. If Evelyn was right, and Torry had no reason to believe otherwise, Torry's bank account would be filling up rather dramatically in the very near future. With the money she had saved over the last few months, she could afford to walk away from Lost Treasures today, and her pride demanded it.

However, she would not quit without giving her notice, without fulfilling her responsibilities. She would not childishly, not to mention unprofessionally, leave in a fit of pique, regardless of how satisfying that might feel. She shook her head. "You can't afford me, Harold. Let me finish out the week, and we'll part ways. I'll always be grateful for the opportunities you gave me, but I won't forget what you did." Torry pressed her lips together and stared grimly at Harold. Her mind was made up.

"Okay, Torry," Harold said. "Thanks for at least giving me the week's notice. You've been nothing but honorable. Too good for this place."

She nodded and left the back room. She'd never heard him utter truer words.

The day passed quickly, as she planned for the next and final display she would design for Lost Treasures. A constant flow of customers purchased clothes and accessories throughout the day and into the evening. Torry was astounded when she realized that she had not only missed lunch, but also dinner. The store telephone rang once again, and Torry picked it up as she finished helping another customer at the register. "Lost Treasures. This is Torry. How can I help you?"

"Why are you there, Victoria?"

"I...what? Evelyn?" Torry finished the sale and moved away from the counter so she could concentrate on the call. "How did you know I was here?"

"Really, Victoria. What a ridiculous question. I am still waiting for your answer," Evelyn said, her annoyance carrying through the telephone line clearly.

"I gave my notice today. I am going to work for the rest of the week." Torry leaned against the wall, idly watching Grace work.

"After what he did to you?" Evelyn hissed.

"Yes. I...it would have been unprofessional to just quit without notice, Evelyn," Torry said in a low voice, not wanting to be overheard.

"Oh, and I suppose his betrayal was perfectly professional?"

"No, of course not. But I will not sink to that level. My reputation is important, particularly after what he did. I'd rather take the high road." Torry sighed. "I realize you disagree, but I feel this is the best way to handle it."

"Hmm, and I suppose you have worked the entire day," Evelyn drawled.

"Well, yes. It's been busy—"

"Thanks to your displays, no doubt."

"And thanks to you, Evelyn," Torry said quickly.

"Yes. Don't remind me. Come outside. Right now." Before Torry could say anything, the line went dead. She looked at the receiver blankly for a moment before hanging it up and turning to Grace.

"I'll be right back, Grace," Torry said and headed to the back room to grab her coat. Walking through the front door, Torry stopped short, surprised to see a silver Mercedes idling at the curb.

The window opened just enough for Torry to see Evelyn, who jerked her head toward the passenger door. "Get in."

Hurrying around the car, Torry slid into the warm interior. "Hi," Torry smiled, happy with the unexpected visit. She was pleased to see Evelyn's lips curl into a smile.

"I don't have long, but I wanted to see you for at least a few minutes. That is for you." Evelyn pointed toward a bag on the floor near Torry's feet. Leaning forward, Torry opened it a bit to see what was inside and salivated as a tasty aroma flooded her senses.

"Mmm. That smells wonderful." She turned toward Evelyn. "Thank you." Not sure whether Evelyn would allow Torry to kiss her, she settled for covering Evelyn's hand with her own and squeezing. When she saw Evelyn lean toward her, Torry quickly leaned in too.

The kiss was slow and sweet, as if she'd come home after a long journey. Torry sighed happily and felt a smile against her lips. Pulling back, Torry smiled into sparkling eyes. "I'm so glad you came by."

"As am I. I have two questions. I have a good friend who owns an art gallery. She has invited me to a showing a week from Friday. Will you attend with me?"

Smiling, Torry nodded. She tried to go to the showings at Jax's work when she could, but with the falling out and the slow mending of their friendship, she hadn't been to one in months. "I would love to."

"Good. I want you to meet her. Second, are you free for lunch on Wednesday?"

"Yes. It's my day off, actually. I'll be changing the displays tomorrow night." Torry smiled again as she thought of her plans.

She didn't have time to paint a scene, but she didn't really need to. The story was famous enough that she believed others would recognize it.

"Well, then. I will pick you up at one from your apartment so you can sleep in a bit," Evelyn said before swooping back in for another kiss, this one a bit more passionate. Torry whimpered when Evelyn sucked on her lower lip before breaking the kiss. "I have to go, darling. I will see you soon."

Nodding, Torry took the food and left the car, waiting on the sidewalk until it had pulled into traffic. A familiar ringtone had her searching the pockets of her slacks for her cell phone. "Hey, Dad," Torry answered with a smile.

"Hello, Torry. How are you?"

Stepping back to lean against the brick facade of the neighboring building, Torry smiled as she answered, "I'm great. I'm at work, but I have a few minutes before I have to get back in there."

"Oh? Are you outside? Isn't it too cold?" her dad asked, concern in his voice.

"It's okay. I have my coat on. So, what's going on? Settled back into work after eating too much for Thanksgiving?"

"Well, you know how your sister cooks for an army," he groused good-naturedly.

Chuckling, Torry agreed. "Oh yeah, I'm looking forward to gorging myself when I'm in town." She smiled sadly, as she realized that she would not see Evelyn or her daughters for Christmas. She'd have to make sure they exchanged gifts before she returned to Rhode Island. If it weren't so early in their relationship, she would invite all of them back home with her, but she didn't want to rush anything. She wondered what Evelyn would be doing for New Year's Eve, whether it would be appropriate to even ask.

"Torry?"

Realizing she had zoned out, Torry said, "I'm sorry, Dad. I didn't catch that." She raised her shoulders up, wincing even though he couldn't see her.

"I asked about your Thanksgiving. I know we spoke briefly, but you were pretty vague about what you were doing. You just said you were spending it with a friend. Was it Jax or Greg? It wasn't Brandon, was it?" he asked in a low voice.

"God, no! Brandon's long gone. And no, it wasn't with Jax or Greg, although Jax did invite me over. It was um, well, I mentioned her before, Evelyn Allbright, the editor in chief of *Trending*. Remember, she's the one who featured my window dressings in her magazine and has been helping me gain exposure so that I can freelance? So, yeah, I spent it with her and her two daughters."

"Evelyn Allbright?" he repeated. No doubt he was looking her up on the web.

A squawk in the background preceded a shuffling sound and her sister's voice on the line. "Torry! Why didn't you tell me you spent Thanksgiving with Evelyn-fucking-Allbright? That woman is famous!"

"Language!" Torry heard her father shout in the background, and she laughed, knowing well how her father felt about cursing.

"It was a last minute thing. She's really great, Katie," Torry said, flushing.

"I bet! She's also gorgeous. I remember when Nana brought her to the funeral," Katie said.

"Yeah. Well, I caught her attention with those window designs I told you about, and we've gotten closer."

"Closer, huh? Is that code for something, Torry?"

"Um, well," Torry faltered.

"Katie, that's enough. Give me back the phone," she heard her dad say sternly.

"We'll have to catch up more. Really soon," Katie said quickly. "In fact, it's a good thing I'll be there in January for your art showing. Oh! But you can tell me everything when you're here in—oh, my God—less than two weeks," she squealed loudly.

A short tussle ensued before she heard her dad say brightly, "Okay! Sorry about that, hon. You know how your sister gets."

"That I do," Torry agreed with a chuckle. "It's fine." She missed her sister, although she was not overly fond of being pumped for information. She knew her sister would be relentless until she got all the dirt. She was also a shameless stargazer, often telling Torry about all the goings-on in the celebrity world. Her developing relationship with Evelyn would be viewed as the mother lode, the perfect blending of all things interesting to her sister.

"Torry, I'm glad you have a new friend," her dad said in a careful voice. "Perhaps at some point we can meet her and her daughters if she becomes more than an acquaintance or a business connection. After all, the last time we met her was hardly under ideal circumstances."

"Oh! Well, yeah. Definitely. We are, it's not, she's not just a professional relationship." She grimaced at her awkwardness. Realizing her dad was waiting for more information, she added, "We're close. Um, I like to spend time with her outside of work, and she seems to feel the same way."

"Cynthia mentioned her," he confided. "She had only good things to say about her, about how she donates her time and money to good causes and is a sharp business woman. She also mentioned that the tenor of their conversations regarding you has changed over the last few months," he teased.

Torry laughed nervously. "Well, I'm glad she likes her. I do too. Like her, that is."

"Good. Good. You sound happier. Certainly better than when you were with Brandon," he said, his voice sounding as if he had bitten into something sour as he said Brandon's name. "I just want you to be happy, honey."

"I know. And I am. I really am." She was surprised to feel herself tear up a little bit. "This is my last week at Lost Treasures. I'm setting up the last window display for the shop tomorrow night. It's...so much has happened so quickly."

"Yes, but you can handle it. You have a good head on your shoulders." After a pause he added softly, "Your mom would be so proud of you. So proud. I know I am."

"Thanks, Dad. I love you."

"Love you too. I'll talk to you this weekend. Don't let your sister get to you."

"I won't. Bye." Hearing his farewell, Torry disconnected the call.

That was unexpected. She wondered whether he had some idea of her relationship with Evelyn. She never could hide anything from him, and she had mentioned Evelyn's name quite a few times lately. If he did know, he was showing his support, and for that, she loved him even more. He obviously was doing his best to make up for the various arguments they had shared and the guilt-trips he had thrown at her after she moved to New York.

Their relationship had gone through many changes since her mom died. Until that point in her life, she hadn't really spoken up for herself. Her mom's death acted as a wakeup call for her. As cliché as it sounded, her mom's death had made her realize that life was precious, and she needed to take control of it. Only she could make her dreams a reality. Her family had sought to support each other while they grieved their loss, but they all had grieved differently.

After sinking into depression and struggling to put her life back together, Torry had returned to college a changed woman. Quiet, serious, she curled into herself as she processed the events that changed her irrevocably. Over time she began to think about her future, a future without her mother. And she had thought about embracing all that her mother had turned her back on—design, fabric, color, art, even Nana. She kept her friends at arm's length as she came to terms with her loss and planned her future, not knowing how else to protect herself, and she had learned how to no longer rely on events to somehow unfold in beneficial ways for her.

Her father had clung to her, calling her frequently and practically demanding that he know everything that was happening in her life. She chafed at his behavior. If Katie hadn't interceded, Torry feared she might have acted out unacceptably. The last thing she ever wanted to do was hurt her dad, but back then she had been struggling, still trying to find her equilibrium. Although she didn't know all the facts, she resented the sacrifice her mother had made for him. She resented the sad look in her eyes she'd seen over the years. She resented not growing up knowing Nana. It took her a long time to release those feelings. New York had helped her to gain perspective.

At least he seemed to have learned from his past overstepping by not pushing her about Evelyn. No doubt he had found more than enough information about her online, and Torry was sure that Katie would tell him whatever she found in the celebrity news. Then there was what Nana told him about Evelyn. She knew Nana and Evelyn met monthly. She wondered whether Evelyn would confide in Nana about their deepening relationship. She wondered how Nana would feel about it.

An interesting development was how at ease her dad seemed to be while spending time with his mother-in-law. From all she knew, he had despised Nana. Yet, after her mom's death, there was a shift in his attitude toward her grandmother, a softening. She came to visit often during the first year, helping out, drawing Torry out of the house, even just sitting in the room with her quietly for hours on end. She had helped Torry immeasurably, and it seemed she had helped her dad too.

If he did have an inkling regarding the nature of her relationship with Evelyn, she was pleasantly surprised that he was not upset over the age difference. Then again, he had been twenty years older than her mom, so maybe he just knew better than to be a hypocrite. Evelyn was only fifteen years older than Torry, but damn if she didn't look younger than her age. Smiling, Torry reentered the shop to finish her shift and eat the food Evelyn had brought her, glad that the workday was nearly finished.

The next day flew by as she rounded up what she needed to change the display and worked the floor, helping customers, answering questions, and ringing up sales. When the doors closed for the day, she became a ball of energy, the familiar feeling of excitement at the thought of creating new displays buzzing through her.

Five hours later, Torry stepped back and expelled a large breath, pleased with the results of her efforts. In the first window, Eliza Doolittle and Henry Higgins danced at the embassy ball. Henry wore a black Hugo Boss tuxedo with tails, a white piqué wing-collared shirt with stiff front, white bow tie and waistcoat. He looked distinguished and elegant. Eliza wore a fabulous white Lagerfeld gown with a modified empire silhouette and stunning beadwork that reflected the lights. Long, white evening gloves and costume jewelry, such as drop earrings and a tiara that held in place an elegant hairstyle, made it clear that they were at a formal affair, but they had eyes only for each other.

The second display reflected the last scene from *My Fair Lady*. Henry sat in a wingback chair, fedora over his face and legs crossed at the ankle, as Eliza stood smiling while she leaned against a doorframe, holding in one hand a pair of men's slippers. Henry wore a three piece Burberry charcoal-gray wool suit, while Eliza wore a floor-length pale pink Balenciaga evening gown of silk chiffon over a satin underdress with a fitted waist and flowing lines.

This is how she felt around Evelyn, the student striving so hard to impress her mentor. Somehow, without her knowing quite how, she had not only succeeded in making Evelyn notice her but also had captured her heart. It was a good thing, too, since Evelyn mesmerized Torry each and every time their paths crossed and after this past weekend she felt chills race up her spine and grinned. She did not want to even contemplate a life without Evelyn. Sure, she could be abrasive and opinionated, but she was also honest and brilliant. Torry was falling in love with Evelyn Allbright.

Yes, these scenes reflected her life well. It was a fairytale come true. Although she did not know what would happen next, she had high hopes for the future. She knew her own heart, and Evelyn's actions made her believe that she was looking for more than a fling. Certainly, she would not have introduced Torry to her daughters if she had no intention of building a relationship with her. No matter what, if Torry had any say in it, she would make sure that Evelyn wanted to keep her around. Even if only to retrieve her slippers.

Chapter Fourteen

A BLAST OF WIND hit the row of windows lining Evelyn's office, rattling the storm panes noisily and breaking her concentration. Glancing at her laptop, she was surprised to see that it was nearly time to meet with Cynthia for lunch. She admitted to herself that she was nervous. She suspected Cynthia knew the nature of her relationship with Victoria, and was unsure if Cynthia approved.

She wanted to move on with her life, and that included being able to bring Victoria with her to the various events she attended without fear that the resulting exposure would somehow affect Victoria's career negatively. She'd spoken to her daughters, and they didn't care about the paparazzi. They wanted Victoria in their lives, wanted everyone to know how they were connected, and Evelyn did too. She wanted to show the world how much Victoria meant to her. That included at Clive's art gallery exhibition tonight. What held her back was the fear that the press would insinuate some unsavory liaison where she promoted Victoria for sexual favors. Their bond was so much purer than the small-minded, cynical paparazzi could understand.

Although true that she and Victoria had attended some of the same events over the last few months, they had not attended as a couple, at least not blatantly. Hillary had noticed their bond immediately at her showing last month. Evelyn's lips curled as she remembered her reaction. The gallery owner's widened eyes and gaping mouth had amused Evelyn greatly, particularly since the woman was normally graceful with her movements and behavior. The flummoxed look remained for several seconds, until Evelyn reminded her that a gaping fish was unbecoming. When Hillary cornered her a bit later, she mentioned meeting Torry briefly at the little resale shop. Evelyn's thoughts returned to that conversation.

"She's the promising artist you mentioned?" Hillary asked.

"If you mean Victoria, then yes. I take it you saw some of her window displays at Lost Treasures?" Evelyn asked lightly, smirking.

"Not only have I seen them, but I spoke to her about them. She is unbelievably kind and modest. And don't think I didn't notice the looks you two have been swapping. She's not merely a protégé to you. I haven't seen that look on your face since Jeremy swept you off your feet," Hillary said gleefully.

Evelyn frowned at the reference to her daughters' father. "Yes, well, I'm sure I have no idea what you're babbling on about. She is a talented artist, and I want to help her receive the accolades she deserves." Evelyn pulled on her chunky necklace several times before realizing what she was doing and allowing her hand to fall to her side.

"Oh, I have no doubt that you want to help her," Hillary said, her hands held out in a placating gesture. She leaned in, a wicked smile adorning her face, warning Evelyn that she was about to be teased by her old friend. "And I bet she just loves helping you too," she said in a lascivious tone of voice, wiggling her eyebrows suggestively.

Glaring at Hillary, Evelyn muttered, "I had no idea you were so juvenile. Do not suggest that we are doing anything untoward."

"Oh, but it isn't me who's juvenile, or should I say, who's indulging in juvenile behavior. Or indulging in a juvenile."

Anger ran hotly through Evelyn's veins, and whereas before she had tolerated her friend's teasing, she lost her sense of humor entirely at the thought of Hillary besmirching Victoria's reputation or intimating that she was too young for her. In a low voice, the one she used to terrorize her employees when they were inordinately inept, she hissed, "Victoria is not an adolescent, and it is becoming crystal clear that she is more mature than one person in particular." She turned away, ready to leave. A hand on her forearm stopped her, and she stared at it with disgust and no little amount of fury until Hillary hurriedly let go.

"Evelyn. I'm truly sorry. I crossed the line. Please forgive my clumsy attempts to tease you. If she is the one causing you to glow and smile more than I've seen in the past decade, more than that really, then I'm happy for you." Her words were delivered softly, beseechingly.

Taking several deep breaths, she allowed the anger to drain out of her, nodding minutely. Feeling a presence at her elbow, Evelyn felt comforted. She looked up into green eyes shadowed with worry. Smiling tenderly, Evelyn said, "Victoria, there you are. Have you enjoyed the exhibit?"

"Yes, but are you, is everything…" Torry's eyes jumped back and forth between Evelyn and Hillary.

"No need to fret," Evelyn cut in smoothly, squeezing Victoria's hand before regretfully letting go. "I was catching up with an old friend is all. Victoria, this is Hillary Patterson, the owner of the gallery." After withstanding Victoria's questioning gaze a few more moments, she watched Victoria turn her attention toward Hillary.

"Ms. Patterson, it is a pleasure to meet you," Victoria said. "Oh! I remember you. It's nice to see you again."

"Likewise. Perhaps we can meet for coffee to discuss showing your work here during the summer. I realize many galleries have contacted you already, but we have a diverse clientele."

"Well, if you are friends with Evelyn, I see no reason why we shouldn't meet."

They had met, and Victoria had admitted to her excitement and nervousness about displaying her works in several media at the gallery in June. An eclectic mixture had attended Hillary's art gallery showing, although not Victoria's friends, Jaxine and Gregory. They were planning to attend her showing at Clive's gallery tonight, and Evelyn knew that she was anxious about the ensuing introductions. Her relationship with Victoria, still so new, was one she cherished. She wanted to take her rightful place beside the woman, if only to provide support to her as she bowled over the art world as easily as she had the fashion industry, but she couldn't, not quite yet. The first step would be gaining Cynthia's blessing.

Strolling out of her office, she gave last minute instructions to her assistants before leaving for lunch. Soon, she would be able to attend any event she wished with Victoria by her side instead of pretending that they were merely business associates, mentor and protégé, professional acquaintances. Frankly, Evelyn was more than done with pretending. Her feelings had formed so quickly and deeply for Victoria that it pained her to live disingenuously in the public eye. By the end of the day, she hoped to have Cynthia's blessing so she could discuss with Victoria what they wanted to do. Soon, they'd be able to make plans for a future shared together.

Entering the restaurant, Evelyn was led to a table looking out onto Central Park. She gave Cynthia the obligatory air kisses before removing her coat and handing it off to be hung up. Sighing as she sat down, Evelyn smiled at her friend. "Cynthia, how are you?"

"Good. Very good, in fact. I'm excited to see what Victoria is showing at the gallery tonight."

"As am I. She wants it to be a surprise. Lord, she's devoted every spare moment toward this showing."

"You mean you've let her out of your sight?" Cynthia teased.

Taken by surprise, Evelyn cocked her head and smirked. She appreciated that her friend was opening up the conversation regarding her relationship with Victoria in such a straightforward manner.

"She's her own woman," Evelyn said in a mild voice. "I wouldn't dare staunch her creativity. The world needs her vision."

"And you?"

"Without question," Evelyn answered with a small smile. "You already know that, Cynthia. Why don't you ask what you really want to know?"

"What is the nature of your relationship with my granddaughter?"

Evelyn felt butterflies erupt in her belly. It was silly, really. She'd known Cynthia for two decades, and they'd been good friends for over three years. If Cynthia disapproved, she would have indicated those feelings by now.

"I'm in love with her," Evelyn admitted, tasting the words she had not dared to utter beforehand. She hadn't admitted such feelings to Victoria, not wanting to scare her away. "I've never fallen for someone so quickly, and I'll admit that I fear she does not feel as strongly as I do. Nevertheless, I'll do everything in my power to make her happy, to keep her with me." She jutted out her chin as determination filled her.

"Of course you will. If I thought otherwise, this would be a very different conversation." Cynthia sipped some water, her eyes focused outside at the passersby for several moments. Finally, she redirected her focus on Evelyn. "You're all she talks about. You and her creations." She smiled widely. "I've talked you up to her father. He seems open to the idea."

With a sigh of relief, Evelyn said, "That's good to hear. I'm hoping we can begin attending events together as a couple instead of business associates, if Victoria is willing."

"Why wouldn't she be?"

"You know she has insisted on making her own way. She doesn't want people to believe her success is due to our relationship instead of her talent."

"Hmm. That is silly. Anyone who sees her work will know how ridiculous the notion is."

"Yes, but she needs to believe in herself."

Cynthia squeezed her hand. "You're good for each other, Evelyn. I've seen her become more confident in her abilities. And happier, so much happier. I'm glad you found each other."

"Thank you, my friend. I am too." Evelyn paused, contemplating how Victoria had entered her life. "It seems serendipitous in some ways. When our paths crossed at the funeral service, I knew she was special. The way she spoke about her mother…but I let that go. Then we spoke of her several times, yet I never followed up on my curiosity of what she was doing, how she was faring. Even after she moved to New York, I failed to reach out, even after hearing about your frustration with her refusal to accept your help. I could have done something about that. I could have offered her a job, worked behind the scenes. Instead, I ignored those fleeting urges and went about my life. It wasn't until she decided to be seen by the masses, until she created those window designs at that little resale shop, that I saw her. Truly saw her. And since then, she's all I see."

A comfortable silence settled over them as they ate, and Evelyn ruminated on their conversation. Maybe she hadn't been ready to see Victoria, not until a few months ago. Or perhaps Victoria hadn't been ready to be seen. If that were the case, Victoria might need more time before she was ready to be seen as Evelyn's consort. If that proved to be true, Evelyn would wait. She refused to lose this priceless treasure due to her impatience.

The day flew by, and Evelyn could hardly wait to see Victoria, who was at the gallery and had been for hours, no doubt flitting around, making sure her pieces were perfectly positioned for the showing. Viewing herself in the mirror, Evelyn smirked. Her ensemble reflected the way she wanted to look, feel, and be—the sensual, provocative woman Victoria brought out in her. She wanted everyone's eyes on her not just due to the fact that she was the Queen of Fashion but also because she was an attractive, desirable woman. And undeniably Victoria's woman to do with as she pleased. She wore a pale-blue, strapless silk wrap with a plunging neckline in the back, emphasizing her porcelain skin and toned body. Countless hours spent with a personal fitness trainer over the years had paid off.

Smoky eye makeup highlighted her ice-blue eyes, and shimmering gloss accentuated her lips. Quirking a smile, she turned away to gather her scarf and purse. Slipping into some

Prada pumps, Evelyn made her way toward the stairs. "Girls! Are you ready to go?" she called out as she passed their rooms. They fell into line behind her, following her down the stairs while chattering away. Once they were next to the hall coat closet, Evelyn nodded at both their outfits—simple cashmere designer dresses—and retrieved her faux-fur coat. "Get your coats. We don't want to be too late."

"Do you think Torry's nervous?" asked Jennifer once they were settled in the Porsche.

"Wouldn't you be if your drawings were being showcased for the first time in an art gallery?" Julie asked rhetorically.

"Well, she'll have us there. I bet she sells a bunch of her stuff tonight."

"Stuff?" Evelyn asked mildly.

"I mean a bunch of her works," Jennifer corrected herself sheepishly. "Did you talk to her today, Mom?"

"Yes. A few hours ago." *After my illuminating lunch with Cynthia.* She'd made sure to let Victoria know that they were free to be seen together as a couple, if she was ready. Her eyebrows furrowed as she remembered how Victoria had reassured her that it was okay, that she knew how private Evelyn was. Victoria had been so gracious with keeping the nature of their relationship hidden, no small feat for the naturally affectionate woman, over the last few months while they navigated the newness of meshing their lives together. It was just another example of how special she was.

"Are we meeting her family tonight?" Jennifer asked.

Evelyn hadn't really thought about it, but Victoria's father and sister would be present tonight, as well as Cynthia. Her girls hadn't met them, yet. "Yes, now that you mention it. I hadn't considered that." She glanced at her girls through the rearview mirror. "They'll love you."

"And you, Mom," Jennifer said with a smile.

"Whoa! Look at all the people!" Julie squealed. They passed the art gallery and pulled into the nearby parking garage. It was indeed quite crowded. The gallery was well lit, and the paparazzi were out in full force, lighting up the sky with the flashes from their cameras. Evelyn's lips curled upward. Victoria could not fail to recognize how talented she was now.

"Ready?" she asked Jennifer and Julie with a smile as they approached the gallery.

"Ready!" they both exclaimed.

They smiled for the cameras before entering the art gallery and passing off their coats. Evelyn accepted a glass of wine as the girls received glasses of sparkling apple cider, and they took their time walking around the gallery to view the displays. Evelyn did not worry that they had not spoken to Victoria. She expected their paths would cross soon enough. She was more interested in enjoying the pieces on display and discussing them with her daughters.

Most of the pieces were new to them. Victoria had shown them some of her sketches, but these were the breathtaking finished products. Charcoal drawings, pencil drawings, acrylic paintings, oil paintings, Victoria had used several media to create her images, and all were divine. She eyed with interest a painting of a shady park bench on a sunny day as the city landscape loomed in the background. On it sat two young girls hunched toward each other. She could practically hear the girls' giggles, and when she peered closely, she could see their infectious smiles and shining eyes. It reminded her of her daughters. She hummed as she studied several pieces nearby which reflected sharp cityscapes and sweet snapshots of life in motion. Victoria had an eye for capturing beauty within everyday life.

Toward the back were the pieces used at Lost Treasures, including the painting Victoria had gifted to Evelyn. To think of all that had occurred since then. So much. Many visitors crowded around the pool scene, commenting on the chaotic partying and the facial expressions of the revelers. Evelyn once more wished she had found a way to pay for the painting.

"Evelyn, you're here!" a well-known voice said excitedly. Turning around, she saw Victoria, her emerald eyes sparking with delight. Leaning forward, Evelyn delivered a kiss to each cheek.

"Darling, you look lovely," Evelyn said affectionately. Her eyes raked over Victoria, her mouth watering, as she noticed every curve, dip, and valley showcased stunningly by the sexy, vintage, emerald Chanel cocktail dress she wore. Although she refused to show Evelyn beforehand, Victoria had divulged that she had brought several vintage pieces back with her from her Christmas trip to Rhode Island. The couture had belonged to her mother. "I cannot wait to unwrap you," she whispered next to Victoria's ear before stepping back to a polite distance. She heard the small whimper Victoria made upon hearing her words, and she smiled genuinely while watching as Victoria hugged Jennifer and Julie before addressing all three of them.

"What do you think?"

"Torry, I really like your work," Jennifer said shyly.

"Thanks. I'm really glad. I've been so nervous! But everyone's been so nice to me," Victoria said. As she watched the woman converse with her girls, Evelyn found herself smiling slightly, sinking into this feeling of rightness.

"Of course they have, silly. They'd have to answer to me, otherwise," a female voice said behind Victoria. As she turned, Evelyn recognized Victoria's sister. Beside her stood their father and Cynthia.

"Katie!" Victoria's excitement was nearly palpable as she hugged her sister. She hugged her father and Cynthia in quick succession before turning back to Evelyn and her daughters. "Dad, Katie, I want you to meet Evelyn Allbright and her daughters, Jennifer and Julie."

"Torry has spoken highly of all of you," Victoria's father said. "Please, call me Bobby."

"Ha-ha, that's one way of saying that she can't stop talking about you," Katie said, giggling with Evelyn's daughters, as Victoria's face flushed an appealing pink.

"Don't embarrass your sister, Katie. This is her big night. We're here to support her."

"I was just teasing her," Katie said. She looked Evelyn in the eye and added, "I really am glad to meet you. I know you've helped Torry, and I'm glad she has you."

"That she does," Evelyn agreed softly, glancing at Victoria and smiling at the soft gaze being directed her way.

"How long are you in town?" Julie asked.

"Only a few days," Katie answered. "We're gonna catch a Broadway show or two, act like tourists."

Evelyn and Victoria had already discussed inviting everyone out to eat the next night. She turned questioning eyes to Victoria, wondering whether she had broached the subject, yet.

"Girls, if you have nothing planned tomorrow, you're welcome to join us while we do the tourist thing," Victoria said before turning to her father. "Also, Evelyn and I talked about all of us going out to dinner together tomorrow night, if everyone's available?" she said, her eyes flittering to each person.

Waiting until everyone nodded, Evelyn said, "Wonderful. I'll take care of the arrangements." This was all working out much smoother than she'd dared to imagine.

"Excuse me. I am so sorry to interrupt," an older woman said, looking contrite. "Torry, someone's interested in the painting of the Newport mansions."

"Oh! Well, that's great! I'll be right there," Victoria said. She smiled widely at Evelyn. "I'll catch up with you later? My friends should be here soon too. I want you to meet them."

"Of course. Go on. We'll be here for a while," Evelyn said. She watched as Victoria struggled not to wave. She only partially succeeded. It was a silly habit that endeared her to Evelyn even more.

"I love that dorky wave," Julie said with a laugh. Evelyn hummed, and Jennifer chuckled. It seemed that Victoria had wormed her way into all three Allbrights' hearts.

"It's the Hansen charm at work," Bobby laughed.

Surprisingly, Victoria's family stuck with them as they slowly wandered around the gallery, enjoying the works. Her girls chatted with Victoria's sister, while Evelyn discussed Victoria's art with Cynthia and Bobby.

Evelyn smirked when Katie sidled up to her and said, "Do I need to have the older sister talk with you, or do you promise to treat Torry right?"

Evelyn turned slowly, raising her eyebrow as she stared at Katie. She was impressed by Katie's ability to maintain eye contact, even in the face of Evelyn's steely gaze. Finally, Evelyn said, "Although I need not answer to you or to anyone, I will tolerate your bravado since you are daring to confront me due to your love for your sister. I hold Victoria in the highest esteem. I have and shall continue to treat her well." Evelyn bit the inside of her cheek to prevent herself from laughing as Katie nodded her head sharply and faded into the background to rejoin the conversation with her daughters.

Once they returned near the front of the gallery, Evelyn heard hurried whispers and excited exclamations, her name bandied around indiscriminately. She was used to it, thrived on it, but hearing Victoria's beautiful voice caused her to glance over, spotting her with a young man and woman. *Jaxine and Gregory, no doubt.* Although Evelyn felt extremely protective of Victoria, she kept her displeasure for the foolhardy friends at bay. Victoria had such a forgiving heart, but she was certainly capable of making her own decisions. If she wanted to spend time with her fair-weather friends, then who was she to object?

"Evelyn, I'd like to introduce you to my friends," Victoria said, garnering Evelyn's full attention. "Jax and Greg, this is Evelyn and her daughters, Julie and Jennifer," she said, as she gestured toward each of them.

With a demure smile, Evelyn leaned in to deliver air kisses to each one. "It is a pleasure to meet you. Victoria has spoken of you often." She did not mention how they had hurt Victoria deeply with their immature words and actions. It was not her place.

"It's a pleasure to meet you," Gregory said effusively. He was dressed in a Hugo Boss slate-gray suit. She nodded. He looked acceptable, and she could easily sense his sincerity.

"I am so glad to meet you," Jaxine said, her eyes wide and voice uneven. Now, she was someone Evelyn did not find very impressive. Victoria's friend since they were children, Jaxine should have stood by Victoria's side, regardless of whether she agreed with her life choices. Still, Evelyn had promised to remain cordial.

"Yes, Victoria mentioned you work at an art gallery. What do you think of Victoria's exhibit?" Evelyn asked in a mild voice.

"It's about time! I've been urging her to get her pieces out there for years. She never thought they were good enough, though. I'm glad you changed her mind," Jaxine said.

Evelyn's eyebrows flew up, surprised by her words.

"Yes, well, her talent should be viewed and rewarded, not hidden away."

"Yeah! You've gotta flaunt what you got. You know what I'm saying Evelyn," Gregory said loudly while nodding his head several times, eliciting laughter from Jennifer and Julie. Although she wanted to laugh, Evelyn barely allowed her lips to twitch. Until she glanced at Victoria and saw her horrified expression. She looked so adorable that Evelyn could not prevent a peal of laughter from escaping her. She shook her head at everyone's frozen expression, rolling her eyes playfully as they erupted into loud guffaws. She truly liked Gregory. The jury was out on Jaxine.

"Quite right," Evelyn agreed amiably as their chuckles subsided.

"So, Torry, what do you think? Do you want to come out for a drink after this ends?" Jaxine asked.

Biting the inside of her cheek to keep her words firmly in check, Evelyn attempted to release the sudden spike of anger. She and Victoria had plans for tonight to celebrate the success of this showing. In fact, Evelyn had prepared the house, spending an inordinate amount of time exercising her seldom-used romantic muscles and indulging in her wish to pamper Victoria with all the attention she deserved. All she needed to execute her plans was Victoria.

"Oh, that sounds great, but tonight won't work. I've been working nonstop to get ready for this showing, and I really just want to relax afterward," Victoria said. "But maybe next week?"

"Actually, I have a suggestion," Evelyn said. "How about you both come to my home next Friday night for dinner? We can become better acquainted." It was easy enough to arrange, and Victoria would be able to spend time with everyone at once. It was quickly settled, and best of all, Victoria slipped her hand into Evelyn's hand and squeezed it as she smiled brightly.

Before Evelyn and her daughters left the gallery, she thanked Clive for having the intelligence to showcase Victoria's works, purchased a piece called *Two Girls on a Park Bench* (against Victoria's wishes, not that she could refuse Evelyn's money as she had last time), and debated which piece was her favorite with Jennifer and Julie. They agreed to disagree. Her daughters' appreciation for art made such debates quite enjoyable. Best of all, just before they left, Victoria leaned in and delivered a brief, heartfelt kiss on her lips.

"Thank you, Evelyn," Victoria whispered.

"Just wait until you get home," Evelyn said with a seductive lilt to her voice. "Then, you will have many reasons to thank me," she promised and smiled devilishly as Victoria's face flushed and her eyes dilated. With a soft tap to Victoria's cheek, she left.

***

The doorbell rang, breaking Evelyn's concentration. Cocking her head, she listened but did not hear any noise. How odd. The girls were with their father for the week, and Victoria had mentioned meeting her friends for drinks. She was looking forward to tomorrow when she would be spending the day with Victoria. Hopefully in bed. Evelyn smiled at the thought.

Since Thanksgiving week, they had spent all their free time together, ushering in the new year, spending time with her daughters, and attending the showing of Victoria's work at Clive's art gallery. Admittedly, it wasn't as much as she would have liked. The demands on her time had not lessened, and Victoria was in high demand now too. It was hard to believe that winter would be over in just a few days.

Hearing the doorbell ring again and what sounded like pounding on the door, Evelyn rose from her desk and made her way to the front of the house. Whoever it was had better have a very good reason. Evelyn stepped back in shock as Victoria pushed the door open wider and stomped inside. Evelyn could not understand what she was seeing. Never had Victoria directed such an irate glare toward her. She had never seen her so upset.

"Victoria?"

"How could you blackball Lost Treasures? You should have discussed it with me. Harold called me up today, and he made me feel horrible. He told me he couldn't get pieces from any of the designers. No one will even talk to him." Victoria ran a hand through her hair, disheveling it as she began to pace.

"Lower your voice immediately," Evelyn responded, her voice frosty. *How dare she come into my home and raise her voice at me!*

"Oh, no. You don't get to speak to me that way," Victoria raged, stepping into Evelyn's space. Evelyn took a step back, shocked. "Why would you do this? I didn't tell you what happened so you would do this!"

"Knowing what I could do to that little resale shop, why did you take the chance of telling me how that vile, backstabbing bug had betrayed you if not so I would exact revenge on your behalf? You must have known after working for over a year in the fashion industry just how ruthless I can be. You knew who I was," Evelyn said, her voice mild even as her heart beat furiously. The dim hallway cast shadows across Victoria's face, emphasizing her anger and shielding her eyes.

"Truthfully, I was afraid to tell you about Harold because you could so easily ruin him, but I wanted to tell you since you are my girlfriend. I needed your support, your advice. And I trusted that you wouldn't destroy him, if only because I asked you not to," Victoria said, her voice full of accusation.

"You never asked me to refrain from acting against that insignificant little shop, Victoria," Evelyn said stridently before turning to lead the way into the sitting room. She took a deep breath and sat on the sofa.

Victoria sat at the far end, back straight and hands balled into fists. "Come on, Evelyn! You knew I didn't want you to bury that shop. I've told you how thankful I am that they allowed me to decorate the windows. You should have told me what you were planning. If it weren't for him, I wouldn't be working with photographers and designers, and my work wouldn't be in that art gallery right now. As a matter of fact, we wouldn't even be together!" Victoria waved her hands in the air, her agitation reflected through her erratic motions.

"Victoria." Evelyn took a deep breath to calm herself. "That pathetic man hurt you. I could not ignore how his business prospered through your efforts, particularly after you left." Evelyn looked at her fingernails, wondering whether she could fit a manicure in for some time on Monday afternoon. "Besides, all I did was spread the word of what he had tried to do. The designers made their own decisions on how to react."

"But that wasn't your story to spread. I told you what happened in confidence—"

"You told the editor in chief of the premier fashion magazine in the world how a nothing clothing shop that had benefited from her actions and the actions of someone she treasures had attempted to capitalize on those efforts in an unscrupulous way. And you told me how your boss had betrayed you. Whether you like it or not, Victoria, I have power you do not yet possess. And whether you like it or not, I will not stand by idly while anyone hurts those I love," Evelyn said heatedly.

Why couldn't Victoria understand? Her ability to destroy anyone in the fashion industry rested on her unwillingness to wield such power too often. In this situation, however, she had deemed it necessary. He had hurt her. He had hurt one of the most important people in Evelyn's world.

"This wasn't your fight, Evelyn. Can't you understand? I have to fight my own battles or else everyone will assume I am hiding behind your skirt tails." Victoria's voice was less irate, but she still seemed upset.

"It is you who does not understand. I will do whatever is necessary to protect my family. You may be just making a name for yourself, but I am well established and well connected. By extension, so are you," Evelyn said softly.

"People will think you're protecting me."

"Is that so bad? Now they'll know that I favor you. It will only work to benefit your career," Evelyn pointed out.

"No, it's not bad. It's just...I want to do this on my own. Make my own way. I want to be worthy of you," Victoria quietly admitted.

Evelyn slid over and lifted up Victoria's lovely face so she would understand how serious she was while stating the next words.

"Worthy of me? Victoria, haven't you been listening? You are the treasure here." Evelyn ran elegant fingers down Victoria's cheek, pausing on her shoulder. "I am not an easy woman to love. Nor do I suffer fools gladly. With my work, I do not have the luxury of trusting people simply because most want something from me. I have been betrayed more times than I care to recount, and I am sad to say, I trust very few as a result. I have divorced two men, and I have two teenage daughters. And yet..." Evelyn smiled tenderly. "And yet here you are in my life. I will always want to protect you. And when someone hurts you, I will strike back brutally so that others will think twice."

Victoria did not seem happy, but she did look resigned.

"You said I am family, that I am someone you love," she said softly, her bashful gaze belying how closely she was watching Evelyn.

"Yes, I did. You are." Evelyn took a deep breath to steady herself, feeling flat-footed. "I love you, Victoria. I did not expect this. I did not expect this at all. However, I refuse to deny that these feelings exist." Evelyn held her head high even as she felt her body flush while she laid her heart bare.

Evelyn sat still, as Victoria peered into her face before pulling her into a bear hug. Her breath caught when Victoria kissed her behind the ear and whispered, "Thank you. I know your heart was in the right place. But please, please let me know next time. It's like when I asked you not to put in a good word for me anywhere. I need to know I am succeeding because of my actions, my talent not yours."

"My dear Victoria, you are. Please, do not question your talents. They are astounding, as are you," Evelyn said. "I am blessed to have you in my life." Not liking the sad look on Victoria's face at all, she added, "Don't leave. Stay tonight." Her heart lurched unpleasantly when she saw Victoria hesitate. Was she still angry?

"I don't know that I'd be very good company."

"Nonsense. If you're still upset, I'd much rather you remain here than leave. In fact, I'll open a bottle of wine. You're not an angry drunk, are you, Victoria?" Evelyn teased. She watched Victoria shake her head before making her way to the kitchen.

Two hours and two bottles of wine later, Evelyn could not stop laughing. Victoria was positively adorable when drunk—smart, emotional, happy, and philosophical. Evelyn found the woman irresistible.

"Stop laughing! I'm serious, Evelyn. Haven't you ever noticed? Don't tell me you haven't. You can pretend all you want, but I know you have," Victoria insisted as she leaned into Evelyn's side.

"Really, Victoria. Don't be ridiculous. Heather does not glower as I do." Evelyn sniffed. "As if she could."

Victoria's laughter filled the room and Evelyn's heart. She loved that laugh, loved being a part of the reason for the laughter. Jazz played softly, the saxophone solo filling the space soothingly. She knew Victoria enjoyed this type of music, and Evelyn was planning to surprise her with tickets to a well-known jazz club over the weekend. Evelyn pulled the woman forward for a sloppy but heartfelt kiss.

"Mmm. You taste so good, Evelyn. I love kissing you." Victoria's face became thoughtful, signaling another round of philosophical debate. Evelyn braced herself, smirking in anticipation.

"Don't smirk. This is serious," Victoria admonished. "Evelyn." Victoria waited a few moments, pulling back a bit and gazing at Evelyn for several seconds with a solemn look before continuing. "Evelyn. I know why you came into my life both times, but I want to know, why do you think I came back into your life?"

Blinking slowly, Evelyn attempted to concentrate on the question. It was difficult with Victoria draped all over her. Turning her head slightly, she assumed a serious expression. "You came back into my life to gift me with your vision. Whether that is embodied through your paintings and drawings, your window display designs and photo shoot ideas, or your writing and philosophical discussions." Evelyn smiled softly. "Victoria, you enrich my life. You make me happy." She paused before saying mostly to herself, "Why did you come back to me? To save me from an unfulfilling, uninspired life. Only you could remove the yearning I have felt for something more." Done with the drunken confessions, she pulled Victoria's sweater off of her delectable body and began exploring her heaving chest with her lips. She always tasted so sweet, so good.

Nodding, Victoria began unbuttoning Evelyn's blouse as best she could without being able to focus well on what she was doing. "As it so happens, you make me happy too. In fact, I believe that I am the fortunate one. I will always feel grateful for the chance of loving you." Victoria kissed Evelyn lovingly. "Let's go to bed."

It wasn't long before they were in the bedroom and Victoria was removing Evelyn's blouse. She ran a hand through silky locks, as Victoria unfastened her lacy black bra and kissed her way toward the side button on Evelyn's fitted wool slacks. She realized that she had missed Victoria desperately over the last few days. It was easy to push aside the longing while immersed in work, but with the woman kneeling before her, gently lifting one of Evelyn's legs and then the other to remove her pants, desire reared up powerfully.

Looking down, she was captured by emerald eyes.

"I love you, Evelyn. I hope you know that," Victoria whispered.

"Mm. I do know, my dear Victoria." Evelyn knelt on the floor so that their knees touched and leaned forward to rest her forehead against Victoria's. "I know."

Epilogue

VIEWING HERSELF IN THE full-length mirror nervously, Torry ran her hands down the sides of her gown. She wore a fitted strapless Isaac Mizrahi silk-faille peplum dress, white with raised black polka dots. A thin, black belt accentuated her hourglass figure. Well, she had hips and her abdomen was flat. Soon she would be in the town car with Evelyn on their way to the last event for Paris Fashion Week. Torry was surprised that Evelyn had asked her to accompany her to the high-profile event.

For the last ten months they had kept their romance under wraps. Although Evelyn had not wanted to hide their relationship, Torry had insisted that she make her way in the fashion and art worlds based on her own merit and not her relationship status with Evelyn. Few suspected anything other than a professional relationship between them, and that had helped Torry to gain confidence in her abilities as she accepted more freelance jobs. She had even published several articles in various magazines, including the one published in *Trending* that she wrote about window designing. She was able to choose her projects, and she was as busy as she wanted to be. The last few months had become particularly taxing, and tonight she was ready to take her rightful place next to Evelyn at one of the most publicized fashion events of the year.

She knew Evelyn was excited. She had learned to read the signs, and though Evelyn was as focused on the shows and designers as she usually was, Torry noticed how Evelyn smiled involuntarily and yanked on her necklace while lost in thought. They had arrived in Paris separately since Torry was working with several of the designers for their fashion shows and photographers as they captured the clothes displayed on the catwalks. Evelyn had appeared tired and distracted. Torry knew better than to ask. Instead, she did what she could to place a smile on Evelyn's face during the rare moments they were able to share together.

Yet, a few days into the trip, Evelyn had begun to relax more. Nothing most people would notice, although Ira had mentioned it at one of the after-parties. He was one of the few people who knew they were together. He was about to move into a new position, courtesy of Evelyn, once they returned from Paris. Evelyn had announced the global move for Natalee Smith with Ira at the helm. The bold colors and flowing, asymmetrical designs had thrust the South African designer into the spotlight over the last six months. Torry was happy for Ira and knew Evelyn had been looking for a way to propel him forward for the past year. Similarly, Heather was foaming at the mouth to become the new Ira. Evelyn had promoted her to be Ira's assistant six months ago, and Evelyn had since declared her former assistant's work adequate. High praise.

Evelyn was very good at maneuvering behind the scenes. After their heated discussion about the blackballing of Lost Treasures, Evelyn had lifted the ban. Whenever asked about the little resale shop, Evelyn would merely shrug and turn away. People understood pretty quickly that, although it was no longer shunned, the boutique was not endorsed by Evelyn or anyone of import. Soon the shop's sales diminished, and now it was an afterthought. Evelyn liked to tell Torry that it was where she had found a priceless treasure she had once lost. Torry smirked. Evelyn could be so mushy at times.

Last night they met for a late meal and then returned to Evelyn's hotel suite for a nightcap. Torry anticipated having to depart to her lonely hotel room soon after dinner. Instead, Evelyn wined and dined her, focusing solely on her during their meal as if she had all the time in the world and cared only to share it with her. Torry, knowing how valuable Evelyn's time was, took this gesture for the gift it was. Once in the privacy of Evelyn's room, she was pleasantly surprised to receive the woman's amorous attentions. They made love for hours before falling asleep, wrapped around each other. Even better, Torry woke up to kisses on her abdomen, causing her stomach muscles to contract.

"Evelyn," she whispered, as her hands gripped the disheveled sheets, trying to ground herself. Looking down, she was captured by glowing blue eyes. A nose nudged her clitoris, making her twitch and arch as she widened her legs. Evelyn lifted Torry's thighs on to her shoulders and dove in, thrusting her tongue into Torry forcefully.

"Ahh, Evelyn," Torry cried out, as she pushed forward to feel more. Practiced fingers rubbed at her bundle of nerves, eliciting breathless whimpers. Evelyn began to hum as she moved her tongue upward and entered Torry with two fingers. Slowly, so slowly, she thrust and rubbed, causing Torry to groan at how wonderful it felt. "Yes, Evelyn. Just like that. Don't stop!"

And she didn't. An orgasm crashed over Torry so strongly that she froze in the air before flopping back on the bed as her muscles continued to twitch pleasantly. She took deep breaths, her eyes mere slits while watching Evelyn wipe her face on the sheets and reposition herself so that her arms were crossed and resting on top of Torry's thighs, her chin propped on them, effectively pinning her down.

"Good morning, Victoria," she purred.

Torry laughed with delight. "What a way to wake up! Come up here so I can return the favor," she said, her hands reaching for Evelyn.

"That's not necessary. Just let me look at you for a moment, darling. I've missed you."

"Me too." With their schedules leading up to Paris, they had hardly seen each other, and when they had been able to coordinate some time, it was never for long. No sleepovers, no private time for the last month. She'd feared that Evelyn might not care as much as she did, and certainly she had seemed to be unaffected by the separation. It was wonderful to hear otherwise.

"I love you, Victoria. Keeping this relationship under wraps has been hard for both of us, although I understand your reasons. But I want you to know that I do not intend to keep our love a secret any longer. Will you attend the gala with me tonight?"

"Oh, I'd love to. What time should I meet you there?" Whenever their schedules had allowed it over the past week, Torry had attended the same functions Evelyn had and joined her while Ira ran interference with those who desired Evelyn's time. Before the rush of fashion week had upended their routine, they had met at least once a week for dinner and twice for lunch during the work week. In addition, just about every weekend Torry stayed at the townhouse. No one thought twice about the shared meals, and few knew the true nature of their relationship except for their families, Jax, Greg, and Ira.

"Torry, you misunderstand me. I want you to go with me. As my date," Evelyn said with a serious look on her face.

"You...really? Are you sure? I mean, maybe we should look at today's paper to see if anyone picked up on last night's dinner first." Torry ran a hand through Evelyn's hair. "I know this has been hard, but I don't want the paparazzi to give you a hard time. They are bad enough around here. I'm afraid the press will go into a feeding frenzy when we go public, and I'd hate to cause you trouble."

"Victoria, I couldn't care less what the paparazzi say about me, and the girls are itching to talk about you to their friends, to show you off, and have you over more often. I feel the same way." Evelyn kissed Torry's hip. "Besides, I saw the papers this morning. There is a wonderful picture of us holding hands while we dined. I plan on requesting a copy to frame," Evelyn announced with a smirk.

Feeling her eyebrows rocket off her face, Torry took a moment to digest the information. "I'd love to attend the gala with you." She smiled brightly with the realization that Evelyn really intended for everyone to know about them. Torry had used her desire to rise in her career without having to rely on the status of their relationship as the main reason for keeping it under wraps, but she also had worried about Evelyn and her daughters. Obviously, Evelyn couldn't care less about what anyone else thought. It was surprising and wonderful. "I love you," she said.

"I know," Evelyn answered easily with a smile. "Let's take a shower. We'll have just enough time for breakfast before we part."

Several hours and three shows later, Torry smiled to herself while taking one last look in the mirror to make sure she was presentable. Excitement coursed through her at the thought of what was to come. As soon as they entered the gala, everyone would know they were together.

A knock on the door broke her train of thought, signaling Evelyn's arrival. Torry opened the door and stepped back to allow Evelyn entrance. She looked fabulous in a form-fitting, strapless, black Prada gown. "Wow," Torry breathed. "You look spectacular."

"Thank you, Victoria. You look quite stunning tonight," Evelyn answered, as she stepped forward to deliver a light kiss. "Are you ready?"

"Yes. Absolutely." She recognized that Evelyn was referring to more than merely tonight's events. They were entering a new phase of their relationship, one where others would know and pass judgment. It didn't matter. She loved Evelyn and would weather any storm to be with her. Although certainly worth it, building a relationship while always checking to make sure no one was suspicious of what kind of relationship they shared had been challenging. She smiled confidently at Evelyn. "Lead the way."

"Hmm. Yes. Before we go," Evelyn reached into her clutch and withdrew a box, "this is for you." She seemed anxious, which intrigued Torry.

With shaking fingers, Torry opened the box. Inside were nestled platinum and diamond drop earrings and a diamond tennis bracelet. Torry stared at them, speechless. She shook her head slightly and blinked her eyes. "Evelyn," she whispered. Sure hands took the box and placed it on a nearby table. Torry felt gentle fingers lift up her chin.

"Victoria, I love you. The girls love you. Will you consider moving in with us?"

Shaking like a leaf as emotions rolled through her, Torry nodded mutely. She watched a large smile cross Evelyn's face and felt her knees weaken. "Are you sure, Evelyn? I love you. You know that. Don't feel you need to do this to keep me with you. I'm not going anywhere."

"I know, darling. And neither am I. This last month," Evelyn shook her head, "I have missed you desperately. Although work obligations may keep us apart at times, I do not intend to go so long without seeing you again, even if it can only be at the beginning or end of the day. I want you with me, Victoria."

Torry pulled Evelyn to her, hugging her tightly. She felt so loved, so fortunate. When she pulled back a bit, strong arms remained wrapped around her waist, supporting her. "Are you sure, Victoria? It will be quite a change. If you're not ready, if I'm moving too quickly, I'm counting on you to tell me. I will not think less of you." Evelyn scratched lightly at the nape of Torry's neck.

Remembering the last time Evelyn had uttered such words, Torry smiled. So much had changed, and yet the feelings were still strong and true. She loved this woman, needed her. Torry was excited to begin this next chapter in their lives, to be able to fall asleep in her arms, to see her every day. "You aren't rushing me. Far from it. I'd love to live with you." She leaned in to deliver a delicate kiss, an affirmation of her dedication to their relationship.

She wore her gifts as they strolled down the red carpet, hands clasped firmly. Their names were shouted from all directions, but Torry only cared that Evelyn was next to her. "I can't wait to tell Jennifer and Julie that I'm moving in," she whispered. Evelyn's smile as she turned toward Torry was captured for all of posterity, the camera flashes indicating the imminent arrival of some stunning photographs in several newspapers the following day.

"This is merely the beginning, Victoria. Together, we will change the face of fashion."

Looking into Evelyn's eyes, Torry believed every word.

The End.

About Jazzy Mitchell

Jazzy Mitchell is a storyteller in many forms: writer, educator, editor, attorney—she tells stories, breaking down complex ideas in understandable, interesting ways. She taught English in the public schools of her hometown for a decade, giving back to the system that had helped her so much. During that time, she trained and encouraged countless students to write poetry and explore their artistic sides. She likes to recount how law school drove the artist out of her, but over time her artistic instincts reasserted themselves.

Besides writing, Jazzy Mitchell is the proud publisher of Launch Point Press and on the founding Board of Directors for OPUS Literary Alliance.

Jazzy lives in Oregon with her wife, three children, and sassy dog, capturing the essence of life's journey in all its wonderful forms.

Connect with Jazzy

Facebook – JazzyMitchellauthor

Email –publisher@launchpointpress.com

Website – www.launchpointpress.com

Note to Readers:

Thank you for reading a book from Launch Point Press. We have made every effort to edit this book. However, typos do slip in. If you find an error in the text, please email publisher@launchpointpress.com so the issue can be corrected.

We appreciate you as a reader and want to ensure you enjoy the reading process. We would like you to consider posting a review on your preferred media sites and/or your blog or website.

For more information on upcoming releases, author interviews, contests, giveaways and more, please sign up for our newsletter and visit us as at Launch Point Press: www.launchpointpress.com and "Like" us on Facebook: Launch Point Press.

Bright Blessings